I0549078

Wilton Place Publishing

Also by Steven E. Browne

The 3by3 Writing Series

Publish Your Book, Now!
Plan, Write and Finish Your Novel - The Workbook
BLOG: https://3by3writingmethod.wordpress.com/
TWITTER: @3by3writer
facebook.com/threebythree.writingmethod

Non-Fiction

The Accident Report
High Definition Post Production
Getting that Job in Hollywood
Video Editing
Introduction to Non-Linear Editing
Film/Video Terms and Concepts

Fiction

Protecting the Source
Holly Would, But Stacy Won't

Rick, Renee, and the Fat Man

❦ ❦ ❦ ❦

Steven E. Browne

Wilton Place Publishing.

All rights reserved.
Copyright 2014 Steven E. Browne

Wilton Place Publishing,
P.O. Box 291
La Cañada Flintridge, CA 91012

"Mark my words, Francois. Sinister forces are at work."

Inspector Clouseau

"You're so wise. Like a miniature Buddha, covered with hair."

Ron Burgundy

Wet 'N Wild

One sunny Saturday afternoon in June, a highly intoxicated spy using the surprisingly common alias of Rick Johnson lost control of his sports car, flew off a steep California cliff, and crashed into the Pacific Ocean. Being a survival expert, Johnson lived through the dramatic plunge and escaped the rapidly sinking vehicle. He spent most of the day swimming against the outgoing tide, climbing a rocky precipice and commandeering a tourist's rented, dented Kia. Then he tore down the Pacific Coast Highway to his destination - the hotel Ritz-Carlton, half hour south of his sunken Lamborghini.

As a result of his tequila-inspired mistake, Rick Johnson missed a very important meeting.

But this is not his story because he's an idiot.

This story is about how I met the woman of my dreams and walked into that hotel lobby at exactly the wrong time.

My name is also...Rick Johnson.

Mojo Trouble

Evelyn deWilde took my dog.

I got a text from her that read: "This relationship isn't working." Her longwinded, misspelled diatribe ended with, "I'm leafing you."

That made perfect sense to me. The previous day I'd caught her doing "deWilde thing" with the neighbor across the street. When I spotted her smushed against his second floor window wearing only her designer glasses, I knew our relationship was over.

But she took my Mojo.

Mojo is my golden retriever. He's really smart and saved my life. I owed him big time. What infuriated me was that Evelyn didn't steal him because of an emotional attachment. She stole my dog because his light brown fur matched her three thousand dollar Lana Marks purse.

It took some time to find them. They were in Las Vegas living with some guy named Saul "The Weasel" Weinstein. After a five hour drive to Vegas from Los Angeles, I stalked the compound, made some inquires of the neighbors and finally made contact. Evelyn informed me it was going to cost eight grand in legal and "handling" fees (I called it dog ransom) to get inside the Weasel's compound. Even then, I would only get two short visits - supervised by Weinstein's bodyguards. The only way I was going to get custody of Mojo was by paying the Weasel another fifteen thousand, in cash.

This was a perfect example of what happens when I get emotionally wrapped up with an attractive woman - the Rick Johnson Curse (also known as the RJC) rears its nasty head. Then all sorts of trouble occurs that always seems to involve mystery motor vehicles, extremely expensive exploits and incredibly intense alliteration.

The most recent RJC attack involved a Burbank bankruptcy, a Rialto restraining order and a complicated court case in *Corona*.

Heck, at least I had my freakin' health.

Wait, let me rephrase that. The *only* thing I had was my health. I'd even lost my dog. But that was all about to change. Martin Luther King had a dream. I had a plan.

* * * * *

I was standing in the shade at the seventeenth tee at Burbank's DeBell golf course with Larry Ford. I'm not really a golfer and Larry's not really a friend. He wanted information about Evelyn. I needed some serious financial support.

Even though I'd started work as a celebrity fitness trainer, it wasn't the solution I'd hoped for. The clients wouldn't exercise, the celebrities were unknowns and two checks had bounced. My newest idea was to get Larry on the greens, circumvent his wife-unit and work some margarita magic. I figured after letting him win and buying a few drinks in the lounge, Larry would get all warm and fuzzy, then I'd hit him up for a loan.

"Tell me something crazy-kinky about this new job," he said, leaning against the cart.

I pulled a driver from my bag and examined it carefully, pretending I knew something about golf clubs. "Nothing to tell, " I replied picking some grass out of the grooves, "All my clients are overweight and lack any sign of a libido."

"You are so lying. Come on Mr. Celebrity Trainer. Give me the inside dirt. What's it cost for a cardio session with a happy ending?"

The guy had only one thing on his mind and it wasn't golf.

"Larry, there aren't any happy endings in my workouts. Besides, I signed a confidentiality agreement longer than your last divorce settlement. My lips are legally sealed."

I watched him walk to the grassy mound, unconcerned. He slammed the orange tee into the ground with authority and placed the small white ball on top of it. Satisfied with his preparations, he looked up at me.

"Buddy, you've got to cheer up. Just because you've been dumped, your dog's been stolen, and your mom's about to be homeless, there's no need to be so miserable. I mean, really, who wants to hang around a killjoy?"

He hit the ball high and wide.

"It'll bounce out," I said, being overly kind. No way he'd see that thing again. "Hey, do you want to stop and have a few drinks after?"

Larry walked down to the cart and shoved his club into his golf bag. "No-can-do. Gotta help Nancy host a barbecue this afternoon. Between you and me, she blames you for Evelyn's leaving. She liked her a lot, you know."

Everyone thought Evelyn was this cute, innocent girl. So did I, until I found her photo album. Besides being quite sexually adventurous (apparently with other people), she liked having her picture taken with them, naked, in erotic poses. I wanted to tell Larry that his wife and Evelyn had quite an extensive and revealing portfolio, but that might have invited further discussion.

"Have you heard from her?" he asked.

I shook my head. Discretion is the better part of everything, especially when nudity is involved. "Haven't heard a thing." If Larry's wife knew that Evelyn was in Las Vegas, she'd probably be on the next flight out to Sin City.

I was running out of time and if Larry wasn't hanging around for post-game drinks, it was time to implement my plan without the aid of alcoholic lubrication.

"Say Larry, do you think I could borrow another twenty grand to save my house and to pay Mojo's ransom? "

From the look on his face, I knew the conversation was over. What was I thinking?

* * * * *

"What were you thinking?" asked my mother.

Mom's eighty-one, but doesn't look a day over seventy-six. She's always irritable and her wrinkles continue to deepen. What do you expect from a sun-loving alcoholic?

Mom thought I was dropping by to say hi, but I was only there to pay her rent. I didn't dare tell her about my money problems, just the dognapping story. If she had a clue that the cash cow had flown the coop, she'd freak and seeing my mother freak is not a positive experience, especially at close range.

She tilted back and forth in her wooden chair with a frantic, unstated purpose, as if the rocker was going to take her somewhere. She focused intently at the far blank wall.

"I told you that girl was up to no good. She was a tramp then and she's a tramp now. No wonder you liked her so much. You'd better get that dog back. She doesn't have a clue how to take care of anyone."

"I know, Ma, I know. I'm working on it."

Mom continued to stare at the wall, rocking like a mad woman, "I liked that damn dog," she said sullenly. "Did I tell you this place stinks?"

"It's the best I can do. I'll bring you some more air fresheners. "

I didn't have the heart to tell her there were tough times ahead if I didn't figure something out real quick. After paying mom's rent at Saki's Sushi Shack, I went home, sat at my dining room table and stared at a pile of unpaid bills that were threatening to topple to the floor. I didn't have a clue how I was going to pay them, much less my mortgage or mom's rent next month.

I spotted a quarter under the table.

"This is a sign," I said to myself.

I reached down and grabbed the coin. On the way up I smashed the back of my head on the table and immediately heard a horrible ringing. It took me a moment to realize the noise wasn't inside my brain, but was my rarely-used landline.

"Hello?" I said, rubbing my skull.

"Is this Rick Johnson?" said a woman on the other end.

"Yes, that's me."

"Please hold for Greg Atsbee."

Oh, now this was just freakin' great. Greg Atsbee, my college roommate, was returning a call from eight months ago. My bankruptcy proceedings were over. I was about to lose my house and Evelyn had pilfered my Mojo. What did *he* want? If it was forgiveness, he'd dialed the wrong number.

"Look," I said, trying to hide my irritation, "I don't know who you are, but..."

"My name is Traye. I'm Greg's Atsbee's executive assistant."

"Well, listen up, executive assistant Traye. I called Greg in July and all through August and got nothing for my efforts. I think it's time to return the favor."

"Rick, let's pretend I didn't hear that, okay? I think you should take a moment out of your busy, unemployed life and chat with the billionaire. He might have a solution for your incredibly severe income deficiency. Besides, I still have to find Bob Clay and that damn Scott DeVore who is apparently lost in some damn Asian jungle."

The mention of my other college roommates along with Traye's insight into my financial situation put a halt to my stubbornness.

"All right," I said reluctantly, rubbing the back of my head, "Put him on."

I heard a few clicks and a new voice came on the line.

"Rick? Rick Johnson? Is that you?"

I wasn't sure if it was Greg. It didn't sound like him. Then again, it'd been years since I'd heard his voice.

"Rick, it's Greg, Greg Atsbee."

"How are you, Greg?"

"I'm fine, Rick. Thanks for asking," came the much too-quick reply. Why was he talking so fast?

"Busy as usual," he continued at breakneck speed. "There's always a crisis around here. How are you? We haven't talked in years."

"Life's good," I lied. "I'm developing a complex exercise program for pregnant, vegan bowlers, my workout clients are lazy and my mother doesn't like living over a smelly fish restaurant. You know, the usual life dramas."

"I'm sure there's a lot more than that going on, which is why I'm calling. I need some help from my old friends."

Greg Atsbee, CEO of a Fortune 500 company, biggest donor to Cayuga College, was asking a favor of penniless, dogless, soon-to-be-homeless, Rick Johnson. Was he high?

"What's on your mind, Greg?" I said cautiously.

Over the years I've developed a serious aversion to performing any type of good deed. It's a sidebar to the Rick Johnson Curse. I actually have an early warning system in my brain whenever I hear the words "could you do me a favor." It sounds like this: "NO! NO! NO! NO!" only much louder.

"I host an exclusive party every year," Atsbee continued, "It's at the Ritz over in Half Moon Bay. I'd

9

like you, Bob Clay and Scott DeVore to join me. You can take my jet. Wives and significant others are definitely invited."

"Well Greg," I said, choosing my words carefully, "I have a lot of work to do on the exercise program. I've got a slew of upcoming appointments and there are probably ten other things I can't think of right now. I'll have to check my calendar and get back to you in a day or so."

What I wanted to say was, "You're a flaming asshole for not helping me when I needed you! And now you call? To invite me to a party? You've got to be joking!"

"Totally understandable," he continued, "I suppose this is a bit of a surprise."

Damn right it's a surprise. Like I'm dying to go to your pretentious get-together in some half-ass town, probably why they call it Half Moon.

Several years earlier I was in an emergency room covered in blood, holding my recently severed finger. After the orderly heard my story he shook his head sadly and said, "No good deed goes unpunished."

That's why I keep favors and acts of generosity at a minimum - self-preservation.

"For what it's worth," said Atsbee, "I have a business proposition for you. Nothing to do with celebrity fitness or dognapping, but I think it could solve some of your current economic and personal challenges."

I knew there was something suspicious about Atsbee's call. First his secretary mentioned my money troubles. Then Greg revealed that he was onto my new job and Mojo's abduction. Was he having me followed? Did I post it on Facebook? Had I been drunk twittering again? One thing was for sure, I wasn't committing to anything, especially to some favor from a fair-weather friend who was MIA when I was SOL.

Then an unexpected jolt of sanity hit me. I needed every penny I could get my hands on and Atsbee had a shit-load of them. I had to take care of Mom. Where was she going to live? Where was I going to live? Why hadn't Greg returned my calls and why was he calling now? Could I trust him? Was he still on the line? What were we talking about? Was there a question I was supposed to answer?

I let the pause hang hoping he'd repeat whatever he said because I had no idea what it was.

"It would be great to see you again," Atsbee finally offered.

Not the information I'd hoped for, but he sounded sincere.

"It's been a long time," he continued.

"Yes, it has," I said.

Then I remembered. Greg wanted me to go to a reunion in Moon Town, do him a favor so I could get my dog back, keep a roof over mom's head and probably lose another finger in the process.

"I'll let you know in a day or two," I said politely.

"I look forward to hearing from you," he replied and the line went dead.

I hung up the phone which promptly slid off the mountain of bills and smashed onto my foot with a loud thud.

Rockin' Renee

I couldn't stop thinking about all the reasons why Greg would be reaching out to me. Then there was the vague promise of a job. What was that about? Why didn't he just send me a check?

I needed a change of scenery to calm my whirling brain so I headed to Gordon Biersch Brewery. I figured that watching a baseball game surrounded by semi-sober strangers was better than listening to my increasingly insane inner demons.

Burbank's Gordon Biersch is a pleasant upscale chain restaurant with a large circular wood bar and high-def flat screens hung above rows of colorful liquor bottles. It's not a local joint, so I wasn't stealing someone's favorite seat. I settled into an empty bar stool, ordered my favorite beer, a Fat Tire, and waited for the Dodger game to start. I purposefully placed the amber liquid off to the side in an effort to keep my consumption to a minimum.

I heard the nearby sound of a woman's laughter. I was tempted to take a peek at who was having so much fun, but I stayed firmly focused on the TVs. I didn't need any more complications in my pretzeled life.

Then I heard a beer glass hit the bar. No mistaking that sound. I swiveled to see if there was a sudsy tsunami heading my way and instead locked eyes with a green-eyed, red-haired beauty with a cute little nose that money couldn't buy.

"Oops," she said, "Sorry about your beer, stranger. I guess I knocked it over."

I watched as the spill spread across the bar. Suddenly the area was attacked by the bartender and was wiped clean in seconds. The attractive stranger slid next to me and insisted on replacing my drink. In another life this would have been a welcome invitation to flirt, tease and potentially end up in some kind of physical entanglement, but I had nothing left. A fresh drink arrived and was placed between us.

"Renee Gunnison," she said, offering her hand. It was warm and strong.

"Rick Johnson."

"Pleased to meet you, Rick," she said revealing a perfect smile. The thought flickered across my mind that she might be a toothpaste model.

She cocked her head sideways. "I wasn't sure if I'd ever get your attention, Rick."

"It looked like you were getting your share," I replied.

"Not from the right person," she said softly, "You're a hard man to impress, Rick Johnson. Should I knock over a few more beers to see if you're still interested?"

"That won't be necessary, Ms. Gunnison. You have my full attention."

"Call me Renee."

I nodded and smiled, took a sip, and waited for a ceiling fan to fall on my head or for her to pull a knife and stab me in my already wounded heart.

"Okay, Renee it is."

The men she'd abandoned seemed disappointed, but realized it was time to move on - she obviously had.

"So what brings you to the Burbank Biersch, Rick?" She glanced around the bar. "It can't be the female companionship. This is pretty much a sausage fest."

"I'd think that would be more appealing to you."

I regretted it the moment the words left my mouth. Sexual innuendo doesn't play well unless a substantial amount of alcohol or recreational drugs have been consumed. I expected her to leave and head to the other side of the bar. Instead, she snuggled up and lowered her voice.

"You know, Rick, just because you're at an all-you-can-eat wienie fest, it doesn't mean you should stuff your face."

I wasn't sure where she was going with this, but I sensed trouble. And something was happening inside my body. Was I sensing excitement or was the dreaded RJ Curse in warm-up mode?

"You probably order off-menu most of the time," I continued.

All kinds of alarms were going off. I was thinking that it might be time to call it a day - move on into the parking lot, maybe out of the area code.

She smiled. A bit too big, a little too friendly.

"You're right, Rick. I am very selective..." she said, raising an eyebrow, "But don't think replacing your drink is an invitation."

My hands went up, palms out, in a defensive move. "Whoa, hang on there, Renee. I do not expect anything from a single beer at happy hour prices. I may be easy, but I have my standards."

That's not what I wanted to say. I wanted to tell her that I was captivated by her emerald eyes...that her subtle scent of Clive Christian, flawless smile and shimmering blouse had me so wrapped up I couldn't think clearly. Thank God I didn't say *that* out loud.

She settled back into her seat. "So, Rick, where's the girlfriend?"

I looked up at the TV, not wanting to make eye contact.

"Moved to Vegas. Spent all my money. Took my dog. She won't be back."

"Ever?"

"Ever," I said, trying not to add any spin.

"Ouch. I guess that means you're back on the market."

She looked into her martini glass and spun an olive around the edge with a plastic toothpick. "What's your dog's name?"

"Mojo." I said.

"He's not one of those Paris Hilton sissy mutts is he?"

"Golden Retriever. Loves everyone."

The conversation ground to a halt. She rested her chin on her pale knuckles. That's when I noticed the scar on the back of her hand. It was a big one. This was not your run-of-the-mill hand through the window or bike-riding scar. The wound must have been nasty. I returned my gaze to her flawless smile.

"What's the matter, Rick? Not in the game?"

I gripped my beer and managed a defenseless shrug. "Let's just say I'm on the disabled list."

"That's too bad," she said, her eyes already saying yes. "What would it take to get you on the active roster?" She popped the olive in her mouth and held the toothpick upright.

"I thought one drink didn't indicate an interest," I said.

16

She shook her head, putting her red curls into motion, and swallowed the olive whole. "I wasn't done ordering."

This was so unfair. A dynamic, spirited woman who was ready to rumble had invaded my comfort zone and I was trying to pick myself up off the mat.

I remember going to the beach when I was a kid. Huntington Beach - the original Surf City; the one that Jan and Dean sang about. I looked out at those waves and knew they were nothing to be worried about. Five minutes into my frolicking I was blindsided by a powerful breaker. I jumped to my feet. Oh yeah, look at me. I can handle this crap. That's all you got? Bring it on, asswipe.

The next swell rolled me like a pebble in a flash flood. The price for my ocean arrogance - three broken ribs, a badly scraped chest and a smashed nose. A person learns from the painful lessons in their life and believe me, I've learned a lot.

"Tell me about this," she said, pointing to the nub at the end of my left hand.

I was surprised. Most people see my missing digit and avoid the fact that I only have nine fingers. They're typically unnerved when I give them a high four.

"I was helping someone get their purse."

"From what, a wood chipper?"

Damn, she was funny, too. I was beginning to like her. A lot. "Some guy stole it," I said, "I chased him. Didn't know he had a knife."

"Hmm." She lifted my hand and examined the wound. "They did a nice job."

"Are you a doctor?"

"No, I just know what it could look like." She put my hand back on the bar.

"What about yours?"

She glanced at the back of her hand. "This? Oh, I dropped a vase in a sink"

"That's a big scar."

"It was a big vase."

"Small sink? "

I was pretty sure I heard her laugh. She got my humor, never a good sign.

I let the conversation slip into silence again. I'd served time in the military and witnessed some pretty ugly stuff. That ragged scar was a battle wound of some kind. But there was no reason to contradict her story. I was confident this fledgling infatuation would fade as soon as the Dodgers took the field.

At the bottom of the third inning she slipped a warm hand on the inside of my thigh. Around the top of the fifth, she deflected two impressive pick-up attempts by a duo of handsome executives. By then I realized it was too late to resist. I rationalized these fleeting moments of pleasure were a karmic compensation for all the crap I'd been through. I decided to let it ride, fully aware that at any time the moment might end and I'd come crashing back to my depressing reality.

Several drinks later, she paid our bill and followed me to my house.

By the time the victorious Dodgers headed to the locker room, Renee and I were barbecuing and kissing in my back yard.

We spent the night together. Talking, about everything.

The RJ Curse

The RJ Curse has been in and out of my life since fifth grade. The first manifestation appeared when I stole a kiss from Jennifer Tenby during afternoon recess. I swear it was one sweet peck on her incredibly smooth cheek. Three hours later, while walking home, I was intercepted by big Ronnie, a.k.a. "Tank." Apparently Tank didn't like my lips anywhere near his girlfriend. (In fifth grade? Really?)

He beat the crap out of me.

Two things happened as a result of that afternoon. I made sure I didn't get anywhere near Jennifer again, and I started taking karate classes. That was a long time ago, but the pattern constantly resurfaces. Still, I refuse to admit defeat. I am a diehard, dedicated romantic. I always come back for more hoping that this time, with this woman, with this relationship, things will turn out different.

I was reveling in my newfound luck at having met this amazing woman, but recent memories of evil Evelyn kept me on the defensive. I could not think I was safe, especially if I was enjoying myself.

I had a few face-to-face mirror discussions with myself during that first day we were together. Pretending to need some private number two moments, I confronted my good fortune head on. These nose-to-nose conversations weren't about the reemergence of the RJ Curse, but revolved around Renee's choice of me as her lover. There were considerable dissimilarities in our backgrounds, our social status as well as six digit difference in our incomes...mine being zero and hers being...well, deep into six figures.

"Rick, she's not sticking around."

I flung my hands in the air. (I can be extremely dramatic when talking to myself.)

"What's wrong? I'm courteous. I shower regularly. I even know which side of the plate to put the fork."

"Hey, keep your voice down. She'll hear us. Besides, you should know that manners and cleanliness are not pluses when you're dating. They're the price of admission. How long do you think she's going to hang around watching baseball in your under-furnished man-cave?"

"It's a sixty-five inch LED for God's sake and that couch is really comfortable. Besides, she likes me."

"The couch is broken. The TV's about to be repossessed, and yes, she likes you...today. Wake up Rick, You're not the pick. You're the opening act, a spring break fling. You're the one they confess about after the wedding."

"It's deeper than that. There's chemistry between us."

"Lust is not deep chemistry. It's a hormonal imbalance."

"You'll see. My luck is about to turn and she's the one who'll prove the RJC is a thing of the past."

"That is the most ridiculous thing you've ever thought out-loud. Don't talk to me again. And clean this mirror. It's filthy."

I know why I liked her - she was smart, funny *and* sexy. I felt good when I was near her. But what did she like about me? I wasn't sure, so when I returned to the couch and settled in by her side, I asked her.

She looked at me with those killer green eyes. "I like your forearms." She ran her manicured nails along my skin. I got goose bumps. "They're strong, but not all muscled. And I like the way you hold me, here." She put her hands on her hips.

Then she ran fingers through my hair. "I love this, too - all wavy, and light, like a part-time surfer. It's different being with you, Rick. It's special. It's been a long time since I've felt this way and I like it."

* * * * *

It was Sunday afternoon, three days after Atsbee's call, two days after Renee had followed me home. She'd only been out of my sight long enough to gather fresh clothes and load us up with groceries. Over those forty-eight hours we'd spent a lot of time chatting, watching baseball and creating tasty, exotic meals as well as some tasty, exotic love making.

Fresh salmon and shrimp had been grilled and enjoyed. We were sipping martinis in our underwear, watching another Dodger game. During the commercials we'd switch between the Travel Channel and "America's Top Chef." On more than one occasion, we found ourselves in a sexually charged wrestling match. Rug burn was involved.

We chatted about music, phone apps, our likes, dislikes, and current headlines. Every couple of hours we'd digress into some kind of revealing story-telling game. The idea of "bizarre conversations" was suggested. Renee went first.

"It was August. I woke up in a Newport Beach house surrounded by a dozen naked people. I was so hung over I could barely see. I had my t-shirt on backwards and was trying to sneak out the door when everyone shouted, 'Goodbye, Renee!' My head did not stop ringing for hours. I drove down the coast to have lunch with my fiancée, but I couldn't get the image of those gorgeous, naked, tanned beach bodies out of my head.

"We were supposed to be planning a romantic Palm Springs weekend away where we could have some alone time and talk about the wedding. The entire conversation was surreal. He was trying to eliminate distant family members from the invitation list and all I could think about was the previous night's debauchery."

"What happened? Did you go?"

"Go where?"

"To Palm Springs."

"Oh, yeah. It wasn't all that romantic. We broke up a few weeks later."

She grabbed her martini and downed it. Then she bounced on the leather cushion a few times. "Okay, your turn."

I decided to go with Atsbee's party invite.

"I'd say my most recent bizarre conversation happened a couple of days ago when Greg Atsbee called me at..."

"Whoa, whoa, hold on there, lover," she said, drawing little circles counterclockwise with her index finger. "Back that one up, right to the wall. Who called you?"

"Greg Atsbee," I replied.

"Greg Atsbee. Called *you*. Here?"

I pointed to my ancient yellow touchtone surrounded by the stack of unpaid bills. "On that very phone," I said.

"Oh, how sad."

"That Greg called me?"

"No, that phone. They sell them without cords, you know. So what did multi-billionaire Greg Atsbee want? A loan? Dating advice for the over-employed?"

"He wanted me to go to a party at the Ritz-Carlton in Half Moon Bay. Do you know where that is?"

"Uh, yeah, I do, Rick. Why would Greg Atsbee invite you to his rockin' celebrity-filled over-the-top summer celebration?"

"Greg and I shared a house in college along with Bob Clay.

"Not Bob Clay the comedian."

"Yep, that Bob Clay. Greg wants to have a mini-reunion at his party. Said I can use his jet. He'll put me and a friend up at the hotel, and he talked about some kind of business deal that could help me out with my finances."

"For real? The Greg Atsbee? Owner of Keysoft?" she said with more than a little doubt.

"That's the one," I replied, perturbed that she didn't believe me, but then again, no one ever did.

"You shared a house with Greg Atsbee and Bob Clay?"

I sighed again. "Yes, I did."

She jumped to her feet, all excited. "Okay, okay. Let's go over this again and see if I've got it straight. Super-tech Greg Atsbee called you, here, on that shitty old phone, offered to put you up at the Ritz, said you could use his private jet, that you could bring a friend, wants to hang with you and the funniest man on the planet, Bob Clay. Then he invited you to his exclusive summer party and he has a deal that might help you out of your incredibly depressing lack of cash?"

I think she got it.

"It wasn't in that specific order, but that's about it. The weird thing is that he knows about Mojo's abduction and my financial situation. Oh, and his assistant is having trouble finding our fourth roommate, Scott DeVore. Seems he's in a jungle or something. I didn't quite get that part."

"Okay, so what did you tell Atsbee?"

"I told him I'd call him back."

"And?"

"That's it."

"You didn't call him?"

"I've been busy."

Renee began pacing back and forth in front of the couch, her eyes focused on the Berber we'd flatted an hour earlier. She stopped and turned, hands on her hips. "Well geeze, forget the Ritz-Carlton." Her arm swept in a wide circle, "This is the room where everyone goes to learn the secrets of personal and financial success. It has so much, how should I put it? Oh, I know - dust."

"Hey, I did the same thing he did for me, nothing."

She leaned in, her hands back on her hips. "Are you out of your freaking mind, Rick Johnson? Greg Atsbee could change your miserable, dismal life in a split second," she stopped, looking slightly embarrassed. "Oh gee, I'm so sorry, Rick," she said in a quiet voice, "That was kinda cruel and really insensitive. Let me put it another way. Greg Atsbee could *fix* your miserable, dismal life in a nanosecond."

"I thought about calling him, Renee, but if the guy didn't help me when I was desperate and losing everything, why would he help me now?"

She looked at the ceiling, index finger placed on her perfect chin. "Oh, I don't know Rick, maybe *he* was busy. The guy runs one of the most successful companies in the world. He probably has more money stuck in his couch than we've made our entire lives. And Bob Clay? Holy crap, meeting either one of them would have me on my knees, and I mean that in a good way." She paused a moment. "Oh-oh. Did it ever occur to you that one of them might be sick? What if this is the last goodbye for one of them?"

"Sick or not, hanging with those guys is not on my bucket list."

"Well, I'm telling you right now, you need a new bucket and a new list."

She fell onto the couch, put her head on my lap and looked up at me with her best puppy-dog expression, which was pretty damn good. "What about me?" she said.

"What about you?" I replied, looking down into her incredibly green eyes. She batted them several times.

"Take me, Rick. I want to go to the fancy big boy party," she said with a wicked grin. "Think about it – celebrities, movie stars, millionaires, free drinks, great rooms to fuck in, exotic food, and awesome ice sculptures. I love ice sculptures, especially ones with vodka pouring over them. This is the biggest, baddest party of the summer."

She sat up, obviously very excited. "Rick, you do know there's more to this coming-out-of-the-blue invite than some stupid dweeb stroll down memory lame. The situation is loaded with questionable motives as well as the potential of high drama and maybe some embarrassing YouTube opportunities. I love that kind of stuff. Let's go. You and me."

"Even though you know what's going to happen?"

"Yeah, yeah," she said brightly. "You'll be distracted, whooping it up with big shot Atsbee and jokester Bob Clay. I'll be left alone, plastered on free, upscale booze. Then all the rich people will start hitting on me, especially the kinky couples who've never done a redhead."

"Couples hit on you?"

"Oh please, Rick. Everyone hits on me. It's like getting invitations to a movie premiere. Most of them aren't worth your time, but you always want to be invited. Where was I?"

"Surrounded by an army of well-dressed sexual predators."

"Oh yeah. So, I'll consider one or two of the more interesting offers, because you must weigh all options when faced with a possible exchange of precious bodily fluids. Then I'll realize I'd better find you before I get into another one of those sandwich situations. I'm not even sure I can bend that far anymore."

"Then it's settled, we're not going."

"Rick, listen very carefully." She rocked her hips ever so slightly and with a hot breathy voice whispered in my ear. "I want to fly with you on a private jet and get laid at an exclusive resort."

She pulled her face away and looked directly at me. I melted a little. "Can you hear me now?" She put a hand on my shoulder. "What's the matter? Busy that weekend? Got better plans? Spending the weekend at Club Costco?"

"It would be like going to my high school reunion where I'm the biggest loser."

That one stopped her. She sat on my faux leather couch, and scrunched her lips together as she figured a new angle of attack.

"Okay, how about this? I'll play the sex kitten in your newly successful life. I'm hot and totally doable. I'll be all about how you're a sex god and insatiable. Does that work?"

Her plan totally appealed to my sense of insecurity. But I had an even bigger concern. She felt the pause.

"Rick, helloooo. This is the part where you said it's a good idea because you think I'm really hot."

"You *are* totally hot, Renee. That's why I'm worried. I'm afraid you'll be swept off your feet by some famous actor or a dashing trust fund playboy."

"Rick, I'm not going to leave you for some rich party animal."

"Oh? Who are you leaving me for?"

She didn't even pause. "Bob Clay. No questions asked. I'm taking that guy downtown and over the tracks."

"Bob Clay is gay."

"I know that. Everyone on the planet saw his crash-and-burn coming out speech. But the guy totally cracks me up." She slowly stopped giggling. "You'll feel better when you find out these guys are as messed up as everyone else."

"Greg Atsbee is not messed up."

"Yeah, right, he invites you to his exclusive summer party after he ignored you during your most desperate time. And Bob Clay? Who knows what he's up to? Trust me, all is not okay with Atsbee or the big funny man. They're probably going through some premature midlife crisis, reminiscing about the good old days that never were, or, what if, just maybe, there was something big afoot? You know, big time corporate intrigue, boardroom drama. Oh...my...God. It sounds like so much fun. Rick, we've got to go."

"You're making all this up."

"Doesn't mean it isn't true."

"Renee, I don't feel comfortable..."

"Rick, you're *never* comfortable. Let's get your cute butt to a real clothing store. I'll buy you a kick-ass tux. We'll pick up some nice shoes and get you a decent haircut. You and I are going to an exclusive, grown-up A-lister party. Then we'll find out what this asshole Atsbee is really up to. And when he least expects it, we'll shake some major coin out of him."

Plane Pain

Following instructions from Atsbee's assistant, I parked behind an unmarked brick building adjoining the Van Nuys Airport. I grabbed Renee's bags from the back of my vintage Mustang and was surprised by their weight. I lowered them to the ground. What was she bringing? Bricks? And why were there double zippers with locks on them?

"These suckers are heavy," I said, hoping for an explanation.

She shrugged, smiled, and planted a wet kiss on my lips that meant more than thanks. My body involuntarily reacted.

"No, seriously," I continued, "What are you bringing?"

She turned and titled her head. She looked like a model posing for a Guess ad. "The usual feminine accessories for traveling to an unfamiliar destination - dresses, shampoo, shoes, guns, explosives, breath mints. It's only a couple days. I'm traveling light."

She grabbed her bags and picked them up as if they were regular suitcases. "For your information, no one's allowed in this airport unless they're authorized. It's perfect for publicity-shy movie stars, egotistical executives and women who'd never get through a TSA security check because of their carry-ons."

"You're bringing contraband?"

"Of course. You always bring contraband on private planes, otherwise, what's the point?"

I had no response to that. I grabbed my Kirkland roller bag and followed her into the elegant terminal.

The room was exquisite, looking like a Beverly Hills living room complete with a fifteen-foot tall chandelier, designer furniture and imported tile.

A gravel-voiced man in a fitted European suit greeted us. "Can I help you?"

"We're here for a flight to Half Moon Bay," I answered. "Mr. Atsbee arranged it."

"You must be Mr. Johnson. Welcome."

His focus shifted to Renee. "And this is?"

"Renee Gunnison," she replied before I could react.

"Good morning to both of you. My name is Daniel. Please, leave your bags. I'll make sure they're properly stowed. Follow me. The crew is ready and waiting."

We trailed Daniel out through smoked glass double doors. Directly ahead of us was a small but sleek private jet. Two men in crisp flight uniforms stood at the bottom of the gangway. A woman in a matching skirt and white blouse was on the other side.

"Captain Edward Langdon is the gentleman to the left of the gangway," explained Daniel. "First officer Dan O'Keeffe is at his side. They'll be your pilots today. Betsy is your flight attendant."

Renee reached the steps ahead of me and wrapped her arms around Langdon.

I was not pleased with this much too-friendly greeting. Obviously I wasn't the only male in Renee's life.

Releasing him, Renee turned to O'Keeffe and shook his hand, then turned back to Langdon. A huge smile spread across her face.

"Ed, how are you?"

Ed kept his military pose, but his stone face broke into an equally friendly grin.

"Renee, you look stunning as usual. How have you been?"

She threw her head back and laughed heartily. "I'm great. How long has it been? At least a year."

"That was some trip, wasn't it?" she said.

"One of the best," he said, still wearing his award-winning smile.

"Ed, this is my good friend, Rick Johnson."

Langdon threw his hand out. Okay, this was a guy who knew how to greet someone. He could have been an actor and unable to fly a damn thing, but he made me feel secure. I liked him immediately.

"Welcome aboard, Rick," said Langdon in a hearty voice that rang of smoky whisky bars and daring escapes, "It is a pleasure to meet you. Any friend of Renee's is a very lucky man."

Renee put her arm around me. "And I am a very lucky woman," she said, patting my chest, "This guy is the best."

Renee's compliment made me smile. Perhaps my concerns about impending trouble were illusions of the past. Could it be that the RJC storms had passed? If this was the way the weekend was going to go, it was going to be an awesome experience. Then again, the Ed/Renee connection bothered me.

"This is our flight attendant, Betsy Holt," said Ed.

"Hello, Betsy," said Renee.

"It's a pleasure, Ms. Gunnison."

I could tell that Renee was done with the runway chit-chat. She looked at everyone, then clapped her hands and rubbed them together. "All righty then. Let's get this party in the air, in a glass and down the hatch. This sunlight is way too bright for my delicate ginger skin."

She ran up the gangway. I followed her and entered the cabin. She sat in one of the white leather seats and swiveled in a circle, pointed toes powered her rotation. "This is going to be so much fun," she whispered excitedly.

I nodded in agreement but confronted her with my concerns. "How do you know Ed?"

Renee looked around to make sure the crew was still outside. "I dated a professional baseball player."

"Ed plays baseball?"

"No silly, he was our pilot."

"Oh, was the baseball player anyone I'd know?"

"Probably, batted .340 on the field but was like .780 under the sheets. Unfortunately he acted more like a free agent than a team player. I also had the questionable pleasure of sitting in the wives' section for the first half of the season. Man, that place is dangerous."

"Cat fights?

"The worst. Foul balls, foul language, foul play. Ed was my player's favorite pilot. Got us out of a couple of dicey situations and to the ball field just in time for warm-ups. Not only can he fly any plane on the planet, he can use a pool cue, fight like a son-of-a-bitch, and drinks like a fish...when he's not in the cockpit...well most of the time. Maybe after the party he'll take us to Chicago. There's a club there we used to visit. There are so many places I want you to see."

Ed sounded like a real life Indiana Jones. I bet he had some wild stories, most likely a few that included Renee.

I took a breath and looked around. There wasn't anything threatening or slightly out of the ordinary except the evidence of extreme wealth.

Something outside the plane caught Renee's attention. She pointed to the oval window. Walking out of the hangar was one of my ex-roommates. Broad-shouldered and strutting toward the plane was Scott DeVore. With his wide smile and triangular shaped torso, accented by a tailored silk shirt, he looked like the next James Bond...villain.

"That must be Scott. I'd recognize Bob Clay," said Renee.

I glanced over to her. "You're right. Bob's a lot bigger than that."

Scott entered the cabin with a look of disappointment. "Learjets are okay, but they're definitely not Gulfstreams. Hey, Rick Johnson! I hardly recognized you."

I stood. Scott grabbed my hand a little too hard, as if trying to impress. That wasn't going to work. I lived with the guy for a year. I knew exactly who he was. A chameleon can change its colors, but a leopard can't lose its spots. This guy was a carnivore and he moved fast.

"My girlfriend, Renee Gunnison." I said, hoping he wouldn't say something stupid. He was never known for being *suave*.

Scott nodded in Renee's direction. In one glance, he undressed her and then dismissed her. Maybe he realized Renee wasn't going to offer him anything.

Betsy entered the cabin, followed by the two pilots. Ed winked at Renee before ducking into the cockpit. That bothered me, but it was just another reminder that Renee was her own person, with past relationships, just like me.

"Can I get either of you something to drink?" Betsy offered, interrupting my mental musings of what mischief Renee and Ed had gotten into.

Renee didn't miss a beat. "Stoli Elite straight up, two olives, please." She threw a sly smile my way. I could tell she'd turned on the party music in her head.

"What can I get you, Scott?" Betsy asked.

Scott checked Betsy top to bottom and lingered in the middle before making eye contact. "Macallan 25?"

"Sure," Betsy replied, ignoring Scott's leer.

"Make it a double," Scott said dismissively to her back.

"So Rick, what about our ex-roommate being a corporate sage?" Scott leaned forward in his seat, keeping his voice low. What was he doing? Renee was sitting right next to me.

"I've heard Greg's incredibly cheap. I'm not sure if he gave anything to the college."

"Scott, they named a building after him."

"Did you ever consider the school *said* he gave them the money? He's their only famous graduate. Maybe they did it for the PR."

"Have you talked to him recently?" I asked.

"We had lunch a few years back. Never got any business. The guy's an expert at playing the nice guy, but he never comes through."

Betsy handed Scott his drink, leaning over so far I swear Scott was going to jump down her cleavage.

"Here you go, Scott. Can I get you anything else?"

Scott took the glass and continued to stare down Betsy's blouse for what seemed like an entire minute, which in Learjet cabin time is like six months. She remained there, allowing him full viewing rights until he tasted his drink.

"This will be fine," he said finally.

Betsy turned to me and started to give me the lean-over, but stopped midway when she realized Renee was watching her every move.

She handed us our drinks and returned to the galley. We hadn't left the ground and I was already done with this plane insanity.

"So what do you do, Rick?" Scott asked.

I considered telling him that I was an art curator, or an investment banker, but I knew he'd Google me the minute we landed. I decide to go with honesty. It'd worked before.

"I'm a personal trainer and I sell gym equipment on the side."

"Impressive," he said.

He was lying. He wasn't impressed in the least.

Renee jumped in before I could continue. "Rick's lined up financing for seven fitness superstores in the L.A. area. His clients are dumping their gym memberships and installing exercise rooms using his custom-made gear. He's so backordered he hasn't had time to open the brick and mortar locations. Now, established gyms are ordering his line of equipment. He's got them coming and going."

I looked over to Renee in silent thanks.

"Bet you never sold Greg anything," Scott said with a crooked smile.

"I will, eventually," I said, piling on to Renee's story. "Sometimes going too fast gets you back where you started in a hurry."

"That's bullshit," said Scott leaning in with unexpected intensity. "I make the call, do the pitch, close the deal, and deposit the check. It's the way of the world, Rick. Winners take it from the losers."

I wasn't getting into an argument with a guy who'd made a career of questionable life choices. Even in college Scott had a habit of having a copy of the chemistry final in his desk or a roofied coed in his bed. He might be raking in the dough, but in my heart I knew he was doing something immoral, illegal or both.

"Pulling down a couple hundred grand in a week is a powerful feeling," he continued, his fist clenched tight in front of him. "Makes you feel alive. Like a warrior. You're not into that, are you, Rick? You're more of a cable TV guy. Use that remote a lot, I bet."

Renee purposefully put her hand behind my head and played with my hair. Then she signaled Betsy that she was ready for a refill.

Scott did the same.

"Nice to see a woman who can keep up."

Renee smiled that killer smile.

"Oh, Scott," she said in a less than friendly voice, "You have no idea."

What's in a Name?

Fifteen minutes from the Half Moon Bay airport, an hour south of San Francisco, the majestic Ritz-Carlton Hotel sits on an ocean bluff surrounded by manicured grounds and a peaceful golf course. Built in the late nineteen-nineties, the high-end resort was designed to blend into the low key community, rather than dominate the landscape. The plan failed miserably.

Renee and I walked into the elegant lobby, following Scott. High ceilings and inlaid floors were barely noticed, overshadowed by an expansive view of the Pacific Ocean directly ahead. Groups of well-dressed people clustered here and there, probably multi-millionaire Atsbee invitees.

"Hey! Guys! Over here!" A booming voice echoed through the large foyer. Every head in the place turned.

Gliding toward us, in a festive, oversized Hawaiian shirt that was so bright it nearly blinded me, was three hundred fifty pounds of grinning Bob Clay, former star of three popular, nationally acclaimed TV sitcoms.

Bob spotted Scott's disapproving scowl and altered his incoming approach. He shuffled toward me with outstretched arms.

"Rick! Hey! Rick Johnson! How the hell are you, RJ?" he shouted.

Out of the corner of my eye, I noticed two men turn in our direction. I didn't think much of it, as everyone was watching Bob's grandiose entrance. Sporting long black overcoats and with scowls to match, they looked like they'd returned from a midnight screening of the sci-fi movie "The Matrix."

I shifted my focus from the dark duo and offered Bob an outstretched hand. He brushed it aside and wrapped me up in a hug that lifted me off the ground like an enthusiastic grandparent greeting a kid. Releasing me he looked at Renee with a devious grin.

"Well, hello, Mama. Could you be the famous and extremely red-haired Renee Gunnison of New York's NYU and international jet set fame?"

Renee was not happy with this revelation.

"How did you know I went to NYU? Have you been Facebook stalking?"

Hands on his hips, Bob struck a pose. "Oh my God, you have to *ask*? Renee, my love, I have so much to teach you about..." He took a dramatic pause and pointed his fingers at his chest. "...Moi! Not to worry, I'm an expert on the subject. Call me Bob. It feels like I know you already...probably because I do." He laughed loudly at his own joke, and then turned to Scott. "Well, it seems our girlfriend here suffers from an abundance of homophobes. Afraid of a little self-discovery, Scottie, me boy?"

"I'm not afraid of homosexuals, Bob. I am revolted by deviant lifestyles."

Bob clapped his hands several times close to his chest. "Way to go, Super Scottie. Hating those who are different is a time-honored American tradition. Ask any Mormon, Muslim or midget. FYI, I happen to find *your* deviant lifestyle more than revolting."

"What would you know about my lifestyle?"

"Oh pleeeese," said Bob, as he circled Scott, "I know everything. I'm a nosy gay man with waaaay too much time on my hands. I figured if I was going to be rubbing extremities with my ex-roommates I should find out who they are. And if you happen to be Pi-curious, unscrupulous P.I.'s are extremely affordable these days."

"You wasted your money," said Scott dismissively, but something about Bob's announcement made him visibly unnerved.

"Au contraire, my balding friend. You're a fascinating character with dark secrets, a criminal income, and mating rituals that are illegal in every country you've visited." Bob straightened his shirt and smiled. "But enough about you, little man. What is the great and powerful Atsbee doing inviting three losers to his annual elegant event? From my extensive research, Renee's the only one here with enough class to qualify as an official invitee."

"Um, thanks, Bob, I think," she said.

Scott shifted his weight from one foot to the other. "I have no idea what Greg is up to having us all come here. Do you?"

Bob looked at the ceiling with his finger on his chin.

"The last time I talked to him I was staring in 'Overland.' Remember that piece of shit? A prairie sitcom for God's sake. Fat men riding horses - why would anyone want to watch such a ridiculous spectacle? Suck me dry if we weren't top ten TV for three years running. Greg called around that time. We had some nice conversations. No matter what you think, Greg Atsbee's intentions can be nothing but sincere and profitable. I'm always hoping for a couple Atsbee coins to be thrown my way, and I'm sure he has a few he doesn't need. Billionaires can be so, you know, rich."

A tall brunette in a tailored business suit appeared from an office door. Walking with an easy grace, she crossed the polished floor and joined us.

"Gentlemen, may I have your attention?"

She might have been attractive and dressed like a movie star's trophy wife, but I knew the sound of a control freak when I heard one.

"I'm Traye, Greg's administrative assistant. It's a pleasure to meet you."

This woman didn't like us one bit. I wasn't real keen on her either.

"You must be Renee," she said, "Pleased to meet you."

Ouch. She didn't like Renee, either. That was crazy. Everyone liked Renee. Had we done something wrong? I knew that Bob's shirt was embarrassing, but I thought gay comedians had a permanent fashion pass.

"The pleasure's all mine," said Renee countering with a voice so cold I felt ice forming on my shoulder. In another time and place this would have been a hair-pulling, eye-scratching cat fight. For some reason, they chose not to engage.

Traye turned to face us. Her delivery turned monotone and sounded like she was reading from a script.

"Welcome, ex-college roommates. Please listen carefully. Greg has left Denver and will be here in about an hour. Tonight's party starts at nine in the main ballroom. That gives you plenty of time to get reacquainted and..." she looked us up and down, "...changed into appropriate attire. Greg would like to meet the three of you when he gets settled, so prepare yourselves accordingly. As a reminder, Mr. Atsbee is generously covering all your expenses here at the hotel, but your personal entertainment needs are..." she looked directly at Bob "...your responsibility."

Bob looked behind him. Realizing there was no one in back of him he returned his focus to the group. "Who? Me?"

Traye stared at him, expressionless. "Robert Clay, you're not the only one who can hire a private investigator. Getting two dozen New York pizzas to a secure set in Hawaii with vials of cocaine hidden in the crust is no easy task, even for a top billed actor."

Bob scanned the lobby as if he expected the police to pounce. Then he returned his focus to us. "Only three people knew about that," he confided, then realized a few more were in on it. "You're right. It wasn't easy, but if you did your research, you'd know that event turned out to be *the* party of the summer. They're still talking about it along the North Shore."

"You're right, Bob," she replied, "They are still talking about it. Not all of it in a positive light. I also know you've had quite a number of other adventures we won't be discussing here. So, although this address is known to many of the local *entertainment* providers, Greg is not paying for any of those services and he does not want you embarrassing him on his special weekend. Is that understood?"

"Got it," said Bob with a wink followed by two thumbs up.

Traye shot Bob a look, and then handed out elegantly addressed envelopes. "Here are my phone numbers. There's also information about tonight's event."

With her business concluded, she turned and headed back to the hotel office.

Bob looked at us with a puzzled frown. "How did she know I hired a detective?"

"Because she had you investigated, you idiot," snarled Scott.

Renee added her opinion. "Maybe you and Traye hired the same investigator. He could be the country's go-to dick."

I was totally unsuccessful at stifling a chuckle, but her attempt at humor was met with stony silence from both Bob and Scott. Maybe Bob didn't like the competition, and Scott, well, I didn't expect anything but disapproval from him. They both turned and headed to the registration desk, making sure they kept their distance.

The two strange men I'd noticed earlier sauntered to my side. I wasn't excited about their arrival, but played it cool.

"Are you Richard Johnson?" said one of them.

I turned to face them. "Yes, can I help you?"

"Your initials are RJ, right?"

What's with that? Couldn't they spell? I took another good look at them. These guys did not belong in this lobby, or anywhere on the grounds. Their clothes, slouched posture, facial scars, worn shoes and questionable dental work indicated a less than cultured upbringing. Call me an elitist, but I believe there is a minimum level of personal presentation required in the registration area of a Ritz-Carlton hotel.

"Could we have a word with you, RJ? Alone?" asked the taller of the two matrix men. He nodded toward an isolated portion of the lobby.

I was more than confident I could take these delinquents if it came to a fight, but then it dawned on me this might be the financial opportunity Atsbee had mentioned.

The shorter of the two raincoat rejects looked over to Renee and gave her a broad smile, revealing a collection of yellow stained-teeth, several of which had left the premises. "Short business 'scussion," he said, with a wink, "We'll bring 'im right back."

The three of us walked to the far end of the lobby.

"Everything okay?" asked the short man in a hushed tone.

It only took me a second to notice the guy had a glass eye. It remained completely motionless while the working one darted everywhere. "No incidents? Nothing suspicious going on? Everything cool?" he continued.

I had no idea what could go wrong with a short flight from Van Nuys, but he was obviously concerned.

"Nothing unusual other than dealing with a flaming asshole." I said confidently.

The short guy nodded as his one eye scoured the floor, walls and ceiling. "Yeah, this place is crawling with 'em. It's like a giant asshole magnet."

The taller of the two handed me a brown envelope with two hand written letters in thick black ink: RJ.

"The instructions are inside. Remember, this job is not to be taken lightly. You don't have a great track record, you know."

The guy had a point. I wanted to tell them that I'd just hit a bad patch in my life and things were improving, but decided not to complicate matters.

"Not a problem," I said, taking the package, "It's under control. Anything else I should know? Are you guys staying here tonight? Going to the party?"

The one-eyed man shook his head. "Fuck no. This place gives me the creeps. It's like 'The Shining,' with more people. Look, RJ you needed a way out of your financial situation. This is it. And keep in mind that there's no way you'd get this cushy gig if you didn't have major connections."

They were right. Knowing Atsbee had advantages. I decided to have a little fun with the men in black.

"It is always important to have vertically oriented social connections that can help your cause and move you to the head of the line. But of course you knew that."

The tall man produced a cell phone. "Stand next to Barry and hold the envelope."

"Why the photo?" I asked, suspecting something sinister.

"Proof of delivery," was the answer.

"Okay," I said, shrugging my shoulders.

The flash nearly blinded me. I waited while they checked the photo. I could tell they weren't happy.

"Barry doesn't like the picture. It looks like he's staring at the ceiling."

They showed me the picture. Barry's eye had taken off on its own and was aimed somewhere above and to the left of the camera. He looked like a madman.

"You're right," I agreed. "We should do another."

"Happens more than you think, RJ," said Barry, "Sometimes it takes fifteen minutes to make a decent photo."

I believed him. The way that eyeball rotated I was surprised any picture came out right. I was going to make a suggestion they should switch jobs and let Barry be in the photo. His eyes seemed to work fine, even if they were a little jaundiced. Again I decided it was better not to get into their business. This second time I smiled broadly. If these guys cared so much about how they looked, I figured I should too.

They checked the phone. Satisfied with the results, Cyclops Barry slapped me on the back. "Okay, RJ we're out of here. Don't mess this up. A lot of people are counting on you. And remember, if you try something stupid like making your own arrangements, a very angry Joey will find you and you will die, very painfully, very slowly." He leaned into me, our noses inches apart. His breath was so foul I nearly choked. "But of course you knew that."

I put the envelope in my pocket and returned to Renee's side. Bob rejoined us as Renee watched the raincoat men leave the hotel. Then she turned to me.

"Those guys look like hit men from 'The Sopranos' and not the ones who survive."

I patted my pocket confidently. "Delivery flunkies from Greg. Sounds like an easy courier thing with a big payday. They acted all tough but they were such bad actors I almost laughed."

"It's about time things started going your way," said Bob. "I've heard that fitness training isn't all that lucrative. Take it home, big guy. Full throttle."

I gave him a puzzled look. Bob seemed to know a lot about everyone.

"Sorry, little buddy, gotta call 'em the way I see 'em. So far you've been between a rock and a hard-on."

He kissed Renee on the cheek. "Later, beautiful. I'm going to my room and hit the dishonor bar." He held a fist to his ear, thumb and index finger extended. "Call me." With that, he left.

Renee glanced back to me. "What do you make of all this?"

"Haven't quite figured it out," I said as Bob waddled down the high-ceilinged hardwood hallway.

"I know one more thing," she said.

"And that is?"

Renee smiled. "There's a shitload of trouble headed our way."

"You think so?"

"Definitely." Her eyes were wide with excitement, "I can't wait."

An Unwanted Guest

Renee and I entered the hotel suite. Our suitcases had been delivered. The air-conditioning was set to perfect. The room had all the hotel stuff - widescreen TV, couch, iPad on the desk, cushy chairs, and of course, the honor bar. Straight ahead was a balcony that looked onto the Pacific. I don't mean a sliver of water around the corner. The words "ocean view" did not adequately describe this vista.

In the back of the suite was a decent-sized guest bedroom with two queen beds and a bathroom decorated nicer than most houses I'd been in. The master bedroom had a gorgeous four poster king bed that allowed a two hundred degree view that traveled from the bluff to the ocean and continued to a golf course fairway.

Last but not least, the master bath had one of those glass showers and a separate Jacuzzi tub with two bazillion water jets.

"This place is as big as a house," I said.

Renee was not as impressed. "It's comfortable, but nowhere near as huge as some suites in Vegas. Check this out. It's Jean Marc XO vodka and some awesome martini glasses. It's been in the freezer, and it has a welcome card."

"Pour me one of those," I said.

She did and handed me the brimming drink. "Did you piss Traye off? Why was she so rude?"

"She's a snob," I said, "She'd rather deal with executives and celebrities than the riff-raff from Greg's college days. She wasn't all that nice when she first called either. " I looked at Renee standing in front of me, martini in hand. "So tell me, lover girl, what do you need this weekend?"

She walked to the wood-framed window and gazed at the Pacific Ocean.

"I want something I haven't felt in years."

I walked to her side. "And that is?"

"I want to feel safe, secure and loved. Do you think you can handle that, Rick?"

I hadn't felt so protective and powerful since I'd been in the army. "I can get you to that place," I said with confidence.

Renee let the moment hang. Maybe she didn't believe me. Maybe she was basking in the warmth of security, or the buzz of the drink. I sensed her shift away from romance.

"I think it's time to look at the package the men-in-black gave you."

"Yeah, I guess we should check that bad boy out." I said, disappointed we hadn't started to tear each other's clothes off. I hoped that would come sooner rather than later. It'd only been a couple of hours since our last entanglement, but she lit me up all the time.

I pulled the envelope from my jacket pocket and peered into the yellow packet. "It looks like an iPhone and a note."

"Dump it here."

I poured a folded note and a white cell phone onto the mahogany coffee table. I picked up the note. Hand printed in block letters, it looked like a six year old wrote it. I read it out loud.

"RJ, go to the party. After the guy from Boeing shows up and gives you a second phone, bring them to the airport. Seventy grand cash will be there. Don't mess this up."

"Seems easy enough," I said, "I'll have Mojo back and mom's rent paid before the end of the week."

Renee took the paper and examined it. She put a hand on her hip, still holding the note, and puffed an imaginary cigar. "Itz a breeze, Mike. Ya zip down the road. Do da delivery. B*ada-bing bada-boom*, you got youseself seventy G's. Den we partee with da penguins and da skirts."

She picked up the device and examined it. "I wonder what they're using it for. It's password protected. Hey, want to see something ridiculous?"

"Sure."

She put the iPhone on the coffee table and pulled another from her pocket "They look the same."

I reached into my pocket and pulled out the phone Renee bought me for the trip. It was a third match.

Renee disappeared into the bedroom and returned with her laptop and a white Apple USB cord. "I bet there's some kind of data stored on it."

The house phone rang. I picked it up.

"Hello?"

"Rick, this is Traye. Greg wants to meet you in two hours. First floor. In the Board Room. No Hawaiian shirts."

"I'll be there."

She hung up without saying goodbye.

"I'm meeting Greg in two hours," I told her, "It's in a room on the first floor and Traye hates Bob's shirt."

Renee glanced at me. "Who wouldn't? That tent is brighter than the sun. Speaking of Bob, see if he's going to this meet and greet. If he is, I'll have to make my own plans."

I picked up the phone and dialed the hotel operator. "Can you connect me to Bob Clay's room?"

"You'd like to talk to Mr. Clay?"

"Yes, I would."

I heard some rustling and then a muffled, "What's with the headsets? Don't you have a real phone around here? These things are fucking toys. Hey Rick, it's Bob."

"Where the hell are you, Bob?"

"In the hotel phone room working on my detective skills. I'm taking the California Private Investigator license test this fall. I figured it was time to do something productive with the rest of my life so I'm changing careers."

"I'm not sure what you mean, Bob."

"Don't you know what a P.I. is?"

"Of course. It's pie without the 'e' on the end."

"Hey, buddy, watch it," he said sternly, "Let's leave the humor to the professionals, okay? Now listen up, I've been training to be a gumshoe investigator for almost four months. I skim Investigator Monthly, drive around looking at stuff, do surveillance on people I don't know. Last month I went to the PI super conference down in San Diego. Got a couple of badges and everything."

"Good for you Bob, I wish you all the best."

I didn't think a Private Investigator was the best career choice for an infamous, three hundred fifty-pound ex-comedian. Then again, I'd never bet against Bob Clay, except on his losing weight or being serious for more than fifteen seconds.

"Bob, were you invited to this meeting with Atsbee?"

"Oh yeah. Got that covered like a wet blanket. But I've come across some very disturbing information that concerns you and Renee. Be up in a minute. Don't go away."

I replaced the receiver and turned to Renee who was refilling our glasses.

"Bob's coming to talk to us," I explained, settling on the couch, "He's discovered some..." I made quotation signs with my fingers, "disturbing information... about us and mumbled something about training to be a private investigator. Apparently he's been listening in on hotel phone conversations."

"He's up to something, digging into everyone's past. I'm not sure I'd trust him. Did he say if he was going to the Atsbee meeting?"

"Yeah, he's going."

The phone rang again. I picked it up.

"Rick, it's Traye. Let me speak to Renee."

"For you," I said, handing her the phone.

After a brief conversation, Renee hung up.

"The Traye bitch-witch wants me to go a freakin' horny-boy mixer while you're playing kiss-ass with Atsbee." She drained her glass.

I gave her the concerned-friend look. "You should take it easy with that stuff. It's going to be a long night."

She shot me a "fuck you" look back. "And you need to lighten up, *Dad.*"

There was a loud knock at the door. Renee nodded. "Why don't you let Bob in while I take care of the evidence." She grabbed the phones and put them in her purse as I crossed the room.

I flipped the latch and turned the handle. The door was violently shoved inward and I was pushed backwards. Rushing into the room was a short, tattooed hoodlum. He slammed the door behind him and pointed a long barreled pistol at me, then at Renee, then back to me. His stained cargo shorts and torn t-shirt combined with the scar along the side of his face made him look like a B-movie bad guy.

"Let's not do anything hasty," I said, holding my hands up.

"Wow, that is a really cool gun," came a breathy female voice.

The intruder and I turned simultaneously.

Renee shifted her weight causing her hips to swing suggestively. "Oh, yeah, that is really, totally cool and it looks, um, you know, big," she said chewing gum, "Hey, can I touch it? I promise I'll be gentle."

I could not believe it. Renee had transformed into a clueless red-headed bimbo.

"No, you can't touch my gun," the intruder growled, "Ya think I'm stupid?"

"Aw gee, no. I thought you were really smart coming in the door like that. It was so inventive and powerful. Creative even. Are you an actor?"

The guy shifted his focus back and forth between Renee and me not sure if I was a serious threat or if Renee was going to grab his piece.

"The phone. Give it," he demanded.

"Holy cow, what are you talking about?" said Renee.

"The phone. The one your boyfriend got in the lobby. Where is it?"

"Boyfriend? Geee, no. My boyfriend's in jail. This guy over there? He ain't my boyfriend. He's just a guy I have sex with."

"Lady, I don't care who you have sex with. Hand over the phone."

"Oh, *that* phone." Renee rummaged around in her purse. "Yeah, yeah, I got it here somewhere. Hold your horses, okay? Geeze, what a mess. I gotta clean this out someday. It's a freakin' disaster."

"Don't try anything funny."

"Oh, no, I can't do comedy." She produced one of the iPhones. "I thought it was a present. I get lots of presents but they're usually jewelry or see-thru clothing if you know what I mean."

The guy grabbed the phone.

Renee twirled a strand of red hair around her finger, chewing on her imaginary gum. "Hey, do you want to hang out? We're having a party. Somebody left some vodka. It's really good."

"I hate that sissy stuff," he said and spat on the floor.

Renee was appalled. "Oh yuk, were you raised in a barn or something?"

"You're a cheeky little bitch, aren't you?"

She made a little hop for no apparent reason. "Yeah, it's 'cause I work in communications," she said in her new voice.

"Well communicate this. Tell that needle freak Joey that he's been cut out of the loop. Somebody else is making the delivery and getting the payoff."

"Sure, I could do that. I'm an expert at that kinda stuff, 'cause you know I work in communications. Oh, I told ya that already, huh, didn't I? Tee hee. So, is Joey in the hotel? He's cute ain't he? Does he have a girlfriend? Bet he does, but who cares, ya know? Most guys don't."

The guy turned to face me.

"RJ knows Joey, don't you, RJ."

I'd never met a Joey in my life, but I nodded in agreement. "Sure, Joey. The guy on the TV show 'Friends.' What's he up to?"

"Not that Joey, you idiot. Hey, wait a minute. You ain't RJ. You got no sideburns."

"Shaved 'em. Last night," I explained quickly.

"Huh." The man squinted. "Damn cheap Lasik eye surgery. Can't see shit. I knew that guy was a crook...but wait...you still ain't RJ."

"What? Are you high?" I said with conviction, "You sure aren't seeing too good. You got totally ripped off."

He took another squint, wrinkling his nose. "No, fer sure you ain't RJ. Yer too good-looking. And you're a jerk. And a fake. I hate fakers, especially when they're trying to steal stuff we already stole."

56

A half empty bottle of vodka flew across the room, bounced off his head and knocked him sideways.

"What the..."

Instinctively I smashed my fist into the guy's jaw with everything I had. The impact stung, but I knew I'd done some serious damage. The gunman staggered but stayed on his feet. He tightened his grip on the weapon. Although he couldn't see a thing, he was about to shoot.

Renee slammed her foot into the back of the guy's leg, then wrapped an electrical cord around his neck and pulled it taut dragging him backwards.

I dove to the ground as two silenced shots ripped over my head and buried into the wall behind me.

The intruder dropped the gun and struggled to pull the cord away from his windpipe. Renee was having her own difficulties. The wire was tangled up with a floor lamp and the shade kept bopping her in the head. She would push the lamp aside, but it would stubbornly return to hit her.

I scrambled to the floor, trying to reach the gun which had skittered under the couch.

All I heard was the sing-song sound of the fight. The guy grunted, the shade bopped, she swore, and thwacked the lampshade aside. Grunt, bop, shit, thwack. Grunt, bop, crap, thwack. Grunt, bop, fuck, thwack.

I gave up trying to locate the gun and jumped to my feet. At the same time Renee released her grip on the cord and angrily shoved the lamp onto its side.

The assailant twisted out of her grasp and staggered backwards. Between Renee wrapping the cord around his neck and his additional twirling, he was in a dangerous situation. The far end of the cord was solidly wrapped around a heavy mahogany desk, but he didn't seem to notice.

The three of us stood there facing each other for a brief moment, then he muttered "You bitch!" and made a colossal lunge toward her.

I wasn't about to let this derelict touch her. I leapt into the air to block him. The electrical cord pulled taught. A sharp snap came from the man's neck and he stopped mid-flight and yanked to the floor. With nothing to intercept, I flew across the room and landed hard on my chest. I turned to see him twitch several times and then he stopped moving.

Renee was panting, bent over, hands on her knees.

"Are you okay?" I asked getting to my feet.

She straightened up, grabbed my drink from the counter, and downed it.

"Thank God I didn't have my dress on," she sputtered wiping her mouth with the back of her hand, "Bastard would have ruined it."

"What would you have done then? Killed him?"

Renee put the glass down, grabbed my shirt and threw me onto the couch.

"Okay, Rick, why was that guy here?"

I opened and closed my fingers, checking for damage. I hadn't hit anyone in years, but the sensation felt familiar. Years-old Army Ranger training stored in my muscles surfaced quickly and was apparently ready for use. Satisfied I was unharmed, I looked at her.

"I don't know, maybe he wanted to upgrade his phone."

Then it dawned on me. No one wanted to kill *me*. The only people who knew I even existed were a half dozen bill collectors. But Renee sure seemed to know what to do about a guy holding a gun.

"Renee, the only reason I'm in this suite is because you started whining about meeting Bob Clay and going to some fancy dress-up party with a big ice sculpture."

She straightened up, offended. "I did not whine. When I whine, you'll know it. And trust me, you won't like it."

"That was definitely a whine. You sounded like a spoiled child."

There was fire in her eyes, but I was sure it was an act, like her gangster impersonation and her baby doll performance.

"You've got it all wrong, buddy," she said, "I merely pointed out that turning down an opportunity to talk to Greg Atsbee was stupid considering your messed up financial situation. Now, tell me, where did you learn to fight like that? Are you on some kind of secret mission?"

"Oh yeah, I got my decoder ring right here. What are you talking about? Who goes on a secret mission? What world do you live in?"

"Nobody fights like that unless they've been trained."

"I was an Army Ranger, many years ago. And what about you? You can kill a guy and be fine sitting on a bed with his body lying five feet away?"

Renee stood up, walked over to the inert figure and kicked him. It wasn't a tap either. She hauled off and ruined the dead man's kidney.

"I was date-raped when I was seventeen," she said, staring at the lifeless corpse, "Every day, for years, I took intensive self-defense classes and later, when I was attacked in a parking garage, I made that man suffer so badly he was barely alive when I left him. Probably still can't walk. I know for sure he can't have kids. Don't get me wrong, I love guys, but I don't put up with their bullshit."

"I guess I've been lucky."

She walked back to the couch and kissed me on the lips. "Honey, you've been more than lucky."

"That doesn't explain how you took on that guy," I said.

"It doesn't explain why he was coming into *your* room," she countered.

There was another knock at the door. Renee and I looked at each other.

"We are going to revisit this discussion," I said. "There are a lot of questions that haven't been answered."

She was all attitude. "And I've got a few questions for you, Mr. Johnson."

I looked down at the lifeless man on the floor. "What should we do with him?"

Renee gave him another swift kick. This time she cracked a rib. "Cockroach. Let's drop him in the bathtub."

It only took a moment to deposit the body in the deep Jacuzzi. On the way back to the living area, she reached into her suitcase and pulled out a mean-looking handgun.

"Hold on a second!" she yelled at the unopened door.

The evening had shifted into something bizarre. Renee had accused me of being the reason for the attack, and then pulled a handgun from her luggage. Who knew what other weapons she'd brought in her super-heavy bags? I wasn't sure who was more dangerous, Renee or the stranger in the hallway.

"You might need this. That other one is a little too big and clumsy."

She turned the gun and offered me the handle. This lowered my Renee fear factor a bit, but I was not happy that she was packing heat. I pulled the clip out of the handle, made sure it was full, then slammed it back into place. "Thanks."

I stuffed the gun in my belt, and pulled my shirt out to cover it.

"Use the peephole," Renee reminded me.

"It's Bob," I said.

The huge comedian filled the entire field of vision of the tiny viewfinder. There could have been an armed gang of jugglers behind him, but there was no way to tell. I took the risk and opened the door. He waltzed into the room with a hint of a drag queen.

"Hell's bells, what took you guys so long?"

Renee answered quickly. "We were in the bedroom, taking care of some, um, personal business." She threw him a wicked smile and added a wink. "You know what I'm talking about, don't you Bob?"

He countered with his own sly grin. "Ohhhhhhh, okay, I got it." He chuckled to himself, and then stopped mid-laugh. His smile disappeared. His expression turned serious and gave Renee a full scan from her shoes to the top of her red head.

My body tensed. I was ready to pull Renee's gun if he made a move toward either of us. I already regretted not checking to see if the safety was engaged.

"Wait a bed-hopping minute," he said, looking angry, but not the least bit threatening. Hands on hips, he struck a pose similar to the one he did in the lobby. "Do I look like an idiot? Wait, don't answer that."

Renee was acting all innocent. I half expected her to start the bimbo act again. "Something wrong, Bob?"

"You guys weren't fooling around. Your clothes are all buttoned right and you aren't acting any more stupid than normal. No way you were doing anything that involved procreation, recreation or deprivation. I didn't just fall of the tulip truck, you know."

"You mean turnip truck," I corrected him.

"Turnip, tulip, it's a fucking truck with something that starts with a 'T,' okay? You guys are up to something and it doesn't have anything to do with the wild thing, or sex for that matter."

Before either of us could stop him, Bob waddled into the master bedroom, looked around, and then rushed into the bathroom. We followed close behind.

"Aha! I knew it!" He said triumphantly, pointing at the inert body. "You *were* hiding something." His eyes lit up. "I am going to be such an awesome detective. Better than Helen Keller and Ironsides combined. But this begs the obvious question - why was that man taking a bath so close to the start of the party? Not only would he be late, his clothes aren't laid out. This is all so wrong. I wish I had my notepad."

"You can use the hotel stationery." I offered. He ignored me.

Renee came to his side. "This idiot barged into our room and threatened to kill us if we didn't give him the phone that Rick got in the lobby."

"Rick got a phone? No one told me there was swag."

"Do you recognize him?" I asked.

Bob bent over and took a close look at the dead man; then straightened up in horror. He put his hands on his face. "Holy crap! I don't believe it!"

Renee's concerned. "What is it? Do you know him?"

"That's my gardener!"

"No way!"

"Naw, I was just kidding. It's a habit I have, making jokes. It's an obsession I can't seem to shake."

Renee was not amused. "Cut it out, Bob. This is serious."

"You're right. This is serious. No, I've never seen this man before in my life," he continued, standing over the man. "From the looks of those hideous shorts, lack of decent hair product and dirt under his fingernails, I'm fairly confident we travel in different social circles. I don't think he's gay, but I've been wrong about that before. Some of these guys are so deep in the closet they never find their way out. Still, I'm not surprised this happened after what I heard."

Bob turned, grabbed our hands and led us back to the living area. "Come on, *chillun*," he said in a fake Southern accent. "Uncle Bob has some amazin' stories to tell ya."

Guns and Drugs

Bob plopped down in the middle of the couch, and patted the cushions on either side of him. Renee and I cautiously sat down. Bob looked at me, then did a one-eighty and raised his eyebrows at Renee. He took a deep breath and sighed.

"This room is awesome. I am so jealous. But I must tell you that even though you have the best digs in the place, you're both in very deep doo-doo."

"We kinda guessed that after what happened," said Renee, "although doo-doo was not the first word that came to mind. Danger was more like it."

"Glad you're on board with the imminent threat thing. It's actually kinda exciting, especially since it has nothing to do with me," he said with a smile. "I told you I investigated everyone before I came."

"I know, Bob and I thought that was creepy–weird," said Renee.

"Hmmm, maybe you know me better than I thought. No matter, it's the cross I must bear as I enter the life of a professional Private Investigator. Anyway, besides the fact that Rick is quite the binge drinker, which I respect and admire, there's something you both should know." He lowered his voice to a whisper. "There's going to be a lot of weird stuff happening tonight. It's kinda unsafe and I'm not talking about STDs or unprotected sex."

"You're kidding," Renee whispered back, her voice laced with sarcasm, "Really? Danger? Here? No way."

"I am so serious, Renee. I wouldn't lie about something like that. Make a joke, yes. Lie, no."

"You mean someone could be killed?" she asked.

Bob nodded, still whispering. "That and worse."

"You mean like what happened to the guy in our Jacuzzi," said Renee.

Bob pointed his finger at her. "That's exactly the kind of thing I am talking about."

She bowed her head and moved in. "Can you be a little more specific?"

"It's a big-time corporate undercover spy international intrigue thingy."

"Bob, spill it, okay?"

"Someone has stolen high level military software embedded in a computer chip. It's like a hot dog on a stick but different," he continued in his hushed tone. "It's here somewhere and the place is crawling with spies, thieves and other types of people with low self-esteem. It's all going down during tonight's party. The place is going to be jam-packed with backstabbing, double-crossing, slime, kinda like a major talent agency."

"Why are we whispering?" I whispered.

"I always whisper when I'm saying something important. That way no one else can hear."

"It doesn't help if we can't understand what you're saying," I said.

"Okay, Bob, cut the whispering," Renee demanded in a normal voice. "Since when did you become Sherlock Holmes?"

Bob's face lit up like a Christmas tree. "I had this life-changing realization that I was overweight and needed to do something drastic. This detective I hired to investigate the three of you was freaking awesome. I fell in love with what he did. It was so unethical and kinda voyeuristic. He did Internet searches, peeped into bedroom windows, combed through public records, went on secret stakeouts, made garbage investigations, did phone taps, wireless intercepts, all the things a private investigator does on TV. Most of it was illegal, of course, which is why I hired the guy. I even tagged along on some of his surveillances."

"You had someone go through my garbage?"

"You threw it out, Rick. That's what trash is, stuff you don't want any more."

"That's not the point," I said.

"Sure it is. And he took some great photos of you and Renee. You have to come over for dinner and check 'em out. Oh, and Rick, I'd buy some curtains if I were you. Might keep those private moments a little more, well, you know, private. That grilled salmon and shrimp looked good, though."

"Come on Bob," said Renee, "What's happening tonight?" She paused a moment. "By the way, I'm taking you up on that dinner offer. I never turn down a free meal, unless it's pasta. Gotta watch the carb intake."

"Fish, chicken, veal, steak? Plan ahead - that's my motto."

"Steak. Rare. And I love candid shots, especially of me. I'll want copies. So what do you know about this military software thing? Does it have anything to do with Atsbee?"

"First of all, Scott's not a real chemical salesman, well he is kind of. He sells drugs."

"Figured him for a sleaze," said Renee, acting all cocky that she pegged Scott from the start.

"What kind of drugs?" I asked.

"Mostly heroin, but he's broke. Like you, Rick."

"Glad I'm not the only one," I muttered.

Renee was confused. "How do you get to be a broke drug dealer?"

Bob looked at the ceiling, as if God was going to help him with the answer. "Umm, the way I heard it, several of his shipments were intercepted. No product, no profits and no money to repay those big loans. Apparently he wasn't borrowing from Citibank, although those guys do have some pretty severe late penalties. Scott's was dealing with bankers of a higher calling. They don't send a bill. They send a couple of heavily armed Juans. Word is that Scott owes big bucks to some gentlemen who have no morals whatsoever. They're worse than reality TV producers."

"Scary," said Renee.

"Tell me about it," said Bob.

"Is that why he's here?" I asked, "To get money from Atsbee?"

Bob turned to me. "Who knows what Scott's up to but it's all going down tonight at the Atsbee's celebrity gathering so everybody is watching everybody. It's like an awkward awards after-party. Oh, and stay away from some guy named Joey the Knitter. He has quite a track record for leaving bodies behind. It appears you two have something in common with him. You could start a club."

Bob spotted Renee's half-finished martini glass on the coffee table. In one motion he picked it up and downed it.

"Shame to let that beauty go to waste. Where was I?"

"Everybody knows about this chip and Scott is trying to try to steal it," Renee reminded him, "You're making all this up, aren't you, Bob?"

"I would never make up such a ridiculous story. It isn't the least bit funny. Now, get this boys and girls. Greg's super-bitch of an assistant, Traye, has teamed up with sex-crazed Scott to intercept the chip. She couldn't invite only him. Greg would start asking questions about why his ex-roommate was suddenly on his guest list. So clever Ms. Torre convinced Greg to invite broke Rickee boy here, and infamous maxi-me as a cover. Oh, and here's another tip - don't use the house phones. People are listening to everything, and they're quite the chatty group. Can't keep a secret to save their lives."

Bob stood up quickly and began to sway. He held his arms out to keep his balance. "Whoa, note to self, get up slowly when drunk and stoned. Although I think I've made that note before." He turned to Renee. "You're going to the pre-party hook-up party, right, Renee?"

"How did you know?"

"I warned you about those phones," he said, then checked his watch. "It's time for me to hit the road. Rickster, I'll meet you in the lobby. Renee, you nuzzle up to the Traye biatch and find out what she has up her sleeves and in her panties. We'll meet at the ice sculpture inside the party."

"Are you sure they'll have one?" I asked.

Bob threw his hands in the air. "You've got to be kidding. Of course they'll have an ice sculpture. They always have one of those stupid things. It's probably an angel or a buffalo or a manatee or something else equally endangered or obtuse. Who knows what it will be this time? Maybe a big rock."

"They don't do ice rocks, Bob," said Renee.

"Aren't we forgetting something?" I asked.

"Naw, we covered everything," said Bob confidently.

"What about the guy in the bathtub?"

"He's fine. We'll throw him off the balcony later."

"We can't do that," I said. "They have people who work the grounds."

"You're right. We could hit someone. We'll figure that later. I'm new at this detective thing. But don't worry, I'm a fast learner. It only took me half a day to learn how to drive a covered wagon. Those things are a bitch to parallel park."

"So I'm on my own here?" I asked.

"Look who's whining now," said Renee. "All you have to do is work the party until the guy from Boeing talks to you. It's not *that* hard. I'll meet you at the ice sculpture as soon as I'm done with the pre-party."

Bob looked at Renee. "You're not going to tell him?"

"Tell who what?"

"Tell Rick. You know. The thing."

I looked at them both. "What thing? Oh, my god. Renee, are you pregnant?"

"Oh, Bob, don't."

"You've got to do it, Renee," said Bob.

"No, I don't."

"Yes, you do."

"Bob, don't you dare," she shot back.

"Tell me what?" I demanded again.

Bob continued to stare at Renee. "The thing she needs to tell you that you should know, but you don't know yet."

"I'm not telling him anything and neither are you."

"You're not going to tell him that Traye hired you to get him to come? You know, I mean come here...I mean to the party."

"You are such a prick. You're going to ruin everything."

"Considering who's hanging around in your bathtub, the weekend was pretty much shot already."

"Traye hired Renee?" I asked.

"Kind of," said Renee.

I slumped onto the couch.

"Come on, kids, this is no time to fight," said Bob. "Hurry up and get dressed. The great Atsbee is waiting to bestow riches on all of us."

"Bob," Renee said firmly.

"Yes, Renee dear?"

She walked to the door and opened it.

"This is your cue," she said, pointing at the empty hallway, "to leave."

"Got it."

Damn that Honesty Stuff

I was extremely unhappy to hear that Renee was working for the corporate ice queen, Traye. By the time Bob had shuffled out the door I'd lost track of how much vodka had gone down between the three of us. Now I was angry and fuzzy.

"It's not what you think," she said returning to the couch.

The words sounded right, but there was no sense of remorse, not even a hint of pleading. That pissed me off. I was there because of her - and now her motivation was completely suspect.

"Why don't you explain it to me, because I get angry when people use me," I said.

She tried her green-eyed stare-at-me trick, but it wasn't going to work this time. Well, maybe it did a little. But I was still mad, damn it.

"I didn't use you, Rick. And I'd like to point out that you were extremely happy with our situation. You even said you were enjoying your life."

"Sure I was happy, until I was told it was all fake and arranged."

"It was arranged, but it was never fake. I made a deal with Traye. All I had to do was get you to come here and attend the party. That's all. Unfortunately, something happened along the way."

This was exactly the kind of trouble I didn't want to get into. Apparently the RJ Curse was alive and well in Half Moon Bay. This one was shaping up to be a real shit storm. It'd started with an assassin. What was going to top that lead-in?

"You said it would be to my advantage to come here. Now I have a dead guy in my bathtub, a gun in my belt and a deranged actor thinking he's the next Mike Hammer. Are you proud of yourself?"

"Hey, it wasn't easy getting around your emotional baggage, Rick. Unfortunately, once I found out who you really were, I was hooked."

"Renee, you have no idea who I am."

"I know exactly who you are." She reached out and grabbed my hand. Her touch caused my anger to evaporate.

"You're loyal, dedicated, and have a clear sense of right and wrong. I've met a lot of people in my life, and I know when I'm with a decent person. I like you, Rick. I like you a lot."

"I liked you too, Renee, until about thirty seconds ago. Let me tell you what I'm going to do. I am going to get dressed and go downstairs and meet with Atsbee. Then I'm going home."

"You're going to need help."

"Then why don't you give me the name of your shrink."

Renee walked away and poured a fresh drink. She kept her back to me as she looked out at the ocean.

"Rick, there's a dead guy in the bathtub of *your* suite. And if you think he's the only one interested in getting his hands on that phone, you really *do* need a shrink."

She had a point. There were probably other undesirables lurking in the hallway and who knows where else. Then there was the minor issue of killing people in your suite. The hotel management was not going to be happy with that form of entertainment, no matter how quiet we were. But it was time to put Renee on the defense, so I could test her true intentions.

"Renee, why don't you tell me everything that's going on? Who are you?"

She turned from the window, drink in hand, and joined me on the couch. She paused a moment, then put the drink on the coffee table and faced me, her hands in her lap.

"Traye called me a week before we met and told me there was thirty grand plus expenses if I could get you to attend the party, dressed appropriately of course. It was a cut-and-dry assignment. Once you entered the ballroom, I could split."

"And how do you know Traye?"

"I don't. I'm on a list."

"What kind of list?" I asked.

"It's like a Paris Hilton, Kim Kardashian party-girl list. I'm nowhere near the top, but I get work. More than you'd think. I can be pretty hot when I work it."

"Those people aren't hot, they're celebrities."

"Think of me as the backup singer. I get paid to be at parties or accompany executives to events. I'm not the lead, but I get the call."

"You're an escort," I said.

To think I believed this wonder woman actually liked me. I felt like such a fool. "I thought you wanted to be with me, not be paid to be with me. The truth is that you're hired to be with people."

"You're right, Rick. I am hired to *accompany* people. But not in the way you're thinking. I don't have sex with clients."

"My personal experience says you're lying."

She thought a moment and shifted her weight on the couch.

"Let me rephrase that," she said slowly. "I'm not *paid* to have sex with my clients. I have that opportunity, but I've placed myself on the no-fly list. Been there since I started."

"What does that mean?"

"You can try, but you can't fly."

"So who do you have sex with?" I asked.

"People I like."

"And lie to."

"I never lied to you, Rick" she said softly.

"You sure didn't tell the truth."

She was on her feet. In a moment the sweet Renee who'd been with me for days disappeared. In her place was a very angry redhead.

"What is your fucking problem, Johnson? You're going to play the saint? You're on fucking probation, you asshole. Never mentioned it to me. Not once. And while we're on this honesty kick, is there someone in this room who has a restraining order against them? Oh, let me look around. There he is. It's you, you fuck! Didn't want to let me in on that one either, I guess. And not only were you in the Ranger program, you were kicked out. Why? Because you *killed* your commanding officer. No mention of that little incident over the past few days. I guess you didn't want to ruin the mood 'cause the hot redhead bitch might stop fucking you if she found out you were a murderer. Oh, and wait, what's that you say? You were followed by the FBI for two years? Didn't tell me that either. Why? Because you didn't know."

"I was followed by the FBI?"

"For two years. Oh, yes. They've got a big fat file on you, Mister Honesty."

Renee headed to the bottle of vodka and took a long swig, then filled her glass and turned.

"You haven't been honest with me from the moment we met, and you've got your big-boy panties in a bunch because I'm being paid to get you here where your life could be turned around for the better. If you looked one inch past your inflated ego and your colossal inability to emotionally connect, you might consider that this is the first time I've allowed myself to be emotionally vulnerable in years. Oh, by the way, I guess you were going to take on our uninvited visitor by yourself, Mister Protecto-man."

"I did want to thank you for that. You saved my life."

"Fuck you!" she said. She turned, threw the glass, missing me by an inch. She left the room. I heard the bedroom door slam.

I guess I didn't play that very well, but I never expected her to go postal. She was the one who lured me to this damn hotel and into an emotional tar pit. I guess I could have told her a few of the issues I'd faced over the past few months.

Then a different thought plowed into my brain like an out-of-control tractor trailer. A person doesn't take two years of karate and then choke a guy to death without some kind of emotional reaction. And you don't just happen to know your boyfriend of seven days has been followed by the FBI...for two years. There was a lot more to her story than she told me.

My emotional shields were up, but wavering. I heard the shower start. An hour earlier I would have joined her, but the thought of the dead guy in the Jacuzzi tub slowed me. And how could she take a shower with him in there? Granted, the bathroom was big, but still, who was this woman who broke down every barrier I'd put up, made me laugh at the worst part of my life and whose personality made me feel like I'd found my soul mate?

What did she say before this insanity started? She said she wanted something she hadn't felt in years. It wasn't about being drunk or anything sexual; I'd remember that. It was that she wanted to feel safe, secure and loved.

I suddenly realized - that's what *I* wanted.

If she knew all that discouraging information and still hung around, she must have liked something about me.

I made up my mind right there to keep my promise and see this new relationship through to the end, even if it killed me. I liked her a lot.

A Little Help from Your Friends

Renee was right. I'd neglected to tell her some of the more unsavory elements of my past because I didn't want to encumber our fledgling relationship...and I liked the sex. I liked her.

Standing in that suite overlooking the deep blue Pacific Ocean I realized I'd been so wrong. This was not the time to pretend I was anything but a flawed man trying to make the best of an extremely challenged life.

Renee had offered me hope and optimism, provided me with more laughs than I'd had in years. She'd been nothing but supportive since we'd met. I needed to fix things with her ASAP.

Before I left the living area, I pushed the heavy couch away from the wall and located the silenced pistol. I grabbed the vodka bottle and was about to head for the shower, when there was a knock at the door.

I put the vodka down, shoved Renee's gun in the drawer by the bed, then checked the silenced pistol's magazine. It was full, minus the two shots the derelict squeezed off before Renee wrapped him up. I checked the safety and made sure it was ready to fire.

Through the peephole I saw a man in a hotel uniform standing next to a room service table covered with white linen. I put the chain lock on the door and opened it an inch.

"Can I help you?" I asked.

"Room service."

"I didn't order anything."

"Compliments of the concierge, Mr. Johnson."

I glanced over my shoulder and spied the half empty vodka bottle Renee'd thrown at our first visitor. Perhaps this was a refill. More of the same brand would be a welcome backup. At the rate we'd been downing the stuff, our supply was not going to last much longer. After tucking the long-barreled gun into the small of my back, I disengaged the lock and opened the door.

"Dank you, sir," said the man in a thick mid-eastern accent. He pushed his little table into the room and closed the door behind him.

He was slow and deliberate, but when he pulled the tablecloth off with some difficulty, revealing a bottle of obviously well-traveled Popov Vodka, I froze. My first inclination was to pull the gun and shoot him right then for bringing a substandard brand into a luxury hotel suite, but I decided to give this awkward waiter an opportunity to leave unharmed. I didn't want another fight to the death when I could be showering with the woman of my dreams.

"That will be fine, thank you." I said making it clear he should leave.

"I am not finished preparing your treat," he replied.

Treat? He really said treat?

"I'm expecting someone. You need to leave," I said quickly.

"My boss will be upset if I do not finish dee presentation."

"Have him call me. I'll explain. Leave everything where it is and get out."

"I do not think you understand," he said in a harsh tone. He put his hand into one of the silver pitchers. By the time he'd pulled the knife out, I was diving to the floor. The blade flew within an inch of my head and stuck deep into the far wall. I reached to my back and grabbed the silenced gun. As I rolled over and came up on one knee, the faux waiter pulled a second knife from another pitcher.

I squeezed the trigger twice and watched two small holes appear in his neck. The second knife was feebly tossed, landing midway between us and the would-be server crumpled to the ground and quietly choked to death, leaving little blood to clean up. It is amazing how military training comes in handy at the oddest moments.

Unfortunately this was not the warm and fuzzy weekend I'd thought it was going to be. Nothing seemed to be going smoothly, except for the constant supply of vodka.

As I rose to my feet I realized the accumulation of bodies in our suite was becoming a logistical nightmare. Luckily, the room was big enough to accommodate guests, even if they were dropping like flies.

I dragged the second would-be assassin into the guest bedroom and lifted the top half of the body onto the closest bed, then grabbed his feet and threw the rest of his weight on top of the pale blue covers. I looked down on the man staring vacantly at the ceiling.

"You are not forgiven," I told him. I hauled off and slapped him hard. I know it was disrespectful and irreverent, but the guy deserved it. I suddenly felt as if someone was watching over me, then the sensation faded. Was I sensing his spirit leaving, heading for the white light? Maybe he took the Rick Johnson Curse with him. I could only hope.

I placed my index finger to my lips. "Don't tell anyone," and backed out of the room.

I checked the hallway door to make sure it was chained and locked. RJ curse or not, I decided it was time to take control of my life. I headed for the bathroom to complete some unfinished business that involved a special lady and a low-flow shower.

Grabbing the original vodka bottle, I took several more swallows and wiped my mouth with the back of my hand.

There was no doubt that Renee was a special person. She was a great lover. She was funny, smart and beautiful. She even liked the Dodgers. A woman can fake an orgasm, but no female can fake enjoying more than one baseball game. Could I trust her? Probably not, but damn, who *can* you trust? The banks? Wall Street? The NSA? The cable company? It didn't matter. I hadn't felt this good since, this alive...hell, I'd never felt this good, ever.

* * * * *

The noise of the shower filled my ears. Steam blurred my vision. The original intruder was resting

80

peacefully at the bottom of the large Jacuzzi tub. At the opposite side of the room was a naked Renee showering in the oversized glass enclosure. A look of concern spread across her face as I opened the shower door. I offered her the vodka bottle I was holding.

"Join me in a drink?" I shouted, not quite loud enough to wake the dead.

"You don't have any glasses," she said over the sound of the water.

Backed against the wall, she looked unsure whether to drink or to duck.

I smiled my best smile and tried to look kind.

"Vodka glasses are overrated." I said, trying to lighten the mood. "We need to talk and drink, not necessarily in that order."

I'd seen her naked quite a few times over the last few days, but was still in awe of her flawless body. Her figure was like one of those soft-porn actresses on pay cable - perfect in every way. Not that I ever watched those kinds of shows.

"Are you feeling okay?" she asked, obviously uncomfortable.

I smiled. "Never felt better. Why? Do I look sick?"

"Let's see, you're holding a half-empty bottle of vodka, there's a dead guy behind you and you're smiling."

I looked at the bottle, and then shrugged. "You've never seen me smile?"

"Not unless you were drunk, about to get laid, or the Dodgers were winning by a dozen runs. Oh, one more thing, you're walking into a hot, steamy shower, completely dressed. These actions do not qualify as being okay."

"I want to apologize," I said, carefully raising the bottle and offering it to her.

She took the vodka, covering the top with her hand.

"What are you apologizing for?" she asked with water dripping from her nose. There was more than a hint of suspicion in her voice.

"For being a self-centered ass. For not telling you how I feel about you. For hiding my past and not taking that guy down the minute he barged into the room."

"I have no problem dealing with idiots who point weapons at me."

"I could have taken him," I said.

"Okay, Rick, that's an impressive list of apologies. Consider them accepted. As for not saving my life, the way this weekend is going, I'm sure you'll get another chance. Now what's with the shower attire? Setting a new fashion trend?"

"I just woke up from a long, miserable nap. I've been sleep-walking for months."

"And so now that you've had an epiphany, you figured it was time to start showering with your clothes on?"

"I had to tell you I was sorry before any more time passed."

Renee put the bottle to her side. "I was wondering if you were going to become the man I knew you could be."

"I'm here, baby."

"Is it safe?"

"It is definitely safe..." I glanced at the man lying in the oversized tub. "I am safe to be around and it is safe to continue to enjoy what's happening between us. I want to say, from the bottom of my heart..."

Renee held her hand up. I stopped my speech as she took a couple huge swallows from the bottle, then let out a satisfied, "Ahhhhhh," and then nodded. "Okay, let me have it, Rick. Tell me what I've been waiting to hear for days."

"I like you, Renee. I like you a lot."

Her eyes widened. "You *like* me. You fucking LIKE me? I practically moved in the day we met. Gave you compliments, helped you shop, I showed you things most men only dream of, convinced you to go to the best party on the West Coast, and you *like* me?" She put her face directly into the full force of the shower, shook her head several times, then turned back and opened her eyes.

"So, shower boy," she said, "Would you like to take a moment and think about how you're going to rephrase that pathetic outburst for our unimpressed recently deceased Jacuzzi guest?"

I laughed out loud. "You're right. I can do better."

"I certainly hope so."

I took the bottle and followed her lead by taking several swallows, then wiped my mouth with a soaked shirtsleeve. I was about to speak, but she put her hand up again.

"Make sure you're ready."

I raised my eyes to hers.

She put her finger to her lips then said, "Don't blow it."

I nodded. She looked me in the eye and squinted.

I took a breath and began.

"What I meant to say is, Renee, I love you and I don't care who hired you or why. Whoever it was, they did me the best favor of my life. You are the most wonderful person who has ever entered my presence. I want us to enjoy each other and I pray our relationship and feelings toward each other continue to grow long past this weekend."

"That's more like it," she said, taking the bottle back. "Now get out of those clothes and show me how much you love me."

Bob's New Job

Renee and I were getting dressed after giving our king-sized bed a grown-up workout. Renee was standing in front of the mirror putting on pearl earrings. She glanced into the living area where I was fixing more drinks.

"Rick, why is there a bottle of Popov vodka on a table and a knife stuck in the wall?"

"Room service," I answered.

"Since when does room service include throwing knives?"

"It's a new menu item. There was a two for one special. The other one is around here somewhere."

Renee walked into the sitting area. Her red dress complimented her hair and hugged her stunning figure like a silk glove. She pointed at the knife handle sticking out from under the couch. "Could that be it?"

"Yeah, thanks," I said, and got on my knees to retrieve it.

"Don't mess up your pants," she warned me.

Back on my feet, I examined the knife. It was a nicely balanced piece. I was lucky it wasn't buried in my chest.

"Not even a service charge," I said.

"You had a visitor while I was in the shower? Who was it?"

I shrugged. "I don't know. Knives started flying before I could get his name."

She looked at me. I could tell she was a little worried. "Where is he?"

I pointed in the general direction of the guest bedroom. "In there."

"Is he sleeping?"

"With the fishes. He won't be making any more deliveries."

She picked up the bottle of vodka absentmindedly and put her hand on the top. She made an odd face. "This is troubling."

"I know," I said in agreement, "People keep trying to kill us."

"Not that. I can't open this. My hands are too slippery. Here, you try."

I twisted the top and it sprang loose. I went to the cupboard and found a couple more glasses. We settled in on the couch.

"What are we going to do with *two* bodies?" I asked.

Renee sighed. "Maybe we should leave them to Bob. He's the one who wants to be a private detective."

I poured two fingers in the glasses and handed one to her. "Great idea. We'll make it his first test."

As if on cue, there was a knock at the door.

"Peephole," she reminded me.

"Got it."

It was Bob. I tried once more to see if there was anyone behind him, but it was impossible. I opened the door. He barged in, all pumped up.

"Chop-chop. Gotta get to work, kids. Can't have a dead guy lying around your hotel room. It's totally unacceptable, at least on this side of the border. We still have *some* standards in America."

Renee flipped her hair over the back of her dress and gave Bob the once-over. "You're going to move a dead body in your tux?"

Bob nodded emphatically. "Of course, love. It's the perfect plan. The suit will be dry-cleaned and mixed up with a bunch of other stuff before anyone thinks of looking for those telltale fibers." He looked out of the corner of his eye and checked himself in the mirror. "I don't believe any of that CSI crap anyway. I think the guys in the crime lab make it up. I would. Hey, I look gooood." He clapped his hands loudly, "Okay, next question. Why do we have a throwing knife embedded in our wall? I didn't get one of those in my room."

"We had another visitor," I said, offering him the bottle, without the benefit of a glass, "This one was partial to knives. Didn't handle getting shot too well, though."

Bob took the bottle, downed a few swings. "You guys really should work on your social skills. Let's take a look at our newest visitor. Where is he?"

"Guest bedroom."

Bob headed there, taking the bottle with him.

"What are you up to, Bob?" said Renee, following him. "Why are you so interested in all this?"

"You don't know me, do you?"

"No, I don't know you at all, Bob, except you were a lot funnier and thinner on TV. But you're growing on me, kinda like a cuddly fungus."

"Usually happens," he muttered, examining the body lying peacefully on the bed. "To quote Robert Palmer, I'm 'simply irresistible.' As for why I'm interested in your latest victim, I already told you, I want to be a detective. I was a dick on TV, a dick to the press, a dick to my fans, why not make it official?"

Renee and I looked at each other and shrugged simultaneously.

Bob put his index finger to his temple. "Incoming brainstorm. We can dump these stiffs into one of those big laundry carts, roll them down the hallway and dump 'em down the chute. Do we have any idea who he is?"

Renee and I answered simultaneously. "No."

Bob put his hands on his ample hips. I was beginning to think this was his signature move.

"Well, let's introduce ourselves, shall we?" He leaned over and started rifling through the dead man's clothing.

"Isn't that illegal?" asked Renee.

"Of course it's illegal," he replied, not stopping his search, "Everything's illegal in this country. Land of the free, you know, home of the brave, as long as you're rich, white, or a politician." Bob pulled something from the man's pocket. "Bingo!'

"What is it?"

"Directions to the hotel and an old wallet."

He tossed the paper onto the body. "Don't need that. I'm already here."

"What about fingerprints or fibers?" I asked. "Aren't you leaving evidence?"

Bob rummaged through the billfold. "Who cares about evidence? We know you guys killed him. I want to know who he is. Maybe we have mutual friends, although I doubt it because according to this Nevada driver's license our visitor is from Elko, Nevada, and his name is Shirley Torcasso. Hmm, what makes me think he stole this?"

Bob examined the dead man's face, and then straightened up. "He doesn't look like a Torcasso." He returned his attention to the wallet. "Oh, look, he's got a credit card in the same name, a condom, a fifty-dollar bill, a dry cleaning receipt, not for these clothes obviously, and a Viagra pill."

"How do you know it's Viagra?" I asked.

Bob shot me a look.

I backed off. "Okay, so you know."

"You are so correct, Rick," said, pocketing the fifty and leaving the room without explanation.

"This is getting us nowhere," said Renee. "We need to get ready for the party."

"I know. What is he doing?"

"I have no idea, but we have work to do."

Bob returned with a huge rolling laundry basket. "It's always important to make positive, constructive and profitable relationships with the help. These two hell-raisers will be well taken care of, if you know what I mean."

"None of this bothers you?" asked Renee.

Bob abruptly stopped fussing with the cart and slumped onto the end of the large king bed. In a matter of seconds, the happy-go-lucky Bob Clay had morphed into a sad, middle-aged man. He rubbed his face with his hands and looked up at us.

"Seeing these dead people doesn't bother me in the least. I don't know them and I could care less about them. After you've experienced a dozen of your closest friends die in your arms from a terrible disease, six more savagely beaten for no rational reason other than they lived a different lifestyle...after your manager has stolen your one true love *and* ten years of hard earned money, you begin to realize life can be downright ugly and unfair."

He paused and looked out the window to the darkening ocean beyond. "You know what, Rick?"

"What is it, Bob?"

"I have lost so much and felt so much pain...I really don't give a shit about anything anymore."

I looked over to Renee. Her anger had been replaced by a concerned frown.

Bob lowered his eyes, his voice laced with grief. "I also came to the conclusion that no one can be trusted and..." he turned toward the Jacuzzi tub. "...a dead body lacks a soul."

Then as quickly as he'd slumped into his emotionally charged memories, Bob's eyes brightened, his body became energized and he transformed into his familiar self. It appeared as if he'd lost thirty pounds and shed fifteen years.

"On the other hand," he continued, "I've known quite a few television executives who never had a soul and they're walking around just fine."

I was beginning to understand that this funny man had been unhappy for a very long time.

"All right. We need a game plan," said Renee, breaking the awkward silence. "Rick, Bob, to the couch."

"Can't I stay here?" whined Bob, still sitting on the edge of the bed. "I'm really comfy."

"No you can't. Get up," she commanded, "I need you both in the living room. Now!"

"Aw gee," grumbled Bob as he struggled to his feet. He walked the twelve steps into the living area. On the way, he grabbed the bottle of Popov, then he plopped on the couch, cradling the vodka like a newborn.

I sat next to him. Renee stood in front us.

Bob looked up at her, hugging the bottle. "Is this going to take long? I'm thirsty."

"Why are you here, Bob?' she asked.

Bob gulped loudly. It was like a sound effect from a cartoon. I couldn't stop from laughing. Being around Bob Clay was like living in a sitcom. He gazed up at her, and I swear he looked like a twelve-year-old who'd been caught masturbating by his mom.

"Renee, I'm sorry I'm in your way. I'm always in the way. Sometimes I'm in the way when I'm on the way."

"Bob. Stop it."

He sat up straight, put the bottle to the side and folded his hands in his lap. "Renee, don't make me leave. I am having the best time I've had in a decade...maybe two. I want to become the best detective I can be. Hanging around you guys is like being in dick graduate school."

Renee looked over his head, deep in thought. Bob waited for her to pass judgment. Finally she spoke. "Okay, Bob. I guess that makes sense, in an odd sort of way. We're going to need some help tonight."

She turned to me. "What about you, Rick? What are you going to do about this phone situation? A guy just tried to kill us."

"Two."

"What does that mean, two? That's not a complete sentence. It doesn't make sense. We have to communicate, okay? Use your words."

"Two guys tried to kill us."

"I know that. I was here. What are you going to do about the phone, Atsbee, the airport, and any other attempts on your life? What is your purpose here?"

I wasn't expecting a pop quiz. Then again, I wasn't expecting room service to throw knives.

I ran my hand through my hair and looked up at her. "My plan is to walk to the party, talk to the guy from Boeing, get the second phone, go to the airport, pick up my money, come back, get you, have a lot more to drink and get the hell out of Dodge."

"And you're doing all this, why?"

That one was easy. "To make seventy grand which will get my dog back, save my home and help my mom."

"Your mom's sick?" asks Bob.

"No, she's short of cash and a little grumpy."

"Been there, done that, over it," he said.

"Rick," demanded Renee, "You're planning on going to the airport even though it's dangerous?"

I had to think about that one. Answering the door had been a life-threatening event, but I was with Bob. I'd never been so entertained, or so much in love. Besides, I'd been trained for danger, not poverty.

"There are several reasons I'm doing this," I said with conviction, counting on my nine fingers, "One, I need the money. Two, I'm helping you do your job by going to the party. Three I want to help my mom.

Four, I want my Mojo back and five, I want to help Bob become a professional dick."

"Thanks, Rick. That's nice," said Bob.

"Don't mention it, Bob," I reply.

"I did mention it," said Bob, "Is that okay?"

"It's fine Bob," I said.

"Stop it, you two. Listen. If we work quickly, we can get Rick to the airport, collect Rick's money, come back, and catch the tail end of Atsbee's party, then I'll call Ed. We can take Atsbee's jet and get out of here. We need to be in a city where the buildings are higher than three stories and have some good clean fun."

Bob liked that idea. "Wow, it's like I can be a dick and then come back and still be a dick. But I have a serious question."

"This I gotta hear," I mumbled.

"What is it, Bob?"

"Why are *you* here, Renee?"

Renee looked directly at me. "I'm here to protect someone I love and make a little spending money on the side."

Bob picked up the vodka bottle and pointed the top at her.

"Are you sure you're not here to make a crap load of money from several different undercover sources and get this guy in a shit load of trouble?"

Renee did not hesitate.

"No."

Bob shrugged. "Okay. Just checking."

Renee continued. "And for the record, Bob," she said pointing at me, "This guy's got himself into a lot more trouble than what's happened tonight and he's done just fine. Besides, I've always wanted to go to

Atsbee's kick-ass party. I took the job because it was an easy way to make some quick cash which I happen to need right now. A lot of things have changed since I took the gig. I want to make sure Rick and I get out of here safely. I have plans for him, and he needs to be in one piece."

"Oh, now this sounds a little kinky," said Bob.

"It is, Bob," she said. "It is very kinky."

A huge grin spread across Bob's face. "This is the kind of conversation I like. Tell me more."

"Settle down, cowboy. I never reveal my intimate plans before they occur."

"And after?"

A frown wrinkled her flawless forehead. "Bob..."

"Okay, okay, but take lot of pictures."

"You can just forget about the sex tweets Bob, but if you want to join our Half Moon Bay danger party, we could use your help. In return, I know some people who could sign off on your detective hours."

"That would be awesome."

Renee started pacing in front of us, just like she did back at my place.

"Okay, so we're all straight on this. Rick is going to do his job. He'll work the party. Bob?"

"Yes, sir," he said, saluting.

"You have to watch out for Rick. Stick close to him and be alert. Don't let him do anything that seems crazy or dangerous."

"Aye-aye, Capt'n."

"I'm going to this Traye bullshit party. You meet the Atsbee and we'll meet at the ice sculpture, get Rick to the airport, pick up our paychecks and we can enjoy the night. Okay? We're all on the same page?"

"Hell, yes!" shouted Bob, jumping up from the couch, which totally impressed me that he could move that fast. He put his hands in front of him. "Let's do it! Yeah! Team cheer."

Renee shook her head and walked away. "No team cheer. Team gets dressed. Then team gets to work."

Bob was disappointed, for about a second. "What about our guests? They've been lying around doing nothing for hours."

"I think your first idea was the best. Put a privacy sign on the door and we'll deal with them after the phone business is completed."

"Should I put the laundry cart back?"

Renee shot him a look that would have killed a thinner man.

"Those carts aren't easy to come by."

"It was five feet away in the hallway. Put it back." She turned and started to comb her hair.

"Geeze, you're so bossy."

Atsbee

The Half Moon Bay Ritz-Carlton lobby had taken on the appearance of an elegant state dinner. Large decorative banners sported the Keysoft corporate logo and colors hung from the ceiling. The entryway had been elevated to Hollywood premiere status. Renee, Bob and I exited the elevator and walked through the lobby with confidence in extreme slow motion, our heads held high, mainly because we were wearing incredibly tight collars. If we looked down, we probably would have choked and died.

Renee was an explosion of red, looking like she'd been dressed by Catherine Hendricks' personal designer. Bob sauntered with an attitude of a wealthy European leader. Somehow he'd gotten hold of a sash that matched Renee's dress. Military medals adorned his chest. I didn't dare ask where he got them and I was sure there was an expensive curtain or tablecloth missing from the hotel. I silently prayed we wouldn't run into an angry soldier.

There was some kind of commotion occurring outside the lobby at the valet station. A man who looked like he'd taken a swim in his clothes was standing next to a thoroughly dented Kia sedan. He appeared to be shouting, indicating with his hands somcone very short, or maybe he was looking for a large dog. I couldn't tell. The employees kept shrugging and shaking their heads. I figured the issue would eventually be worked out, but the guy had to rethink his grooming choices. Someone should have told him that long sideburns were out of style and weren't coming back any time soon.

We walked among the well-dressed attendees heading toward the party entrance. Heads turned as we passed. Several people pointed at Bob's blindingly white sneakers. Somehow he knew exactly when people were looking at him. He nodded and waved at every opportunity. The King of Comedy had returned...sort of.

Renee stopped in front of the large sign that announced we'd arrived at the entrance to her meeting room. She turned to us with an alluring smile.

"Okay, guys, best of luck with Atsbee." She gave Bob a hug. "Get as much information as you can and keep your eyes open. There are bad people here, people with guns and knives."

"And they're not afraid to use them," Bob added.

"Exactly," agreed Renee. "And Bob."

"Yes Renee, my sweetness"

"Try not to do anything embarrassing."

"Not quite my style," Bob replied, pronouncing his words much too slowly.

"You finished the vodka, didn't you?"

"Me? Never touch the stuff. Destroys your liver."

"Make the attempt, Bob, okay? We're trying not to be obvious."

He took a breath. "Well, in my humble opinion, a bright red gown is not the best approach when subtlety is the goal. I think you are going to be very visible in the sea of black tuxedos and pastel gowns. But, being the professional that I am, I will make an attempt at acting extraordinarily sublime," he said. "By the way, the two of you must stop killing the guests."

Renee glared.

He nodded at her attempt to silence him. "I know. I know. It's a touchy subject. But we can't always ignore our past. Try not to plug anyone in there, okay? There's a lack of bathtubs on this floor."

Renee gave up and turned to straighten my bow tie. "Don't let Bob distract you. You both need to be on your toes."

I nodded. "Done and done. And don't tell Traye about the iPhone, the note, or our two visitors."

"Do I look like an idiot?"

Bob gave her the once-over. "Honey if you're an idiot, I'm a monkey's uncle. Luckily for the sake of this discussion, I am an only child."

Renee stared at him again, but it was going to take more than an evil eye to shut him up.

"You see, if I'm an only child, then I don't have any brothers and sisters, and as a result I can't have any nieces or nephews, so..."

"I got it Bob, okay? It just didn't fly. Not even worth a chuckle. Too complicated and obtuse. Put that one away."

He nodded.

She hugged us both again. "I'll meet you at the ice sculpture as soon as I'm done. See if you can milk Atsbee at the meeting."

Bob smiled. "Oh, Renee, I love it when you talk dirty."

With a quick turn that spun her gown into a flash of red, she disappeared into the room.

Bob turned to me and whispered. "Just so you know, it's going to be one crazy-ass night…"

He looked around and scanned the well-dressed crowd milling at the ballroom entrance. "And I liiiike it."

We only managed to travel a few feet along the flag-draped hallway when Scott joined us.

"Scott," exclaimed Bob, as we continued the polished walkway, "I thought you'd be licking Greg's asshole by now."

"Don't you worry, unfunny fat man. I won't ruin your slim-to-none chance of getting back on television. I know you're here to suck up to Greg for his entertainment connections, but it's not going to work. He has so many problems you are not even a consideration. I happen to have inside information on the guy."

"Of course you do, Scott, because you're still fucking Atsbee's supreme slut assistant Traye," countered Bob, not reacting to Scott's jab. "Guess those Thai girls don't scratch that bottomless itch, do they?"

We arrived at the meeting room before the verbal war could escalate. I opened the door and let Bob and Scott go first, confident the meeting was not going to be easy or pleasant.

Tall, refined, and tan, Greg Atsbee sat with one leg resting on the end of a long mahogany meeting table. Behind him stood a broad-shouldered man with a scowl on his overly large face. I figured he was a bodyguard, but it was hard to take him seriously. The guy had a horrendous bowl cut. He looked like Moe from "The Three Stooges." I silently hoped Bob didn't start making Supercuts jokes or some other reference to the guy's embarrassing appearance. He was too easy a target.

But Atsbee - I was impressed with him. He came off as a man who commanded attention and respect. In his Armani tux, immaculately pressed white shirt and striped silk bow tie, he looked like the leader of a six-billion-dollar company; regal and dignified. His Italian shoes had to be hand stitched. I almost choked when I recognized the Hublot Tourbillon Solo Bang on his wrist. That watch costs more than most luxury cars.

Atsbee shifted his weight to the floor and greeted each of us with a firm handshake.

"Scott, Rick, Bob. Please, have a seat."

Bob and I sat next to each other. Scott kept an empty chair between us. Bob sniffed his underarms as if a lack of deodorant was the reason for Scott's distance. I scanned the room from one end to the other. My gaze lingered at the impressive display of food that sat atop window-side credenza. Fresh flowers stood in tall vases atop gleaming pedestals that matched the teak table. On the other side of the spotless windows were the distant whitecaps of the Pacific Ocean.

Bob looked at Scott, then me, then broke into a grin. "If there ever were three guys who didn't belong together in one room, it's us."

Scott glared back. "If there was ever a fat ass that didn't belong in this room, it's *you*."

Bob stuck his tongue out.

It was at that moment that I realized that Bob Clay was the biological reason humans can't read each other's minds. If another person was exposed to what goes on inside of Bob's head, they'd burst into flames or immediately become comatose.

"This meeting shouldn't take long," said Atsbee, acting like nothing unusual had occurred, "Obviously I have an important event to host, so please listen carefully. You'll have time to think about my offer and spend a little more time together at this evening's event. I believe tonight's party is the best one so far."

Atsbee's presence filled the room as he walked in front of us. "Asking the three of you here was not easy for me, and I'm humbled to say I need help from each one of you."

He looked out the window as if there was an answer hidden in the distant cliffs. I knew he was lying. He'd never been humble in his life.

"I know I could have kept in touch, what with today's technology, but my entire being was focused on Keysoft's success. That phase is over and my life is changing rapidly."

Bob's hand shot up like an energetic student. "Do these rapid changes have anything to do with a new TV show that perhaps could star your ex-roommate?"

Atsbee smiled like an understanding parent. "Bob, please. This is important."

Bob lowered his hand quickly. "Okay, carry on. I'll wait."

Atsbee paused. There was something troubling him, but it was only visible in his eyes. His posture, his clothes, and his voice were still those of a proud leader. It dawned on me that I knew nothing of the man before me. We'd been apart for so many years, I had no idea who he was or where he was going with this little lecture sold as a friendly get-together.

"I know all of you. I heard how you reacted to my call. I've lived with you. And believe it or not, I trust you, a lot more than you trust each other. I brought you here to ask you to do something unusual. Not together. Not for very long. For about two weeks. What I'd like you to do is follow me, be at my side, as an observer."

"What possible reason could I have to follow you around like some kind of lost dog?" demanded Scott, his voice laced with anger, "I have my own life, my own future. You've ignored all of us for years."

I didn't understand Scott's aggressive attitude. If he'd traveled here from some distant jungle, even if it was to do an evil deed or trash Atsbee, why argue with the man? It made no sense.

Atsbee kept on rolling. I think if a giant humpback whale had jumped out of the Pacific and crashed through the window, I don't think he would have stopped.

"What I am asking from you is simple and direct. I need you to observe me during the next two weeks, and then you tell me."

"Tell you what?" Scott sneered.

"I need to know what you've seen, what you've experienced, what you've heard. It is important for me to understand what is happening around me from one's viewpoint. Each of you has plenty of time on your hands, and I'm a rich son-of-a-bitch. I'm offering you three hundred thousand dollars for the two weeks of observation and another full day of relating what you've seen. Your expenses will be covered during this time of course."

His eyes connected with each of us, one by one.

"Bob, I'm asking this as a personal favor. In return, I'll get that television pilot moving. I know the people who can make it happen and Keysoft can be a sponsor, so that's a win for you. Scott, you don't like me, and that's putting it mildly. I think you'd get a kick out of seeing what a fucked-up life I live. The cash could be a big help considering your current situation."

Atsbee took a breath and was about to say something, but changed his mind.

"Rick, not only do you need the money, you need a break from your miserable life. No offense."

I shrugged. "None taken."

Scott abruptly stood up. The moptop man behind Atsbee went on full alert. His hand moved to the inside of his jacket. I was certain that if Scott made a move toward Greg, the guy would have shot Scott dead.

I watched Scott's eyes shift to the bodyguard. He stopped his forward momentum and stood his ground, but his anger was unchecked. Hate poured from his entire being.

"Atsbee, you might be richer than everyone in this room. You might have an army of mindless lackeys who'll do whatever you want. But you do not own me. Asking me to be your dog-on-a-leash is totally insulting. If you knew me, you would never have asked me to come here."

Scott turned and burst out the door.

I looked over to Bob in amazement.

"Gee," smiled Bob, "was it something I said?"

Atsbee watched the door close, then turned back to us.

"Scott's under a lot of pressure and has a lot of challenges that could take a turn for the worse."

"You mean like meeting his bankers in a dark alley?" Bob had no empathy for Scott.

Atsbee smiled, but his expression wasn't one of amusement. I'd call it whimsical, like he'd thought of something funny. He didn't let us in on it.

"Scott could become a very wealthy man by the end of this evening or he could continue to make poor choices."

Atsbee was talking in riddles. I'm sure if he wanted us to know what was going on with sulky Scott, he would have said it. Actually, I was glad he didn't. I couldn't care less about Scott or his banking problems. I had to get to the airport to collect some much needed cash. If Atsbee wanted to play dumb about my delivery assignment, it was fine by me.

"Okay," said Atsbee, wrapping things up, "Think about what I've said and get back to Traye so she can make the proper arrangements." He clapped his hands loudly. "So, how do you feel about my offer? Any thoughts?"

Bob stood up and stretched. "Greg, I'm as bored as a gay man on a Mormon cruise. Count me in on the little tour. There is one thing, though."

"And that is?"

"I don't want to ruin your generous offer, but you realize that my hard-to-ignore presence and world-wide reputation could tarnish your squeaky clean image."

Atsbee laughed hard and put his hand on Bob's shoulder. "Everything's fine, Mr. Clay and I appreciate your concern, but damage control is already in place. Okay, guys. It's time to party. Responsibly."

"Like I know how to do *that*," Bob muttered.

Observations and Emotions

Bob and I left the meeting room ahead of Greg and Moe-the-bodyguard. We pretended to head for the restroom, letting Greg and Moe walk past us. As soon as Greg entered the open hallway, a swarm of tuxedoed tech groupies descended on him.

As the Atsbee mob moved toward the party, Bob turned and stared at me wide-eyed like he was on coke. "Did you see what I saw back there?"

My stomach was in a knot. "You mean all that food?"

He nodded, his hand on his chest. "I'm dyin' here, Rick. My body requires thousands of calories daily to maintain my girlish figure and I am falling behind on my Weight Gainers schedule. Let's get back in there and chow down before the help packs it up for their kids."

We snuck back into the meeting room and attacked the finger food with little modesty. With the heavy wood doors closed, we weren't particularly concerned about social graces. Bob crossed my personal boundary when he sneezed all over the pâté. His allergic reaction was probably a result of the sweet-smelling bouquets on either end of the serving area. Decorative but pungent, they reminded me of Hawaii. Nevertheless, I decided to skip that side of the presentation. There were plenty of other tasty choices on my side of the long row of food – sushi rolls, fried mystery things, tiny meatballs in dark sauce, spinach triangles, and expensive fish.

We weren't totally insensitive to our lush surroundings. As we gobbled the fancy finger food, Bob nodded at the ocean, his mouth full of something orange. I'm guessing it was salmon roe.

I squinted and peered through the twilight haze and spotted a ship – a long tanker. It seemed to be moving south. My mind drifted to the boat and wondered if sailors on tankers ate finger food. Could they see us? Should I wave?

What was I thinking? It was time for another reality check. I performed a quick emotional review which resulted in an unusual discovery. I was happy. Holy crap. I'd already been attacked twice, my girlfriend appeared to be some kind of escort and had just killed someone in my hotel room. Despite the craziness, these last few days had been totally entertaining and certainly more fulfilling than discovering that deWilde had dumped me, banged my neighbor and stolen my dog.

In addition, my new lover seemed to like me. My comedian friend made me laugh. I was drinking for pleasure, admittedly way too much, but it was no longer to forget and tonight's dinner was on the house...and some of it was on the floor. But this was not the time to wander around in a pleasure zone. An unexpected calamity could be lurking nearby. It usually was.

I grabbed Bob's arm. "We have to get out of here and meet up with Renee. I'm supposed to be working the party."

He looked at me and started to choke. Then he tried to swallow. That didn't work. He washed everything down with a glass of vodka and recovered nicely, pounding his chest with a fist.

He made a gross sound, clearing the rest of his blockage. "Aaakk."

I looked at him and shook my head.

"Sorry about that," he said, "You're right. We should get to the party. We have to find out if it's everything they said it is."

"And if it isn't?"

"We'll have to do something about it. Come on, let's hit it."

* * * * *

I should have known Atsbee's party would be over the top. The ballroom was a sensory overload of sound, smells, color, music and voices. Strobe lights, fifteen-foot-long banners, costumed servers, and music assaulted our senses. The expressions on the guests' wide-eyed faces hinted that a rainbow of drugs had been consumed by most.

At the back of the room was a triple-wide staircase that rose to a stage where a fifteen-piece band played. Above the band was a painting of a spectacular mountain sunset.

Scattered among the guests were costumed performers that mirrored the unusual "Oscar Night in Yosemite" theme.

"What's with the campground motif?" asked Bob.

"Didn't you read your invitation?" I countered.

"Fuck no. I didn't even get an invitation. Traye called me and told me to get my ass down here." He nodded at an elderly man sporting a long white beard. "What's Santa Clause doing here?"

I looked at the bearded character holding an old-school camera. "That's Ansel Adams."

"From the Adams family? I don't remember him."

"No, he was a famous photographer."

"He looks like a homeless guy I knew who hung on Hollywood Boulevard. Who's the party planner, Yogi Bear?"

"Greg loves two things more than technology: Hollywood and Yosemite National Park. He decided to put them together this year as a party designer smash-up."

"Well I guess that explains the panhandler with the camera."

"Bob, Ansel Adams is the guy who took all the black and white pictures of the park. He's an icon."

"Is he related to Amy Adams?"

I didn't answer. Instead, I scanned the crowd again. Mingling with forest rangers and hikers were actors dressed as Rhett Butler, Scarlett O'Hara, the Marx Brothers, and Katharine Hepburn. Gowns worthy of a red carpet event were interspersed with an occasional Bette Davis or Julia Roberts look-alike. I wasn't convinced all the celebrities were fakes. Atsbee was known to be close friends with more than a few A-listers on both coasts. Celebrities usually wanted access to the latest tech toys, if only for bragging rights. Atsbee not only had the ability to provide these devices, his company invented most of them.

Guests, servers and entertainers continued to pour into the room.

Bob leaned into me. "The Greg man sure knows how to put on a show. He looked all prim and proper in our meeting, but I have on very good authority that he's turned into a party animal. He doesn't like to share the spotlight either. I like that in a person. I wonder if he picked that up from me."

I patted Bob on the back. "No doubt about it, Bob. Without your lead, he'd merely be another run-of-the-mill high-tech billionaire."

"Damn straight, Skippy."

I did another visual sweep of the room, looking for someone who might be identified as a Boeing employee, whatever that might look like. Off in the distance, on the right, towering above the crowd was a block of sculptured ice. Lit from the ceiling, the mountain of blue was a replica of the famous Half Dome of Yosemite National Park. Above it circled a miniature blimp and hang gliders.

I turned to tell Bob to keep an eye out for Renee, but he'd vanished into the sea of tuxedos and gowns. Undaunted, I worked my way through the beautiful one-percenters toward the base of the ice sculpture. Edging past talkative groups of guests, I caught phrases and clusters of words. Most of the comments concerned something about Atsbee's impending demise at Keysoft. The only hushed tones seemed to be seductive invitations to after-parties or offers of physical entanglements.

Drinks were waved, tipped and spilled. Subtle craziness was evident everywhere. I recognized an attractive B-level actor cornered by two teenage girls and a middle-aged woman. The trio was delighted that the unsteady celebrity was taking the time to stare at their barely concealed cleavage and listen to their conversation. The women appeared to have a plan for him and he was not resisting.

I passed several costumed servers and watched them on their rounds. In a moment of clarity I realized that the actors patrolling the room were not merely performers and food attendants. They were informants, eavesdropping on loose-tongued, braggarts who thought that this event was about them and their life with Atsbee.

Catching on to this use of the servers emboldened me. I took yet another visual sweep of the crowd. Most of the people looked unfamiliar, but I would have expected that. These were associates of the famous Greg Atsbee, a cool, powerful leader of the corporate and tech world. They were definitely not the friends of a bankrupt celebrity trainer from the oft-forgotten San Gabriel Valley.

My focus stopped at a familiar face. Oh this was not good.

Fifteen feet in front of me, in a shimmering white Fred Leighton dress covered with what appeared to be real diamonds, was my ex: Evelyn deWilde. Purposefully standing under one of the down-shooting spotlights, she looked like an angel. It was an excellent disguise. Then my mood changed and my heart leapt. Could Mojo be stashed somewhere here in the hotel? This might be the best thing that'd happened since my recent afternoon shower adventure.

Standing a few feet steps to her side I recognized the "Weasel" from Las Vegas. Overweight and balding, he looked like a taller version of an unattractive Danny DeVito.

I had no need to reestablish a friendship with a woman who'd nearly ruined me. And although I sorely wanted to find out if Mojo was nearby, I knew getting near Evelyn was fraught with danger. She was my bad luck charm incarnate. She always made me feel inferior without the slightest effort. But I was determined to stay on track and get my delivery fee. The rest would fall in to place.

I could hear Evelyn's voice above the music and noise of the crowd. I wondered if my brain was tuned to her frequency, or was she really that loud?

"Oh. My. God. Rick! Over here! Rick!"

Yes, she was really that loud.

She moved in my direction. The crowd parted. She grabbed my hands and held them as if we were about to play "London Bridge." She smiled. It was an unkind smirk compared to Renee's.

"Rick Johnson. I *never* expected to see you here tonight. Are you lost?"

Of course I was lost. I was wandering around Half Moon Bay in a new tux and thought I'd drop by the Ritz to crash a party. Was she nuts? Oh yeah, I forgot. Of course she was. Was I the only one who knew this fact?

My brain started forming questions. Where was Mojo? What was *she* doing here? Did her Vegas millionaire know Atsbee? Did she? Did they fly here in a private jet? Did the "Weasel" make a living at gambling, or is there something more sinister involved? Was he good in bed? Was he better than me?

At least I'd won the hair game. The guy was a cue ball.

I took a deep, cleansing breath, in an effort to be kind and gentle. "Greg invited me along with my ex-roommates Scott DeVore and Bob Clay. Where's my dog?"

Evelyn gripped my hands tight and her eyes narrowed. She made a point to touch my truncated finger. "Mojo's in Vegas, remember? You have to get Saul his money if you want to see him, remember? Did you say Scott's here?"

"Yea, he's here somewhere. He's been overseas, working on some kind of import-export business. He's getting rich, I think," I said, voice steady.

"That's interesting. Really? Scott's here?"

I'd just answered her question. And why was she so interested in a guy I'd only mentioned a few times?

I pretended to look for him in the crowd. "Yes, I saw him myself. We flew up here on Atsbee's jet."

Evelyn seemed to drift off. There was something about Scott that made her try to think. I knew it wasn't going to work. In a moment she was back with me.

"Rick, you look absolutely different," she said with her scary grin. "I'd introduce you to Saul, but he's involved in a dreadfully serious business discussions about some silly North Korean tech stuff. I don't understand any of it. What I *do* know..." she covered her mouth and chuckled loudly, "is that Saul makes a lot of money. I like that in a man. Probably why you and I couldn't stay together. By the way, he's absolutely in love with Mojo. I'm sure you understand. You liked him too...Mojo I mean, not Saul."

I managed to control my temper. "Mojo is a great dog," I said, "It's a little annoying that you stole him from me."

She rolled her eyes. "Oh Rick, I didn't steal him. He wanted to leave that depressing place you called home."

"He didn't seem to mind it."

"He told me himself he wanted a major upgrade in lifestyle. I totally understand dog talk. By the way, are you here with anyone?"

"Yes. I met a wonderful woman. We've been having a lot of fun."

We take turns killing people in our hotel suite. It's a blast. You should try it sometime. Maybe you're next.

"Where is she? Did she come tonight?"

"She's at a private pre-party. She'll be here in a bit."

"Well, that's wonderful. I heard you weren't doing so well."

Well you did have me arrested, stole my dog, and the bankruptcy was due to your crazy spending. But I didn't say any of that. The last time I lost my temper near her I spent a week in a very unsanitary jail.

"Okay, well, I'm going to get back to my friends," she said, pulling away. "Are you staying at the hotel?"

"I'm in the Ritz-Carlton Room."

It was like someone hit her over the head and pushed her back. "Well, that is...wonderful. Greg must be very impressed with you."

"We're talking about a few projects. It seems promising."

She didn't seem so distant all of a sudden. "I hope it works out with him. He's a very influential man. Maybe we can spend some time together if you get the money for Mojo. We're on the second floor. If you want to visit later, let me know."

I managed a smiled. "Of course, Evelyn."

"Great seeing you, Rick." She kissed me lightly on the lips, then did a twirl so her dress inflated. She re-entered the circle of light where the jewels threw reflections into the air like a disco ball. I watched her meet up with her weasel man in a passionless embrace. Behind him was a strange looking geek with huge sideburns. It took me a second until I realized it was the same water-logged man I saw yelling at the valet an hour ago. This guy seemed to be everywhere.

I turned, took one step and nearly collided with a ruddy-complexioned, red-haired man in a wrinkled, dark purple tuxedo.

"Hello. I'm Jordan Bateman," he said, with his hand outstretched. I tentatively offered mine. Bateman grabbed it and shook it too hard. I was not entirely comfortable with this stranger's forceful introduction. I figured I should play nice, but stay ready for anything. This could be another deadly surprise attack or another financial offer.

"Hello, Jordan. I'm Rick Johnson."

"Good to meet you, Rick. You look familiar. Did you ever work in the Seattle area?"

"No, I'm afraid not. I've never been north of San Francisco."

"I could have sworn I worked with you back at Boeing. You know, the airplane company, Boeing? No matter." He reached high in the air as if stretching.

"Sorry, muscle cramp," he explained. "How do you know Greg?"

The word "Boeing" jogged my senses. This was my man, but nothing had happened. Bateman didn't offer me a phone or a spy camera or lead me to a secret side exit. If he was doing anything on the sly, he was keeping it from everyone, including me. I did a quick look above the crowd. There weren't any obvious vantage points to hide a sniper. The distant stairway and stage in the back of the room seemed a remote possibility, but the area was teeming with guests and waiters; hardly a reasonable staging area. I silently wished Bob was here to back me up, but he was nowhere in sight.

My focus returned to Bateman. "Greg and I went to school together," I said.

Smiles were growing on the guests' flushed faces. Conversations were becoming louder. I noticed someone drop a champagne glass and pretend it never happened.

"You and Greg must go way back," said Bateman, maintaining direct eye contact.

Was this guy prying, or qualifying? Did it matter? He was the Boeing man, but he wasn't dressed right. Who wears a purple tuxedo to a formal event? This wasn't a high school prom.

Bateman was not distracted by the other guests' actions. Even the couple trying to swallow each other's tonsils didn't draw his attention.

"Any wild stories?" he continued, "From college, I mean?"

I shook my head. I felt extremely uncomfortable around this guy. He was sketchy, suspicious.

"No stories to tell," I said. "It was pretty dull."

Bateman chuckled. "I bet he has a few. Everyone does. Did he ever tell you any?"

This was not working for me. I shook my head again and smiled, wondering how long the game would last.

"Every time I saw Greg, he was working, studying or running for student government. The man was a saint the entire time we were together. So unless things have changed..."

Bateman stared directly into my eyes. There was no kindness in his expression as he continued to force the conversation. "Sounds like the same guy to me. He doesn't stop, does he? What do you do, Rick?"

"I'm in the exercise business - private contractor. I also design and sell personal-improvement equipment. It's a growing business."

Bateman acted like he hadn't heard a word I said. "Yeah, well, I'm still in advertising. Got some profitable contracts thanks to Greg. Hey, you wouldn't happen to have an iPhone, would you?"

This was it. I eyed the man carefully. It was go-time.

"Actually, I do," I replied.

"Could you show it to me?"

I pulled the phone that was delivered in the lobby and held it out. Bateman did not even look at it. He produced his own phone and pressed a button. His phone revealed a graphic that looked like a target. Two X's were in the center of the design.

"This looks very good," he said. He offered me his phone. "I think you'll like this one. It's a perfect match, don't you think? My guess is that the two of them together would work much more efficiently at the airport, don't you think?"

The phone he offered looked identical to the one in my hand and the one I brought with me.

"I think you're right." I said, guessing that was the right correct thing to say. I took his phone.

"Don't you want this one?" I asked, thinking this was supposed to be some kind of trade.

A look of panic crossed his face. "Are you fucking crazy? Don't give that thing to me!" he snarled in a low voice. "You need them both, you idiot."

Bateman straightened up and smiled as if nothing had occurred. "It was a pleasure chatting with you, Rick. Take care of those phones. I think you'll enjoy their added features."

He turned to leave, and his eyes met mine again. Something changed. He looked around, and then grabbed one of my lapels and leaned in.

"Stay away from Joey. He's here. In this room."

Bateman disappeared into the crowd.

I pocketed the two phones and made a mental note to put Bateman's phone in my right pocket because I thought it was the "right" one. The lobby phone was in my left pocket because it was "left" to me, and my phone was in my pants pocket, because I didn't want to get confused. It was time to get to the ice sculpture.

Costumed characters continued to circulate the room eavesdropping on everyone, but now I viewed them less as performers and more as undercover agents. I moved past a group of young executives arguing over the merits of natural versus implants and finally arrived at the bottom of the flared staircase.

As I looked up at the incredible mountain of ice that towered over the party, someone bumped into me, hard.

I heard a mumble that I assumed was an insincere "sorry." The guy was gone before I could discover what he looked like.

It took me a moment to realize my pocket might have been picked. I immediately stopped and checked. One, two, and three phones. I had them all as well as my wallet. I came to the conclusion that the guy was just an insensitive jerk and headed for the bottom of the giant ice sculpture.

Bob's Olympic Event

Getting to the distant iced Half Dome was harder than it appeared. I worked my way between people, squeezing through small openings and clusters of partiers. I'm not much of a hugger and don't enjoy being in close quarters with strangers, so the constant rubbing against unfamiliar individuals was uncomfortable. I felt someone grab my ass. I turned to locate the culprit, but no one looked guilty or interested. Checking my pockets, I made sure I had all my phones. Locating all three devices, I continued on my journey.

Then I spotted something out of place. In the middle of a sea of inebriated humanity, standing by himself, was a very different Bob Clay. Lost and confused, I think he was shocked that no one acknowledged his existence. I was fairly certain this crowd was not his demographic audience. My bet was that no more than half a dozen people in the room had seen a Bob Clay performance. Most of them *knew* about Bob's comedy routines as well as his spectacular rise to fame and well-publicized crash, but not what he looked like or how he did it.

The sad Bob moment didn't last more than a couple seconds. His melancholy expression evaporated like water in the desert and was replaced by a broad smile. He snatched a fresh martini from a passing tray and muscled his way into a group of strangers. In a matter of seconds he was the center of attention. He said something, put his hands on his hips, threw his head back, and the entire circle laughed heartily. With his ego sufficiently renewed, Bob departed the circle and headed in the direction of Half Dome.

I followed him to the base of the ice sculpture and watched over his shoulder as he stared down at a group of miniature fishermen placed alongside a vodka-filled river. He shifted his gaze upward to a row of branded vodka bottles frozen inside the block of ice. He smiled and shook his head.

"That is so Greg," he said to no one in particular. "Product placement at his own party."

Bob turned to find me facing him.

"Hey, little buddy. How the hell are you?"

"Let's go, Bob. We're on our way to the airport."

"What are you talking about, Rick? Check out this ice sculpture. I told you it would be here." He folded his hands and rested them on his protruding stomach. "I'm sorry my friend, but I can't leave now. I have a reputation to ruin." Then he pointed at the crowd. "Take a look at the delicious opportunities out there."

I didn't have time to explain that I needed that money and I wanted my dog back before something terrible happened and that my mother's apartment smelled really bad. We had to get going.

"The man from Boeing contacted me. We're on our way to the airport."

Bob's eyes opened wide. "Are you freakin' nuts, Johnson? It's dark out there. Besides, this crowd is full of horny, rich men and a lot of them live quietly on my side of the street, if you catch my drift. If you're thinking of leaving the grownup playground, you're on your own."

I couldn't tell if the vodka Bob consumed had begun to affect him or if he'd ingested something more potent. I did know he had less than pure thoughts in mind as he pointed at the crowd and played a version of "Eenie *Meeny Miney Moe.*"

"I thought you were on my team, Bob. Remember? 'Team Rick'?" I walked around in front of him and blocked his view. "And what about wanting to be a world-class detective along with your love of new adventures?"

"Those are extremely important priorities and they come right behind hanging at the Ritz, drinking free booze and messing around with rich, gay executives."

"I'll give you three grand."

"Make it four," he countered, craning his neck to see around me.

"Thirty-five," I said.

"Done," said Bob. "But we have to come right back. The airport's only a few minutes away. Deal?"

"It's a deal. But what's with the needy greedy game, Bob? I thought you were rich."

Bob leaned in. "I was. Don't you remember? My manager stole almost everything. I managed to stash some cash but I'm hardly rubbing elbows with the rich boys. I can't even get a meeting with Andy Cohen. It's bad enough I had to leave my marigolds to grovel for another TV show, and now I'm going to be your freelance wingman for a measly four grand.

"Thirty-five hundred Bob."

"Thirty-eight."

"Stop it. We're done with the bargaining." I hoped this argument wouldn't continue, because if I didn't get to the airport and grab the cash, I could never pay him or anyone else. Hell, I didn't even have cab fare to the airport. My plan at that moment was to hijack Atsbee's limo or grab a hotel shuttle.

Bob was lost in thought, or in a brain fog. Whatever was wrong, I knew he wasn't firing on all cylinders.

"Okay," he said, "but I gotta get a refill before we go, 'cause, ya know. I live on the edge. I'm that kinda guy. It could be a long trip."

"It's ten minutes away."

"Yeah, but if we run out of refreshments, it'll feel like years.

Bob turned and scooped a glassful of vodka from the stream, capturing one of the small model fishermen. He looked down into the cup. "This guy's too small," he said, and tossed the figurine back. He looked at me and shrugged. "Catch and release."

He took a huge drink, placed his glass beside the river, and pulled out a silver flask.

"Bob, what are you *doing*?"

"Working my twelve steps."

"Drinking vodka from a stream is *not* part of the program."

He looked at me seriously. "You can never work the steps unless you drink first. It's a rule. I should know. I've worked so many steps, I'm on the tenth floor and still climbing."

"We have to leave, Bob. Now."

I glanced to the side of the ice mountain and spotted Bateman sitting in a chair with a vacant expression on his face. I took a few steps in his direction and then stopped. It was obvious he was gone from this world. Protruding from his chest was what looked like the end of a metal knitting needle. I watched as a pair of gloved hands appeared from behind the drapery and pulled him out of sight.

This did not bode well for my immediate future. I quickly returned to Bob who was still refilling his glass from the stream.

"This is the best fishing spot in the world," he mumbled.

Over Bob's shoulder, I spotted two massive linebackers in black suits with wired earpieces and bulges on one side of their chests heading directly toward us. They were moving fast, parting the sea of Atsbee. I'd already received two iPhones that appeared to contain valued-added content, so I had no intention of hanging around to find out why these descendants of Bigfoot were heading my way.

"Bob. We go. Now!"

"What *is* your problem, Rick?" said Bob, without turning. "You worry too much and you should do something about those forehead wrinkles. I know a great Botox guy. He could make those plow lines disappear so fast, it would be like your head was hit with a frying pan."

I left him talking to himself, dove beneath the table skirt that surrounded Half Dome and scampered underneath a line of serving tables, dodging electrical wires, empty wine boxes and table legs. Near the end of the maze, I flipped the tablecloth and popped out on the employee side.

My head smashed into the bottom of a serving tray. A surprised Groucho Marx watched his salmon-covered crackers fly into the air. I brushed crumbs and bits of fish off my jacket then glanced toward the entrance. I was going to make it out easily, and for a moment, I reveled in my cleverness.

A flash of red caught my eye. It was Renee, flanked on either side by two undesirables. Behind them was Scott, giving orders. Even with that split-second glimpse, I could tell she was not going willingly. One of them had his hand suspiciously on her back. I was sure there was a gun involved or she'd be taking this guy on. And Scott? I knew he was up to something unsavory. But messing with Renee was going to get him into a lot more trouble than he expected.

Pushing my way through the last few incoming guests I headed for the exit. I'd made a commitment to Renee and I was not about to let slimy Scott screw it up.

I burst into the lobby and spotted another suspicious duo hankering for a fight at the far end of the corridor. I proceeded in the opposite direction, the same way I saw Renee being pulled.

Around the corner, at the end of the corridor, was an emergency exit that warned of an alarm sounding if opened. The sign was a total lie. I exited the building and peered into the darkness. Thank God the half-full moon illuminated the area. Renee was being pushed down the path between the hotel and the ocean side bluffs. Her red dress flowed in the gentle night breeze.

126

Then I saw what I needed - a maintenance golf cart with empty wine boxes strewn across the small flatbed and keys in the ignition.

I casually strolled around it with feigned disinterest, and then jumped into the driver's seat. Starting the engine, I realized this was an awesome find. The electric cart was nearly silent.

I aimed the stealth vehicle down the path and was about to get away unnoticed when I caught sight of a person running at me.

My mind raced. I started making up some bullshit story about why I was stealing the hotel's cart when I realized it was Bob. Despite frantically pumping his arms, the heavyset comedian wasn't traveling much faster than a walk.

I let off on the accelerator and the cart drifted to a halt.

Bob stopped and bent over, his hands on his knees. "Don't...leave...me."

"They took Renee," I whispered loudly, "Hurry up. Get in."

"Who took her?" he wheezed.

I pointed down the path. "Some of Scott's goons. Get in."

Bob, still panting, looked up and beckoned me. "Back it...up."

I shook my head. "I'm not putting this thing in reverse. God knows what kind of noise it'll make."

Bob stumbled the last few feet and fell into the flatbed, knocking empty wine boxes onto the ground. His hand rose from the back making a feeble wave.

"Go...you..." he gasped. "We...save...girl."

Renee was between the two men, being dragged down the path where it curved toward the bluff.

I stomped on the accelerator and the cart started moving. The warm summer wind blew through my hair and the sound of waves could be heard crashing on the nearby shore. It was a great night for a golf cart ride, but my appreciation of the balmy evening was being ruined by the threat of Renee's demise.

Bob grabbed the back of the passenger seat and pulled himself closer.

"What happened in there?" I asked, my foot pressed to the floor.

"A couple of ugly-ass guys built like refrigerators came up to me. Asked where you'd gone," Bob sputtered. "I'm sure they were packing heat and not the good kind. I told them you were in a meeting with Atsbee and they tore off into the kitchen. I guess that's where he was."

I watched as Renee and her captors stopped near the edge of the cliff. One of the men had his arm outstretched. I assumed there was a weapon in his hand. A small rise on the side of the path caught my attention

In the Army, I'd experienced firefights in foreign countries that resulted in the horrible deaths of my friends. I'd been threatened with rape in a county jail and I'd had been attacked on a public street by a crazed mugger with a huge knife, but the thought of Renee being in danger was the most frightening feeling I'd experienced in years. I also knew that charging two armed men on a slow moving golf cart was not a smart idea.

I pulled off the path and parked behind the small rise. I got out of the driver's seat and came to Bob's side.

"I'm going around to the side of this knoll. When I give the signal, drive over the hill and aim directly at those guys. That should create a distraction. I'll come from the opposite direction and take them down."

I figured that Big Bob would not be perceived as a threat. I could do the dirty work attacking from the flank.

"You mean I get to drive?"

"Yes Bob, that's what I said. Now pay attention. Drive the cart directly at them. That should give us the advantage of surprise, but wait for my signal."

Bob hopped off the flatbed and rubbed his hands together. His childish enthusiasm did not give me much confidence. I got the sinking feeling that he didn't care about rescuing Renee. He just wanted to play with the car. I didn't have time to think of another plan. It was all I could do on short notice.

"This is going to be awesome," he gloated, "It'll be the charge of the heavy brigade."

"Bob."

"Yes, my good buddy, Rick, what is it?"

"Wait for my signal," I said.

Bob saluted. "Yes, sir."

I crouched low and headed around the side of the small hill. Words were being spoken, but the nearby breaking waves muddled their meaning. The dark figures were partially lit by the rising half-moon. I silently hoped that they didn't see me heading their way.

I was guessing that if these goons were intent on hurting Renee, they'd have already accomplished the deed. Perhaps there's something else going on - a renegotiation of her deal - or was she trying to talk her way out of a difficult situation? Maybe they thought she had something they wanted – the phones, perhaps, or maybe they were into physical misdeeds.

It is a little known fact that hired crooks can be creepy and exhibit extremely poor manners at these types of functions often deviating from their original purpose because of poor training or, sometimes, a total lack of crook discipline.

I was nearly in position when I caught a glimmer of movement to my side. Backlit by the building's accent lighting. I saw that Bob had moved the cart to the top of the rise and was leaning forward as if readying for an attack.

Suddenly he let out a howl and started drifting down the grassy hill. Aided by his hundreds of extra pounds and the incline, the cart quickly accelerated. I watched in amazement as Bob's diversion worked. The men were startled, and turned to find where the inhuman sound was coming from.

Bearing down on them in the semi-darkness, Bob began weaving back and forth, presumably to avoid potential gunfire. The two men were dumbfounded, not understanding what was coming at them.

I burst into a run. The man farthest away took several steps toward Bob, peering into the darkness trying to decipher what was heading his way. I aimed my attack at the slime ball holding Renee. I hit him at a full-on run and slammed him to the ground. We wrestled, each of us trying to control the weapon in his outstretched but immobilized hand. Renee walked over to us with a calm demeanor and violently kicked him in the ribs. That sudden blow slowed his resistance and broke something inside his body. A second kick knocked the gun out of his hand.

"You ripped my dress, you skinny shit," she snarled.

The other assailant continued to walk toward Bob, unaware of the commotion that was occurring behind him. Confused by the large cart driver, he waited too long to make his decision. By the time he realized Bob's intent was to literally run him over, he turned and tried to dodge the cart. Bob had gravity on his side, and with a quick twist of the steering wheel, Bob hit him with the right front fender. The impact threw the man to the side and he tumbled onto the manicured grass. Bob spun the wheel again as the limping man struggled to his feet. Before the guy knew it, the front of the cart was on him and he was about to be run over again. He ran straight ahead trying to outpace the golf cart.

"Run!" yelled Bob, half standing in the small cart, "Run you smelly evil piece-a-shit!"

I grabbed my bad guy by his jacket and pulled him to his feet.

"All right, Mr. Big Shot, let's get you into some light and find out who you are."

I glanced to check on Renee. During that moment, the stranger pulled away. His cheap suit ripped at the seams. Slipping from my grasp he ran up the path. I was left holding a shredded piece of poorly made jacket.

At first I was angry at losing the little cowardly turd, but then I realized that the raid had been a success. Renee was safe.

Bob was still chasing his quarry in tight little circles. After several more turns I watched the man become disoriented, reverse his direction and run straight off the cliff. There was no sound. No scream. The guy simply headed full steam toward the ocean, then dropped out of sight.

Bob stopped the cart and walked to the edge of the bluff. He peered over the brink for a long time. Then he returned to the car and drove to us. He seemed upset.

"You saw that, didn't you?" he said pointing his thumb over his shoulder. "The guy ran right off the cliff. All he had to do was stop."

"How's he doing?" asked Renee, attempting to straighten her disheveled dress. I could tell from the tone of her voice, she didn't really care about the guy. Maybe she sensed Bob's grief and was trying to get his mind off the fact that he'd just murdered someone.

Bob looked back at the bluff, then turned to us. "It's pretty dark down there. I couldn't really tell. One thing's for sure, he's not coming up the way he went down."

"It's okay, Bob," I said. "Hop on the cart and we'll go to the airport."

Bob looked puzzled in the pale moonlight.

"We're leaving another body behind?" he said.

"It's how we roll, Bob" I said, "Third one tonight."

"It seems awfully unsanitary."

"Are you volunteering for the job?"

He thought for a second. "No. I'm front line assault. I don't do cleanup or windows."

"Okay, then," I said. "Let's move."

Renee stood her ground. "Hey, party boys. I'm over here. Remember? The girl you were supposed to rescue?"

"We already did that," said Bob, brushing grass clippings from his sleeve.

I walked to her side. She looked even more alluring in the moonlight. Was I on some kind of drug? Why did I find her so irresistible?

"Come on, Renee, let's go to the airport. It'll be fun."

She put her hand up and shook her head. "Rick, I like you more than free drinks, but I'm not riding in *this* dress on *that* thing. You can forget it."

"What's the difference? It's already ruined."

"Doesn't matter. I have to go back and change."

"You have no idea what's waiting for you in there," I argued.

"Rick, I am going back to the room and putting on something more suitable for combat. Then I am going to get myself a real motor vehicle, not some Toys R Us reject."

"Hey, don't talk about Betsy that way," whined Bob.

"You're kidding. You named it?"

"Ah, no, but I thought I'd try it out for size. We could use it as a code name...like we have to find Betsy."

Renee stared at him.

"Okay, that idea needs some work. Come on, Rick, let's get to the airport. Maybe we can break into the bar on one of those planes."

"Why don't you meet me in the lobby?" said Renee.

I looked back at the hotel. "I don't think that's a safe place for me right now...or you either. I've had two security details try to nab me."

Renee shrugged. "I'll be fine. You're the ones with the phones that they're probably tracking. I'll meet you at the airport. Just don't do anything stupid on the way."

"Renee, are you sure you're okay...going back there?"

She paused and turned, obviously annoyed. "I'm fine, Rick, but I didn't like being set up like that. If I get my hands on that bitch Traye, I'm going to rip those fake hair extensions out of her freaking head."

"What happened?" I asked.

"I was mingling with the single hotties and you know, I get a little distracted by broad shoulders and blue eyes. Damn, I get fooled by those colored contacts every time. There I was, flirting with the rich boys and all of a sudden these goons decided it was their turn to dance. Thanks for catching up with me."

I picked up the man's gun from the ground.

"Here, you might need this."

"Thanks," she said in a softer tone.

"Be careful in there," I said, "I don't want you to get hurt."

"Listen, Robbie Rescue, I took care of myself long before you turned my life upside down. I think

I'm capable of changing my clothes and getting a decent ride to the airport."

She lifted her dress and headed back to the hotel, then stopped and turned again.

"That didn't come out the way I wanted," she said. "I wanted to say that I appreciate what you did, but I can take care of myself."

"Understood. We'll be at the airport."

Bob climbed into the cart's driver's seat. "I love watching couples working out their differences. It gives me hope that someday I too might find someone who will come to my side, preferably my right side. It's a much better angle for..."

"Shut up, Bob. Let's get this mission over with. The sooner we get rid of these stupid phones, the better. They've been nothing but trouble. Move over."

"What? After the incredibly dangerous stunt work I just performed?"

"Bob."

"Okay, okay. But I'm driving after we do the airport shuffle."

He climbed out of the cart and circled around the back. I grabbed the wheel and jumped into the driver's seat. Bob sat in the passenger side. I felt the car tilt in his direction.

"I've got a friend who lives a few miles up the coast," he said. "We can chill there after we're done with this silliness."

"I thought you wanted to go back to the party."

"Can't. Those big guys were evil beings, and they smelled awful. If they aren't going to have a dress code around here, they should at least have an odor code. Who wants to be near a stinky criminal? What is this world coming to?

Unfair Fairway

The ocean side of the hotel was lit with accent lights. Music drifted out into the night. Renee was walking the asphalt path, heading back to the main building. I wasn't sure if that was the right decision, letting her go there alone.

"Do you think we should help her?" I asked Bob as she disappeared into the building.

Bob turned to face me. "I think it's time she dressed herself. Besides, have you ever tried to fight someone wearing an outfit like that? It's absolutely exhausting."

"I meant should we go back with her to make sure she's safe?"

"If you knew what I knew, you would immediately deny knowing anything about what I know, but you certainly would not be asking that particular question to anyone I know. What did you say again?"

"What did *you* say?"

"I asked you first."

I couldn't be playing Bob's word games. I moved on to the next subject as I started the cart and headed along the path toward the golf course.

"Are you telling me Renee is not an escort?"

Bob burst out with a guffaw so loud it startled me. He covered his mouth, chuckled a few more times, and put his arm over my shoulder.

"Not even close, Rick. And trust me on this one: Renee Gunnison will be more than fine. You have no idea what she can handle. Well, I guess you have *some* idea of what she can handle. Wink, wink. Nod, nod. But your troubles are a tiny flaw in a fifty-carat diamond."

"Bob, I get the feeling you're leaving something out."

Bob ran his hand through his thick, dark hair. "Of course I'm leaving something out. I always leave something out. It's a rule of all entertainment, politics and child-rearing that you never, ever tell anyone the entire truth except on one occasion."

"And that is?"

"When you want someone to think you're lying."

"So, Bob..."

"Present and accounted for."

"You *are* going to tell me."

"Sooner rather than later," Bob promised, putting his feet on the tiny plastic dashboard.

I turned the wheel, left the cart path and aimed down a long fairway. "How about during our picturesque drive to the airport?"

"What, are we close friends again?" he asked, "We must be, now that we're battling the agents of evil side by side."

"We were always friends, Bob, even when you tried to seduce me back in college."

"I wasn't trying to get with you, Rick, I was merely being friendly. If I was trying to seduce you,

138

you'd be at this hotel with me, not Renee." Bob pointed straight ahead, "Onward, Rick Johnson! May you avoid many late payments with the money you earn tonight."

The fairway looked relatively flat in the dull moonlight. The thought passed my mind that Tiger Woods might have played a round here. Or maybe he just played around here.

Bob sat up, turned and looked back at the hotel disappearing behind us. "Wait a minute. Where the fuck are you going?"

I grinned. It took him long enough to figure out we weren't driving on a road.

"Doing a little bit of bushwhacking," I said as I leaned back in the hard plastic seat. "The cart path crosses the entrance road up ahead. I saw it from the limo when we drove in."

Bob slapped me on the arm. "Well, aren't you Mr. Dan Danger, going rogue on the dark scary golf course."

He was right. I was taking risks again and it felt good. Evelyn had made me so gun-shy I'd become afraid of my own shadow. I felt as if the RJ curse had been lifted. I wanted to stand up in my little green cart, spread my arms out in the warm summer wind and yell, "I'm on top of the cart!"

Instead, I looked over to Bob. I needed some answers from the answer man.

"Bob, you seem to know a lot about what is going on. What's the story with Renee? She's not your everyday woman."

Bob returned his feet to the low dashboard and clasped his hands behind his head, trying to get comfortable.

"You are a perceptive individual, Rick. Renee Gunnison is a different type of female. Actually, you should know that tonight she's a freelance government agent working on a complicated corporate espionage case. However, I happen to have a zillion informants myself. I am in the know and I am on the go, albeit my current pace is incredibly slow."

Bob was a spy too? Was this a new administration recovery program? Hire every unemployed person as an undercover agent?

"You work for the government?"

"Oh, no. They're all thieves and scoundrels. I have much better sources - the staff at E! Entertainment. They are a much more trustworthy group of people than any government acronym."

"E! Entertainment tracks government agents?"

"If they're sleeping with celebrities, you bet your peter, Mr. Paparazzo. Renee Gunnison has an impressive record for bedding famous people and she has excellent taste I might add. She could be a successful producer if she decided to switch careers. She's got the contacts, dirt on nearly every important power player, nerves of steel, and lies like a son of a bitch."

"Why are you telling me this, Bob?"

"Are you going senile? You just asked me."

I turned the wheel, and followed the gentle curve of the fairway, chugged past the tee and aimed for the next green.

"I thought Renee's job was to get me to go to the party."

"Ah, my friend, that's when it started. Traye hired Renee to make sure you got your stubborn butt here. But then Greg got wind of something more sinister and he overbid Traye and hired Renee to make sure you didn't get hurt in tonight's undercover double-double-crossing mess. I have to admire your curvy girlfriend. How she got Atsbee *and* Traye to pay her is a stroke of sheer genius. Unfortunately, she violated the number one rule of a spy."

"Getting her cover blown by an unemployed comedian?"

"No, my bankrupt friend, she fell in love with a handsome fitness trainer who likes to drive around in little green golf carts in the middle of the night. If she doesn't crack this espionage ring, her career in the spook business is finished, kaput, down the drain, end of the line, fired, *hasta la vista, finito...*"

"Okay, Bob, enough. I get it."

I aimed the cart to the left, crossed over to the adjoining fairway and skirted a sand trap with a small rise that led up to its edge. As I made the turn Bob grabbed onto the small plastic handle to avoid falling off his undersized seat.

"Hey, signal those turns, will ya?"

"There are no signals, Bob."

"Then use your words."

"How long has Renee been in the spy business?" I asked.

"Since college. Her party-girl cover was a perfect ruse."

"I've been played, haven't I, Bob? Come on, tell me. I can take it."

"Look, what I am going to tell you only a few people know. Do not, I repeat do not mention this to her or anyone else. Agreed?"

"Agreed."

"Renee lost her parents, a brother, an uncle, an aunt, and two cousins in a Pakistani terrorist attack when she was a college sophomore. She was supposed to be with them, but she stayed back to finish a school project. She was devastated. You know, I remember when I was nineteen..."

"So do I, Bob. You were at Cayuga, and I think you broke the school record for sleeping with the most people on campus."

"Ah, the good old days, where have they gone? Oh, I know, to my waist. Anyway, Renee turned into this super patriot. Here's another fascinating factoid; Renee Gunnison has saved more lives than most doctors I know. But she has a problem."

"Me?"

"Apparently we all have *that* annoying issue. More importantly, she has a habit of wrecking things. She only gets hired on important cases because she's a disaster in the making. Her involvement always causes huge amounts of collateral damage. When she's working a case, she inevitably gets into deep trouble, looks like she's about to blow the entire gig, but somehow she gets the job done. No one quite understands her method. But they're usually upset when they find out how much it cost."

"She kills innocent people?"

"No, she's pretty good about choosing the right targets, but she's wrecked cars, houses, motorcycles, small planes, large boats, expensive dresses, and more than a few mansions."

"Well, that's part of the job, isn't it?"

"Ah, no, Rick. That is not part of any job."

"Okay enough about her - what about the airport?"

Bob shrugged. "It's not going to be pretty, but the weather should be nice."

"So far it's been pretty ugly everywhere else we've been." I replied.

"I liked the ice sculpture."

I laughed out loud. "You didn't even look at it. You only saw the line of frozen liquor bottles and those little men in the vodka stream."

"They were so cute. I took a couple. Couldn't help myself. I hope no one saw me."

A blur of brown metal flashed in front of us. I turned my head following the image and realized I was looking at the taillights of a big, fat, late model Bonneville. The clumsy car tore up the fairway as it tried to stop on the dew-slicked grass.

"That is the second ugliest motor vehicle I've seen," said Bob.

"What's the first?'

"This piece of crap," he said watching the monster car as it started to turn. "I don't think they're going to miss the next time."

I turned the steering wheel and aimed for the rough. Bob held on to the dashboard with both hands.

"If my calculations are correct, they're going to have a problem on the way back," I said.

"Come on, Rick. What're you gonna to do? Outrun them?"

"Not quite."

I entered the rough and turned again, driving parallel with the fairway. Between Bob's extra weight and the resistance of the longer grass, our forward progress slowed considerably.

Bob took a nail file from his pocket and examined the back of his hand. "I think this is a mistake, Speed Racer. We are outgunned, outflanked and out powered. I'd say we've been totally outed."

"Watch and learn from the master."

"I saw the movie, Rick. Obi-Wan is defeated by Darth Vader. Became this kinda ghost thing. Not a smart career move. Tell me you're not a man with delusions of being a super-hero using a puny golf cart and a ripped tuxedo. I like you Rick, but you're no Jackie Chan. My guess is that we're going to end up being a hood ornament on an unappealing car. I'll just *die* of embarrassment."

"No one is going to die."

"Tell that to the guys back in your suite."

"The folks in that car think they're on a racetrack. They're in for a big surprise."

"So far they've been on top of the surprise pile, and I'm not expecting the tide to change any time soon. Hey, do you think my nails are too long?"

The roar of the V8 engine startled us.

"Geeze," said Bob, not looking up from his manicuring chores. "That is way too loud for a Ritz-Carlton golf course, especially at this time of night."

Grass and dirt flew into the air as the car's wheels dug into the ground. The wide-grilled rust bucket began moving forward, gaining speed.

Bob stared at the oncoming car. "The fact that I'm going to be hit first is totally unfair. You drove. You should die first. I'm sensitive about these things, you know."

I continued aiming the cart down the rough, peering into the semi-darkness. I knew what a small mound on the edge of a fairway meant - a sand trap and I was going to our little cart on the other side of it.

The car's high beams lit us up.

"We're doomed, I tell you," sighed Bob as he held his hand in the glare of the car's headlights. "I knew I should have taken care of my affairs."

"I thought you were broke."

"Oh, you're right. I meant I should have had more affairs."

"There'll be plenty of time for that, Bob. They have no idea who they're dealing with."

The cart's front wheels passed behind the small mound of grass. The Bonneville's headlights illuminated the top half of us like the Christmas tree in Rockefeller Center.

Bob continued to work his fingernails as the car careened toward our little cart. Then the Bonneville hit the front of the rise. The dented grill rose in the air and then dropped, plunging us back into a moon-lit semi-darkness. Sounds of twisting metal and broken glass came from behind the rise, then the overly loud engine went silent.

"What happened?" asked Bob.

I spun the wheel in the opposite direction, again throwing Bob off balance, and aimed the cart inland toward the access road.

"They hit the lip of a sand trap, then the front of the car pitched into the depression. They thought they could just drive over that little hill but they were sadly mistaken. They're going to take a couple of penalty strokes for that one," I said. "Shall we go to the airport, Bob?"

"Yes, sir, we should fly to the airport in our trusty, um, our sturdy, our slow-as-crap...you know, Rick, I got nothin'," said Bob, returning his nail file to his jacket pocket. "But from now on I'll have to call you....The Cartmeister."

"I'd rather you didn't."

"Cartman?"

"You stole that from South Park."

"Magna Carta?"

"Gotta do a lot better."

"Final offer - Master Cart."

I smiled as the tiny vehicle bounced off the grass and we headed for the main highway.

Par for the Course

Even without Bob weighing it down, our little maintenance cart wasn't built for speed. It wasn't built for comfort. It definitely wasn't built for the highway. The only thing that vehicle was supposed to do was putter around a golf course, and that was four miles behind us.

I wasn't particularly worried about driving the green mini-monster down the main road of Half Moon Bay. Long before departing for my idyllic weekend on the coast, I did the required Google search on the location.

Less than an hour's drive south of San Francisco, Half Moon Bay is a land that time had forgotten. Not as cool as Malibu, Hawaii, or even Pismo Beach to the south, it is far from the interstate and not really considered a must-see tourist destination. It's a sleepy community with a few restaurants and cold Pacific waters.

Money, recognition and even photogenic shorelines were assigned to the better known coastal areas to the south – Big Sur, Carmel, Monterey, and San Simeon. Even on a Saturday night, the town's twelve thousand residents are usually sleeping, drinking at home or in a bar or procreating in an attempt to replace the young residents who constantly leave for the promise of big money and excitement of city life. The only legitimate jobs with a potential future in Half Moon Bay were at the Ritz.

I turned into the airport entrance and headed for the parking lot. Soft circles of light from rusted streetlights dotted the pothole-filled access road. A flimsy gate at the end of the parking lot was conspicuously open, inviting me to drive onto the runway. We bumped our way onto the tarmac. I drove about twelve feet and came to a stop. I wasn't going anywhere near those planes. I figured whoever wanted me to be here would make their presence known.

Bob put his pudgy hand to his forehead, shielding his eyes from the glare of the overhead lights. "I love getting out in the evening with the stars above you, a good friend at your side and the Ocean breeze in the air. It's a shame that strangers have to ruin that unique experience trying to run you down with their pitiful late model car. On the other hand, it is important to get the sense that death is always close by. Makes you feel humble."

I laughed out loud. "You? Humble? Come on, Bob. I *know* you."

"Hey, I said it makes *you* feel humble. Not me. Okay fearless leader, what's next on your to-do list?"

"We wait."

Bob crossed his arms. "For what? The train? We left the party of the year, were almost run down, drove a deserted highway without an open bar in sight, to sit around and stare at million-dollar planes full of booze and food?"

"They said I'd be met here."

"Looks kinda quiet," said Bob as he reexamined his nails. "You never know, that might change. I'm kind of regretting we didn't bring our clubs. I've never played that course. I hear that it is quite serene in the daylight without the cars and abductions."

A black town car tore through the parking lot, onto the runway, and skidded around to the front of our cart, pulling a perfect one-eighty blocking our path to the jets.

"Wow. That was an awesome move," said Bob. "A bit over the top, but I'm always a sucker for grand entrances."

Scott stepped out of the town car and stood behind the open door, using it as a shield.

Bob started chuckling. "Scottie looks like he's doing an episode of Hawaii Five-0, except they have good-looking actors on that show."

"Okay, assholes. I can't believe I had to chase you all the way out here. Hand over the phone," said Scott.

I sat perfectly still and considered the situation. I had Renee's gun tucked in my waistband, but Scott had the forethought, or cowardice, to hide behind the car door. On the other hand, Bob and I were sitting like oversized children on a kiddie park ride. Driving away would be a joke. Running might be faster, but equally as foolish. If I was going to have any kind of future with Renee, I needed to give Scott one of the phones. It seemed like the only thing do to.

The problem was, which phone? There was the phone that Renee bought me, there was the phone I got in the lobby, and there was the phone that Bateman, the man from Boeing handed me, and they all looked the same.

Despite Scott's impressive entrance, Bob was treating him like a child which was totally ironic as Bob was incapable of being an adult.

"Scott, do you have any idea what kind of trouble you're going to get yourself into?" Bob said, "This is not a game. Well, it is, kind of, in an odd sort of way, because when Traye met you in..."

"Shut your trap, fat man. I know exactly what is happening here. This situation is bigger than you. Hand it over, Rick."

Bob wasn't finished. Actually, I don't think Bob was ever finished.

"Oh, Scott, lover of Asian children, Traye's got you spinning in little perverted circles. There are at least two other evil groups working here tonight and they're all in Traye's pocket. If you get anywhere near those planes, you're going to be a sad bad man, more so than you are now."

"You don't know what you're talking about, blimpo. One more word and you'll be a dead groundskeeper in a tux."

Bob nodded, lowered his head and whispered. "Give the asshole the phone. He deserves it and more."

I whispered back. "Are you keeping something from me, Bob?"

"Why do you keep asking me that?" he shot back. "Of course there's more to this than what I've told you. There's always more. It's like an episode of 'Lost.' Just give the spy the phone."

"Scott's a spy, too? What is this, a secret agent convention?"

Bob nodded. "Duh. What do you think this stupid annual gathering is? Didn't you wonder why it wasn't held in New York, San Fran, or my fave, Las Vegas? They buy and sell information here all night long. And it's next to a kick-ass, unmonitored airport on the Pacific Ocean. Come on, Rick, how many times do you need, have a gun pointed at you until you realize this is undercover central? You're the only person here who isn't on someone's payroll."

"I guess I didn't get the memo on my spy fax. But isn't it wrong to give our enemy the secret phone?"

"Give him the damn phone, you idiot!" shouted Bob, which caused me to jump. Then he returned to his whispering. "Do you know which one is which? I hope you kept them in different pockets."

"Yeah," I said, thankful that I took care of that issue already.

"Give him yours, the one you brought with you."

"Won't he know the difference?"

"Look at him. He's an idiot. Have you ever known a broke drug dealer? The prick can't do anything right."

"The phone, girls," demanded Scott. "You can kiss and make up after I leave."

I got out of the cart, walked the ten feet to the town car and handed Scott my phone. I desperately wanted to rush him, put him in a headlock and choke him until he decided to change his ways, but I knew in my heart this guy would continue to make bad decisions. I tossed him the phone from about five feet, then backed away slowly, being careful not to turn. If I was going to be shot by this dickwad, I wanted to look him in the eye while he did it. I learned a lot in the

Army. One thing was that it is extremely difficult to kill someone who's staring at you, especially if they know who you are.

"You're a loser, Rick. I would have expected more resistance, but nothing's changed. You're still doing nothing, accomplishing nothing."

Even as I backed away my impulse was to reverse course, throw him onto the asphalt and break a finger or two, but my military training came back in gushes. You only take on an adversary like Scott when the odds are in your favor. I knew there would be a time and place to confront him when he wasn't holding all the cards.

Bob made a move to get out of the cart. Scott shifted his aim. "Go ahead, fatso, give me an excuse."

I kept my eye on Scott as I continued to back toward the cart. "Don't move Bob," I said quietly. "And don't do anything funny."

"You're taking away my entire reason for living," he complained.

I could tell he wanted to mess with Scott as much as I did, but now was not the time.

"Let me rephrase that. Don't do anything threatening."

"That's better," said Bob under his breath, "Now can I tell him what an idiot he is, teaming up with the psycho bitch from hell?"

"No, he'll find out soon enough."

"Okay, have it your way." Bob looked at Scott, who was getting back into the town car. "Have a great night, Scott. Say hi to Traye for me."

I could tell that Scott wanted to shoot Bob, but we all knew starting a gunfight here would draw too much unwanted attention, from all directions, not to mention the possibility of damaging some very expensive planes and setting a lot of volatile jet fuel afire.

Then I heard the roar of a familiar car coming from the access road and it put a smile on my face. This time it would be Scott's turn to face the wrath of the dreaded Bonneville. The wide sedan tore through the parking lot and bounced onto the runway. Apparently crashing into the sand trap damaged the car's muffler, because it sounded like ten Harley-Davidson motorcycles.

"Wow, those guys are good," shouted Bob, covering his ears as the car swerved along the tarmac. "I wonder if they have sand in their shoes."

Scott slammed the town car's door shut, and with a screech of tires sped past the golf cart, past the Bonneville and into the parking lot. Both Bob and I pointed in the direction of the town car.

The Bonneville never stopped moving. It circled us, in a much larger arc than the town car, and with a screeching of tires followed Scott to the coast road.

Bob and I sat in the little golf cart, in silence, under the beam of the nearby streetlights.

"They'll be back," Bob finally muttered.

"What makes you think that?"

"Jesus, Rick, don't you know anything?"

"Apparently not."

"They'll be back, because you gave Scott your phone."

"How do you know? They all look the same."

"It's a pretty high-tech process. I'm not sure you'll understand it."

"Try me."

"I marked the bottoms of the phones with a sharpie back in your room. You gave him the one that said RP for Rick's phone. I could see it from here."

I pulled the two remaining iPhones out of my pocket and examined the bottoms. Marked in black I read - "SP". The phone that Bateman gave me had nothing written on it. Obviously Bob didn't get a chance to draw on that one.

"Let me guess," I said, "Spy Phone."

"Nice work, Rick."

"Way to go, Bob. Very clever."

"Yeah, I'm a real dick, aren't I?"

"Then why did they follow Scott? Why didn't they ask us for the phone or search us, or run us down?"

"It's like when a dog sees a rabbit. If it runs, then it must be caught. Totally instinctual. Not a lot of thought involved, especially with us pointing at Scott. They made the assumption that he took everything they wanted."

"Hands in the air!" came a voice from the darkness.

"Oh geeze" moaned Bob, putting his hands up. "This is why I like public transportation. It's much more civilized than these private landing fields. People get so weird when they think no one's watching. I've seen some pretty bizarre stuff when I was out sleuthing."

"I thought you didn't have any cases or even a license."

"Didn't stop me from spying on people."

"You did say this place was crawling with spies. I guess you fit right in."

"I said the *party* was full of spies. Not the damn airport. Airports are supposed to have pilots and stewardesses, Starbucks, tacos and bars, not idiots driving in circles pointing guns."

Two men in black turtlenecks and black pants approached us slowly, handguns at the ready.

"These are probably our guys," I said.

"I wouldn't count on that, little buddy. They look like bad guy rejects from a 1980s James Bond movie. They can't be *my* guys, because I prefer my men smaller, unarmed and much more submissive. And wrinkled turtlenecks are a definite boner buster."

Somewhere down the row of planes, one of the jets started its engines.

Bob sighed. "We need a better car," he grumbled, "One with doors and a gas tank."

"How do you know they're bad guys?"

"Anyone who points a gun at me qualifies."

"Shut up!" said one of the turtlenecks.

"Okay, okay, don't be so bossy!"

Runway Runaway

The two men stopped five feet from the cart.

"Why are you here?" asked turtleneck number one.

"I was told to come," I said, my hands still in the air.

"By who?"

"Don't you mean by whom?" said Bob in his best condescending voice.

"Shut up, asshole," snapped turtle two.

Bob shrugged. "I'm simply trying to help. You see, English is my first language. I happen to speak it fluently."

"Hey," turtle one said, lowering his weapon, "I know you. You're that comedian on TV. What's his name, Jerry Seinfeld."

"Never heard of him," Bob snorted, "Must be on late night cable. I'm Bob Clay."

"Oh, right, Bob Clay. Hey, your programs are still on in Korea."

"Really? What do you think?"

Turtle two was annoyed at turtle one's groupie talk. "Cut the crap, Lorenzo. I'm working the thin one. Besides, that guy's not even funny. Have you ever seen any of his shows. They stink."

"Sometimes jokes get lost in translation," explained Bob.

Turtle two raised his gun.

Bob ducked his head. "Okay, okay. I'll be quiet."

Turtle two turned to me. "Who told you to come *here*?"

"I got a note. Do you want to see it?"

Bob started doing his whispering thing again. "What is this? Elementary school? Don't show them your note."

Turtle two motioned to me. "You. You're coming with us. Get off that thing."

"Don't go," said Bob, "It's dangerous. You know they have no scruples if they don't appreciate good comedy."

"This is the job, Bob."

"No, it's not," he argued.

"I'm telling you it is."

"And I'm telling you it's not. I know more about this than you do."

I climbed out of the cart. Bob was not being helpful, and I was determined to get my seventy grand.

"Atsbee told me there was a special assignment for me and I'd get seventy grand for it," I said.

"Atsbee doesn't use people who wear dated sportswear. Didn't you listen to him? The job is to follow him around and make a report. This is totally different."

"Why didn't you tell me this earlier?"

"It's complicated, but I'm sure we can work it out."

Horns blared, tires squealed and the sound of the scary Bonneville came from the direction of the highway. The two guards looked at the open gate. The parking lot was empty, but the noise was growing increasingly louder.

Out of the darkness, a white SUV raced down the line of parked jets. Following behind it was the wide-bodied Bonneville. In last place was Scott in his sleek town car. The SUV swerved and aimed directly at the two turtlenecks. They raised their guns. The Bonneville broke from the line and headed on a different tack still aiming at the guards. On the other side of the SUV, Scott accelerated, but he was playing catch-up. The two guards ran off toward a nearby turbo jet.

I spotted Renee at the helm of the SUV. Her red dress had been replaced by a fashionable black Nike V-neck T-shirt. She slowed the SUV as she pulled up to the cart, but didn't completely stop. I jumped onto the running board and put my arm inside the open window. The door was locked.

"Hang on for a second, lover," she said, pressing everything in reach. "I don't know where the damn buttons are."

"Nice car," I yelled, hanging to the inside of the door as she started to accelerate, still pushing buttons. "Where'd you get it?"

She didn't look at me, but stayed focused on the asphalt ahead with an occasional glance at the dashboard. "I borrowed it from the hotel."

"Borrowed?"

She smiled that beautiful smile. "Stole."

She pointed to Bob and yelled out the window as we passed by.

"Learjet. Last one. End of the line."

Bob raised his hands as if to say, "What about it?"

"GO!" she yelled.

Bob realized what she was saying, fumbled with the ignition and managed to get the cart started while Renee headed toward the opposite end of the runway. I was still hanging onto the door, feeling a little foolish.

"I can't find the lock. Climb in!"

I pulled myself into the car and tumbled onto the passenger seat of the SUV.

"What's going on?"

"Car chase," she said, as she accelerated quickly and headed to the far end of the runway.

"I know that. I mean, what is going on?"

"It could turn into a plane chase."

"Stop it. I want to know why you're here and why we're heading the wrong way...we *are* heading the wrong way, aren't we?"

"Ed's going to pick us up at the other end of the runway, but before that can happen, we need to get rid of the two cars and the idiots with wrinkled turtlenecks. Geeze, did we drop into a black hole of fashion or what? Do their mothers know they are wearing those stupid things?"

"Who's Ed?"

Renee pointed over her shoulder toward the other end of the airport.

"You remember Ed. He's our pilot, the guy who brought us here. Unfortunately, flight attendant Betsy didn't get the call. I know it's against federal regulations, but these things happen when there's an escape involved. I'm pretty sure he didn't file a flight plan either, mainly because we don't know where we're going."

"Why would Ed do that? Isn't it a requirement to file a flight plan?"

"We'll do it later. Besides, Ed works for the highest bidder, which at the moment is me. He's actually an excellent negotiator. Not so good at strip poker."

"What about our having a romantic evening: going to an exclusive theme party, great room, and wild sex. The ice sculpture is melting as we speak."

Renee looked at me. "Are you serious? This is way better than a party filled with stuck-up spies, computer geeks, and a fake ice mountain. I thought we checked the wild sex off the list at least twice today."

She was right. We did do that and this action was much more fun than Atsbee's party.

"Okay, so tell me, after we escape, have a few beers in some real city, then where are we going?"

"To Bob's hideout."

"Bob has a hideout?"

"Yeah, that's where he hides out. Hang on."

She slammed on the brakes, pulled a one-eighty, and ended up facing the opposite end of the runway.

"What's with all the car stunts?"

"Gotta practice. The police get mad if you do it in a school parking lot or on a neighbor's lawn. I had to draw these hopeless amateurs away from the plane."

I looked down the long stretch of runway.

"Are you sure you know what you're doing?"

"Of course..." She turned and smiled. "...not."

The other two cars turned onto the runway and aimed at us.

"Here they come," I said.

The Bonneville and town car headed down the center of the runway, side by side. Behind them, the Learjet had reached the end runway and turned toward us.

"They're going to charge us." I don't know why I said this. It was totally obvious.

"I kinda figured that would happen," Renee replied.

"Do I get a say in what happens next?"

"Nope," she replied, and stomped on the accelerator. I was pushed back in my seat. My hands flew to the dashboard to brace myself.

Renee moved the wheel slightly to the left. Instead of aiming at the decreasing gap between the two oncoming cars, she focused the SUV directly at the Bonneville. The ugly brown sedan moved slightly to the side, and Renee adjusted again. The faces of three men were lit by our headlights.

The man in the back seat reached over and grabbed the steering wheel. The Bonneville swerved out of the way. Renee turned the wheel to the right and we shot through the open space between the cars and headed for the Lear at the far end of the runway.

The town car slammed on its brakes, leaving a trail of blue smoke, but it took a while to slow down on the greasy landing strip. For a moment I thought he was going to tip over.

Renee and I jumped out of the SUV as soon as we arrived at the Lear and ran up the extended steps. We quickly retracted the stairs and sealed the hatch. The engines whined and the plane strained against the brakes.

"Get strapped in," Ed yelled from the cockpit.

Before we could reach our seats Renee and I were thrown back. I pulled myself and glanced out the window in time to see the ground drop away and the town car rip beneath us, missing the wing by inches. Once the Lear leveled off, Ed entered the cabin.

What was he doing? Had Ed lost it? We couldn't be climbing this fast, this steep on autopilot.

"Who's flying the plane?" I moaned.

Ed looked at me like I was a crazy man. "First officer Dan is at the controls," said Ed calmly, "You remember him, don't you Rick?" He turned to Renee. "That was fun. What'd you do this time, Renee? I want details. Did you get it?"

Renee struggled to sit up. "Oh, Ed, you know I can't kiss and tell on an empty stomach."

"I will," came a voice from the back of the plane.

"Bob, you made it!" exclaimed Renee.

"I always make it...fun," he said, holding a bottle of champagne in one hand and a cluster of empty glasses in the other.

As Renee began to tell Ed what happened over the past several hours, the Learjet lazily banked over the town of Half Moon bay, then, without warning, it went into a steep dive.

Sittin' Around

I found myself sitting on a metal folding chair, in some kind of old storage shed. My hands were duct-taped together in my lap. My chest and feet were taped to the chair. A single naked light bulb in a protective wire cage dangled on a single electrical wire above my head. The light threw harsh shadows onto the greasy, concrete floor.

Sitting across from me was an extremely frustrated Renee, wrapped up in the same gray strips of tape.

"This is not a comfortable situation," I said, stating the obvious.

Renee agreed. "Who would have thought the damn plane would malfunction? I thought we were home free," she grumbled.

"Apparently not," I said, examining the small room. "They didn't even clean the place for us. I mean, we're the guests."

"It smells like a high school locker room doused in fish oil."

I wanted to ask why she was familiar with that particular scent, but I let it go. I managed to pick up a few clues about our location from the equipment lying on the metal shelves that surrounded us.

"From the paint and propellers I'd guess it's some kind of boat repair shop," I said.

Renee didn't care for her surroundings or my clever deduction. "This is disgusting, far worse than your place. Look at the floor. It's a mess."

She was right. There was nothing clean or sanitary about the room, but I was more concerned about Bob and Ed than the condition of our makeshift prison.

"Did you happen to notice where they took the others?" The foul smell irritated my sinuses and I couldn't rub my nose.

"They came in the building with us, but I didn't see what happened to them."

I stared at Renee's hair and troubled face. Her once coiffed locks were totally disheveled. The moist coastal air had caused her curls to tighten. A red swirl covered one eye, giving her a Superman look. Despite being tied up in that tiny room I felt like I had more control over my life than ever. During the past twenty-four hours I'd taken on two assassins, chased a couple of thugs around a golf course and almost escaped in a private jet. I was just starting to get back into action mode. Even in this grease-covered storage room, I knew there was a way out. I just had to find it.

"What do you think they're waiting for?" I asked, scanning the shelves for something that could free us.

"Beats me. If they wanted to kill us they had plenty of time. Maybe their boss isn't here or he's at the party."

I nodded and continued searching. Being held in a tiny storeroom seemed technically wrong and highly unplanned. There were several jets lined up on the nearby tarmac. Plenty of vehicles were available, including the van that brought us here. If these guys wanted to leave, or take us somewhere, the opportunity certainly existed.

I looked up at her.

"Can I ask you a question?"

"Do I have a choice?"

I smiled. I had her exactly where I wanted her...kind of.

"Tonight, out there on the golf course, Bob said that you worked with..."

Renee glared at me. "Rick! Ssshhhh." It wasn't a request, but a command.

"Okay, different subject. I was wondering, are we still...?"

"Still what?"

Geeze, I thought, what an attitude. It wasn't like she had anything else to do.

"I guess I'm wondering if..."

The door opened and one of the turtlenecks poked his head into the room. We both glanced at him. He looked back over his shoulder.

"They're not going anywhere," he said, then closed the door, leaving us alone again.

I waited a bit to make sure the guard didn't unexpectedly return.

"May I continue?"

Renee was still not happy about the situation. I understood. It wasn't a comfortable chair, the room was a mess and I would have preferred to be somewhere more romantic if she had to be tied up.

She glared at me. "I'd rather you didn't. This isn't the time or the place. The room could be bugged."

I looked around the room. "I never thought of that."

"There could be cameras too," she added.

"I guess that eliminates having a little, you know, *us* time."

"Rick, it doesn't work if we're *both* tied up."

At least she still had her sense of humor.

"You're right," I said. "Okay, not mentioning any specific names because of our potential viewing audience...after this blows over, can we pick up where we left off...I mean in a personal sort of way?"

Her expression softened. It reminded me of a few Jennifer Aniston films I'd watched. Aniston always had this scrunched-up expression when she was about to deliver unpleasant news.

"Rick, liking the same baseball team is not enough to keep us together."

"Come on, Renee, we can make a go of it. I know you like me and I like you. If I got us out of here, would you reconsider?"

"Reconsider what? Our entire relationship is based on false assumptions and hidden agendas. You're broke, for God's sake. I'm a professional liar. It's part of my job description. Considering my current line of employment, I don't think a relationship would benefit either of us. I travel all the time and where I go and what I do does not allow texting or goodnight calls."

"But we're great shower buddies. We could save on water."

"That was then. And this is not. Bob put a wedge between us by revealing everything."

"I won't tell anyone, besides, he didn't tell me everything."

"It was more than enough. And the way things stand right now, I might have to find another line of employment."

"That's great. You can find something less strenuous. One with dental benefits and reasonable hours. We could work on our résumés together."

"Rick, there is no 'us' in the future."

"Who saved you from those guys outside the hotel? Who took on the knife-throwing clown? Who made you moan in the shower?"

"That wasn't a moan. That was a groan."

"Sounded like a moan to me. Admit it. We make an excellent team."

"Rick, you have a probation officer and your job is to help fat faux-celebrities lose weight."

"Not all of them are fat."

She drilled me with that emerald stare. "I'm not your girlfriend and this is not your kind of work."

I decided to stop trying to patch up our relationship and returned to examining the room. With all the crap on the shelves it was hard to tell what was what in the harsh light.

I spotted a glimpse of a small window behind one of the racks, but it was too small to crawl through, even if the shelves were slid from the wall. My focus moved to the ceiling. I silently berated myself for not noticing the excellent escape route above me. If all went well I'd be out in a matter of minutes. First, I had a few more questions for my lover, who appeared to be shying away from a personal commitment.

"May I speak candidly?" I asked.

"It seems there's no stopping you."

"Are you willing to make a deal for your freedom?"

Oh-oh, I'd pissed her off.

"Are you insane? You're making a deal for my freedom?"

"Ssshhhh. No, I'm not insane. I have anger issues, a stolen dog and severe financial problems, but I am not crazy."

Her eyes opened wide, then her original reaction dissipated and her expression went all squinty. "You honestly believe you can get out of here, all taped up like that?"

Hadn't she been listening? "Renee, I can get me out, but if you're ending our relationship, there's no reason to bring you along."

She sat up straight. "You're not going anywhere."

I let the moment settle, waiting to see what she had to say.

"You really want a relationship based on lies?"

"Everybody lies. Bob lies, Atsbee lies, you lied, I lied, Clinton lied, Donald Trump lies. But you lied about your job because you were doing your job, which is to lie about your job. I get it. It's okay."

I think I lost her on that one.

"You see," I continued, "lying is not a deal-breaker."

I got nothing but a blank stare.

This would have been the perfect time for her to profess her undying love, and then we could have escaped together, hijacked a car and disappeared into the night, laughing and kissing and some other fun adult stuff. But that didn't happen. So I told her what I was going to do.

"Renee, I'm going to leave now. Since we're not an item, you'll have to find your own way out."

"You're not going anywhere, Rick. That's duct tape. You're stuck in a filthy closet, and no amount of bullshitting will get me to say I love you so that in a few hours you can die happy in a crappy warehouse."

I smiled. "If you're trying to spare my feelings, don't worry. I know you love me."

"I have nothing more to say on the subject."

I looked at my bound wrists. "You know, there's a funny thing about duct tape."

"There's *nothing* funny about duct tape."

"It can be snapped, if you know how to do it. You should spend some time searching YouTube when you're not working. You can learn so much."

I raised my forearms in front of myself, lowered them, and rested my hands on my thighs.

"You're sure you don't want to make a go of this relationship? Buck the trend, take a leap of faith, let the power of love work its magic?"

Renee hesitated and then frowned. "Rick, don't get me wrong. I do love you. I love everything about you, including your fucked-up past, your sun-bleached hair and the delusional idea that we can be a cute couple living in a white picket fenced house and have sex in the chandelier. But we can't. It's not in the cards. Besides, I don't think this is the most romantic situation to try to convince me to be with you."

"Are you free tomorrow?"

She didn't respond.

"Renee, you don't always get to choose your moment of truth. You sure you don't want to give us another try?"

She stared at the ceiling and then looked back at me, her head cocked to one side. "We did try. Look where it landed us. It's over. And if you want honesty, these are, probably, our last moments together. We have no future."

"I know you're wrong, but I had to ask."

I raised my forearms, closed my eyes, and with a *snap!* the tape around my wrists remained stuck to my skin, but the ends dangled from my outstretched arms.

I set about pulling the rest of the tape from around my ankles and chest, ignoring her. I worked quickly, knowing that at any moment someone could open the door.

"Rick?"

I could see she was upset, but it was time for me to get a move on.

"Can't talk now, Renee. Gotta get going."

"They'll find you."

"Maybe, but they'll have to do a lot of searching in some uncomfortable high Sierra back country."

"They'll find you and then they'll kill you."

"Renee, if you're not going to be with me, what difference does it make?"

I carefully climbed the metal racks that rested against the wall. The skylight hadn't been used for years, and it took a few moments to get the latch unhooked. I grabbed the edges of the opening and pulled myself up and out, onto the roof.

Angry Fist

Leaving Renee in the storage room was not such a terrible idea. With the skylight open, I was sure the fashionably challenged turtlenecks would ignore her and try to find the missing captive—me. I was the one they wanted. Renee would be safe for a short time, but I had to figure a way to get her out, fast. I didn't know how many additional turtlenecks were in the building, so there was no way I was going to barge in the front door and survive, let alone free Renee.

Standing on the roof, I scanned the area. Once my eyes adjusted to the semi-darkness, I could see I was in a small industrial area wedged between the end of the airport and the Bay. About three blocks long, the complex was a mosaic of one-story shops and garages. In the distance I could make out the line of private jets.

I considered the airport as a possible escape route, but knew it was surrounded by a fence and offered little help in terms of getting Renee out of danger. Besides, the car stunts that had occurred earlier might have attracted curious law enforcement officials trying to figure out what was happening in their sleepy little airport.

Two roads led away from the area in opposite directions. There was no activity, no movement in either direction. Saturday night in Half Moon Bay;

who would be hanging at a marina area on a Saturday night? Even the boats were silent.

Then I heard it. Off in the distance there was party noise and I thought I saw what looked like Christmas lights and a cluster of parked cars. Was that music? Could it be a local bar? If it was, I knew exactly what to do. Nobody loves a knock-down, drag-out fight more than a bunch of rowdy drunks on a Saturday night.

* * * * *

The Old Princeton Landing was a low-key drinking and music establishment in a small single-story building. Neon lights proclaimed there was plenty of Bud Light inside and yet the building was as bland as soda water. I walked up to the gray wall, its paint peeling under a low porch. A weathered flyer on the wall proclaimed it to be "The Coastside's Biggest Little Music House."

I opened the door. The odor of beer and sweat hit me like a blast of bad air, but I continued on. I made my way past several overweight drinkers huddled over steins of amber brew. With my grass-stained tuxedo, I was not blending in with the jeans-and-sweatshirt crowd. I hoped the idea of helping the desperate rich guy might work in this situation, especially if I worked the idea that a damsel in distress was close by.

There was a small stage at one end of the room. Half a dozen tables sat in front of the performers. Between the tables was a postage-size dance floor. Two couples rocked back and forth, making out to the music. At the other end of the room was a bar along the wall that faced several pool tables.

Moving deeper into the bar, the smell of fried food made my mouth water and my stomach ache. I would have liked nothing better than to sit down and enjoy some hot fried chicken and a couple of beers, but I had work to do. I approached a guy who was vacantly staring at the band.

"You know anyone here?" I hoped he didn't think I was an annoying interloper and ignore me. It turned out he was a friendly drunk and could care less who was asking what. He answered without turning.

"Shit, yeah. I know these people. Hell, I think I know everyone here, except that weirdo over there."

He nodded toward a man leaning against the wall dressed in slacks and a nice upscale sweater. He, like me, did not belong here. He reminded me of how Bob acted for those few moments back at the Ritz; standing alone in a crowd of people, looking lost.

"Betcha he's from the Oceano Hotel down the street. Probably thought this was a pickup bar and had no idea it's a local joint. But ya never know, he might score. Some chicks love out-of-towners. No strings. No names, git my meaning?"

I nodded. I've never been that kind of guy, but I'd known plenty of people who loved the one-night sneak-out thing.

"So who is the grumpiest, meanest person in the room?" I asked.

My new friend stood up a little straighter and craned his neck back and forth. He turned around and looked in the direction of the pool tables.

"See that big guy who's about to take a shot?"

It was dark, but I could see the man shooting pool was about six-six and weighed maybe three hundred pounds. He would be a perfect sidekick for my rescue raid. If he had friends the same size, my plan was going to work like a charm.

"Yeah. What about him?"

"He's been thrown out of this place a couple of times. He broke up Cameron's Pub a couple of months ago. Hates everything and everybody. I'm not going to point him out, because last year he broke a guy's finger for doing exactly that. I was standing right next to the poor fella. Came up and asked him if he was the guy who pointed him out. The fool said yeah, with a really bad attitude. The guy didn't say a word, grabbed his finger and snapped it like a twig. I wouldn't go near him if I were you."

"What's his name?"

"I don't know his real name. He goes by Tank."

Terror gripped my body.

I thought I was on my way back to an exciting life, using my newly recovered military skills, but the thought of confronting my decades-old nemesis brought my forward motion to a grinding halt. Why is it that a grown man resorts to the fears of a child?

I was about to vanquish the RJ curse, but it turned out I was more comfortable dodging knives or fending off armed assassins than asking a fifth-grade bully for help—a guy who probably possessed the very skills I was desperately in need of. Talking to Tank was more terrifying than being water boarded.

After a few moments the lump in my throat subsided and the tightness in my chest loosened. I forced myself into putting my emotions aside for the sake of another: Renee.

I reexamined my situation. I figured I had a few advantages. This group of heavy-drinking Americans would most likely help me if they thought their turf was being threatened. If Tank was as mean as this guy'd said, he might help me free my friends. It was time to prove my love, my commitment and my ability to lie through my teeth.

I waited until Tank was done with his shot, then walked up to him.

He gave me one look up and down and laughed heartily. It was not a friendly laugh. "What the fuck is this? A penguin?"

Oh that was original, Tank. Apparently he hadn't changed, but I was on a mission. Tank was either going to help me, or kill me, but at that point I was not going to back down.

"Tank, it's Rick Johnson, from fifth-grade. Remember me?"

Tank looked like he'd been asked the circumference of a circle. His eyes glazed over and I thought he was going to turn to stone. Finally, Tank returned and his eyes regained a semblance of sanity.

"Oh yeah, Johnson. I remember you."

One side of my brain was sure he was going to hug me. The other side screamed he was going to pick up where we left off, and start pummeling me. I was careful not to move. Summoning all my courage, I made up my mind that if Tank came at me, he was going to have a pool cue sticking out of an orifice it wasn't designed for.

"What are you doing here, Johnson?"

"Gotta problem, Tank. Big one. I need your help."

"You see I'm busy here, right?"

It was go-time.

"Tank, ya gotta stop. These assholes have my friends and my girlfriend tied up in a shed about a quarter mile down the road. I think they're some kind of foreign terrorist operation using the airport and they're armed."

"Terrorists, huh? Then how the fuck did you get here?"

"Broke out." I held out my arms. "Look at the glue from the duct tape. Tank, I wouldn't be in your face if it wasn't important. They said this town was an armpit and they couldn't wait to get out of it because they said everyone here was stupid and the place was full of dumb Americans."

I thought that embellishment would help my cause. Tank was thinking again, and it wasn't a quick process. At that point I wondered if he had some kind of brain damage and maybe I shouldn't have talked to him at all.

His buddies were staring at him...and me. I started to get a nervous feeling in the pit of my stomach, like something big was about to go down. I figured that I could take Tank, but if they all joined, things were going to get ugly.

"How many guys?" Tank asked.

"Four, maybe six."

"They got weapons?"

I nodded. "Handguns, a sniper rifle and a couple of automatic rifles with some kind of foreign language on them."

I tried to make the situation sound as dangerous as I could without appearing ridiculous.

"And they're all wearing black turtlenecks." I added.

"Turtlenecks?"

"Yeah, the shirts that go up around your neck and you wear them skiing."

"I know what turtlenecks are, dumbass. We've seen these guys around town all day. They got your friends?"

"Yeah. Said they were going to kill them and my girlfriend."

There was another pause. I had a feeling that I'd made a mistake.

"You know, Johnson..."

I relaxed my body. I figured if I dropped Tank and one other guy, the others might think twice about coming after me. But if all four of his friends came at once, I'd have to run.

"You always were a straight shooter."

Tank jumped on top of the pool table, blocking his friend's shot, and shouted.

"HEY, EVERYBODY. SHUT THE FUCK UP! WE GOTTA PROBLEM HERE."

Our Gang

Tank whipped the entire bar into frenzy although he did destroy the pool table stomping his boots all over the felt. The most gratifying part was that he believed me. He got a saloon full of people who didn't like him to think they had to get their asses out of their comfy drinking chairs and save the world, all for me.

In a matter of minutes, I was leading a crowd of forty people through the industrial area of Half Moon Bay. Tank and his friends were on either side of me. One step behind were the bartenders and the band. This motley group of drunk Half Moon Bay residents fanned out across the street, ready to beat the crap out of anybody wearing a turtleneck.

I don't know where he found it, but Tank carried a metal baseball bat in his hand.

"You know Johnson, if this raid is a bust, I will personally ram this up your ass. These folks want action, and I'm gonna give it to them one way or another."

I heard some familiar clicks and glanced behind me. Weapons were being pulled from purses, waistbands and pockets. I didn't expect to be leading an armed posse, but I should have known that this group was most likely armed. I wasn't prepared to see over three dozen. And those were the ones that were visible. Who knows what other weapons were still hidden.

We arrived at our destination. Splinter groups fanned out from the main gathering to cover the back exits of the building. People hid behind garbage cans - like a plastic tub would stop a bullet and surrounded the building. I was unceremoniously pushed to the back of the crowd as the most aggressive of the group followed Tank to the front door on their mission to defend truth, justice and the Half Moon Way. The band quietly retreated to the street. Musicians are not usually leaders of the pack, especially when gunplay is involved. Except rappers, of course.

After a few slurred words of warning that were not only unintelligible but lacked both a subject and a verb, the metal door was flattened with a coordinated shove by four hefty Half Mooners.

Three men in black turtlenecks turned, and looked extremely dismayed. They must have heard us coming, but I guess they assumed a group of local ruffians searching for some Saturday night fun would never choose *their* door to demolish. The sight of the large intoxicated crowd, along with a dozen guns poking through the entryway, was more than they bargained for. Without a word, they turned and ran out the back.

I raced into the storeroom and found two empty chairs with duct tape hanging from them. The skylight was open, but unless Renee was hiding in a paint can, she was long gone.

I'd really made a mistake this time. I honestly thought I could get back before anything happened to Renee. I should have brought her with me.

Was it the fact that she wouldn't commit to me? Was it the fact that she doubted my abilities to escape? At the moment when I was about to scale those shelves, I had no doubt that she would be safe and I was making the right decision.

I remember a few of my friends who'd had fights with their girlfriends or boyfriends and walked out. In some of the stories, they'd left a person they'd cared for in a vulnerable situation—drunk in a bar, kicked out of a car late at night, or left them walking home. I'd done worse. I silently swore I would never leave her in such a susceptible condition again. Even though Bob said she was more than capable of taking care of herself, the danger was real and none of us are perfect. I had to find her.

I inspected the floor around her chair. There was no sign of a struggle in the grease, but the ends of the duct were straight, with no ragged ends. Renee didn't escape. She was cut loose.

Returning to the main room of the shop, I found Bob and Ed retrieving their wallets, phones and other personal possessions from a Folger's coffee can in the center of a table. I pitched in and gathered my belongings surrounded by jubilant, inebriated rescuers.

"I thought they stole my little vodka men," sighed Bob, kissing the small figurines.

"Um, Bob? Don't," whispered Ed. "People are watching."

Bob continued doting over his little men and didn't look up. He thought he was playing hard to get with a group of admirers. "Should I sign autographs?" he whispered.

"I don't think so," said Ed, "and I think you should tone it down. We're not in West Hollywood, you know."

Bob looked up and checked the people near him. They were all holding guns, totally bleary-eyed and waiting for something to happen and it was not Bob signing autographs.

"I forgot," Bob said quietly, "Gay doesn't always travel well outside urban areas."

Bob looked at the ceiling and pretended to whistle as he slipped the dolls into his tattered tux pocket. Then he raised his hands high in the air.

"I want to thank all of you. You saved our lives. That was awesome. People of Half Moon Bay, you rock!"

Cheers replaced the awkward silence.

Ed dusted off his pilot's cap and placed it on his head. "Impressive rescue, Rick," he said and put his hand on my back. "Your backup is a little unusual, but it worked."

I was on to the next issue.

"Did you hear anything about where they took Renee?"

Ed was shocked. "She's not here?"

I walked around the small room hoping to spot something that could give me a clue as to where she was taken. "I left to get help. She wasn't here when I got back."

"That's not good," said Ed.

"Tell me about it." There was nothing in the room except bits and pieces of boats.

The rescue crowd had become bored and thirsty. They'd searched the building and found nothing of interest. Some of them were disappointed they didn't find turban-toting terrorists or a stash of high-quality drugs, but I'd accomplished part of my goal. Bob and Ed were safe. I had the phones and my personal possessions, but I was missing the most important part—Renee.

Bob, Ed and I were swept up in the exodus. As we passed through the opening where the front door once stood, Tank arrived at my side. We headed down the street toward the bar. The half-moon was still semi-bright, like everyone walking down the street.

"Where's the girl?" he asked.

When I was in fifth grade, Tank was a foot taller than me and a hundred pounds heavier. In my dreams, I imagined I would pass him in height, weight and fighting prowess. Six-foot-three Tank still towered over me. He's got me by at least one fifty, but I was sure he wouldn't last a minute if I challenged him. I think it worked out for the best.

"Someone took her, Tank. I have no idea where."

"Whatcha gonna do?"

I was puzzled why Tank was interested, but I told him my plan anyway.

"I'm going to have a chat with one of the turtlenecks and shake them up."

"I'm with ya, Rick."

I didn't trust Tank. I knew he'd come through for me, but he was the guy who beat me silly when I was an undernourished fifth grader. What kind of person does that?

Ed joined the conversation, not caring that Tank was listening.

"I'll call a local limo that Greg and I use," he said as he walked with us. "We can start looking for Renee as soon as he gets here."

Bob was at the head of the mini-mob, strutting down the street, making new friends that he'd never remember.

I was relieved no one in the rescue party was hurt. The turtlenecks weren't so lucky. When I spotted them I could tell they'd been introduced to some local justice. From the looks of scrapes on their foreheads, cheeks and necks, I assumed they've spent some painful face time with the asphalt.

The atmosphere inside the bar was heady and euphoric. It felt like a rowdy saloon from an old Western. I worked my way through the exuberant crowd to get to one of the turtlenecks. Tank followed me. Before I could open my mouth, Tank was in the guy's face.

"Where's the girl?" he snarled, pushing his baseball bat into the guy's nose.

The bruised man didn't move. He was too scared. The crowd noise increased. Everyone was drinking heavily and Bob was the leader of the pack, pouring shots and making toasts.

"They took her to a beach house," the turtleneck said. He started to tremble. I didn't envy him. Besides being incredibly mean, Tank had really, really bad breath.

The unruly patrons jostled the other turtlenecks. I hoped someone had called the police, or those guys were going to be torn apart.

"Where's the beach house?" yelled Tank, pushing the end of the bat against the man's nose.

"Montara," stammered the injured man, "Somewhere north of here. They wouldn't tell us exactly."

"Who took her?" I yelled.

"The others. They made a call. Got instructions. They said you'd be coming and they needed a better location. They said someone would let you know where she was and then you'd walk into a trap."

"Got enough?" asked Tank.

I nodded and backed into the crowd. We were running out of time and I was certain the police would probably be arriving any second. I didn't want to be in the position of explaining this situation to my probation officer. I gave Ed a sign and slipped out the door. He joined me outside a few moments later with Bob in tow. Bob a had stolen bottle of Stoli from the bar hidden under his jacket. He pulled it out and took a drink.

"That place was completely crazy," he said, as we ducked around the corner of the small building. He offered me the bottle. "Here take the bottle, Ed. Rick, let me have the phones."

Unhappy with this request, I shook my head no.

Bob was insistent. "Come on, give 'em up, buddy. We have to re-mark them. You can watch. I promise I won't take your precious time-consuming, income-draining electronic devices."

For some reason, I thought this was a good idea. I nodded to Ed, who reached for the vodka. Bob was reluctant to give up the bottle, and actually tried to hold on to it until he realized he couldn't do both, hold the booze and take the phones.

Bob rubbed the markings off the bottom of one of the phones, then numbered them one, two and three, but in the process of marking them he'd mixed them up. At that point I had no idea which phone was which. I probably could have figured it out from the opening screens but looking from the outside it was a crap shoot which was which.

I said nothing. It was done. I had bigger problems.

"Hopefully Scott will return with your phone before someone important calls," said Bob. "Otherwise he'll know we gave him the wrong one."

"Bob, no one calls me."

"That's perfect."

Apparently Bob didn't care that I had no friends. Then again, maybe that was a good thing.

The limo pulled up to the bar. We piled into the back.

"Guys, this is Barry," said Ed.

Before anyone could give Barry instructions about where to go, the front door of the limo flew open. Tank jumped into the front seat and closed the door behind him with a slam that shook the car.

"Okay, I got more information from that skinny little rat." Tank reached over to the back seat, his hand outstretched. "Hi, I'm Tank."

Bob grabbed Tank's hand. "Bob Clay, detective-in-training."

"Ed Langdon, pilot."

"Cool. Great to meet you guys. Rick and I go way back. Right, Rick?"

"Yes, we do, Tank."

"We gotta get your girl now, right?" he said, still playing the concerned hero. "Not to worry. My boys are getting their car. It's down the street. It'll take them a minute. They forgot where they parked it."

Bob, Ed and I looked at each other, not sure what to do. Finally I spoke.

"What information did you get, Tank?"

"Your gal is in a house in Montara, on a bluff. There are four guys. They've got weapons and they're dressed in turtlenecks like that fag I just beat the shit out of." Tank stopped, remembering Bob's public revelation of his gay lifestyle, "Oh, geeze, sorry Mr. Clay, no offense intended."

"None taken," shrugged Bob.

Tank smiles. "Cool. I liked your show."

"Thanks."

The long reach of Bob's celebrity was everywhere.

"That's it?" I asked. "That's all he told you?"

"There are only twenty houses in Montara like that. We'll find her if we have to bust into every one of them."

I think Tank was excited about the chase. It didn't matter who or what. If he were a dog, his ears would have been perked and his tail wagging, jumping up and down, saying, "Come on! Let's chase something. Now! Hurry!"

"What do you think, Ed?"

"I don't know," he replied. "Renee's usually the one calling the shots. I'm more of a transportation coordinator. I'm concerned about Dan, though. It looked like the equipment malfunction might have been faked."

I was interested in this information. "You think the plane might be okay?"

"I'm hoping. Not so sure about Dan. It's not like him to disappear without checking in."

Tank jumped all over this. "You guys came in one of those private planes. I love planes. I have about a dozen at my house."

"That's impressive," said Ed, obviously not believing a word.

"Yep," said Tank proudly. "Big ones."

Ed's phone lit up.

"Oh-oh," said Ed, looking at his screen, "It's Greg Atsbee."

Tank was impressed. "No freakin' way. You know him? I thought he was dead."

How did Tank get that idea?

"I always wanted to meet that guy," Tank continued, enthusiastically, "He's amazing. They've made a couple of movies about him. Wasn't that guy from Titanic in it? You know, Leo Decapitated?"

"What are you talking about, Tank?"

"That guy. You know. He was rich and had parties and liked that girl, what's her name, Oh, I know, Daisy. And he drove a big car, too. An old one."

Back in college Greg always complained about this problem, but I hadn't heard it said in years. Certainly not so elegantly.

"That's a different guy," I said, "The guy you're talking about was called Jay Gatsby and he lived back east on Long Island about a hundred years ago." I stopped there. Trying to explain that Gatsby was a character in a novel to a drunk Tank would only confuse him.

"Yeah, that's the guy I'm talkin' about. So you do know him?"

I nodded. It was the best I could do.

"Put him on speaker," I told Ed.

Ed pressed a button on the phone. "Greg, I'm here with Rick, Bob, a guy named Tank, and Barry from Executive. We just got out of a little scrape, but we're all fine."

I jumped in. "Greg, it's Rick. Renee's in some kind of trouble. Do you know where she might be?"

There was a pause on the other end. Ed and I looked at each other, unsure what the break in the conversation meant, but we both sensed trouble.

Ed muted the phone. "Something is off with Greg."

I agreed. "It's like he's hiding something," I said, "It could have something to do with Keysoft. He's leaving the company. Everyone was talking about it at the party."

"That's what I heard," added Bob.

"I've heard it too," said Ed. "Do you think all this drama is related to his being fired?"

I merely shrugged. Ed unmuted the phone. "Any idea where Renee might be, Greg?"

"Meet me at the hotel. I have information you'll find valuable about her," was the reply.

"That's not good a place for us," I said. "We've already had a few incidents there."

Ed muted the phone again. "How about Greg's place in Moss Beach? It's up the road a few miles. If something goes wrong, we're only twenty minutes from the Bay Area and it's close enough so he can leave the party and get back before anyone misses him.

He's always taking private meetings during these things."

"Is it safe to meet there?" I asked.

"Any place is fine with me," said Bob, "As long as no one shoots at us, ties us up or tries to give us another fucking iPhone."

"I'm with ya, buddy," said Tank, a little too loudly, "But not that way."

Bob Gets a Promotion

Meeting at Atsbee's house wasn't a great idea, but it was better than going back to the hotel and was definitely safer than the airport. We couldn't stay long. I had to find Renee and yet, I had no idea how to do that. If Greg didn't have information about Renee's whereabouts, we might have to do it Tank's way: go door-to-door.

Greg Atsbee's fortress-like brick house with its circular driveway made me uncomfortable. Located next to the ocean I was sure there was a cliff on the far side of the building. What also concerned me was that the grounds were most likely enclosed by some kind of protective barrier. Privacy works both ways. It might serve to keep the unruly riffraff out, but it could also trap the occupants.

Greg met us at the front door. Barry drove the limo to the far end of the circular driveway and parked so the car was aimed down the long entryway. I liked the idea of our transportation being nearby and ready for departure.

We passed through thick wooden doors and entered the marble entryway. This was no Orange County cookie-cutter home. A lot of thought, planning and cash had been put into the construction of this mansion. Everything appeared to be of top quality and extremely solid.

Following Greg to the back of the house, I glanced into the other rooms as I passed, looking for tell-tale shadows or other evidence that people might be lurking nearby. There was no sign of anyone, not even bowl-cut Moe the bodyguard. I sensed there was some kind of security in the large residence. I didn't believe the great and powerful Atsbee would leave himself that vulnerable.

We entered an enormous room. The entire ceiling and ocean-facing wall were composed of a single, curved piece of glass. The lighted front lawn, majestic oak trees, stars, moon, and the light reflecting off the distant Pacific were visible from almost every corner of the room.

"Very impressive," I said, in a half-hearted attempt to be cordial. "But we don't have time to socialize, Greg. I need to find Renee."

Atsbee was still playing the elegant, aloof CEO. "I understand you've run into some trouble this weekend," he said.

"I don't think you heard me," I replied with an edge to my voice, "I need to find Renee. She's in trouble."

"Have a seat, Rick," said Atsbee, picking a cigar from a wooden case resting on a small hand-carved pedestal. "You're going to need some information before you run off into the night, not knowing where you're going or who you're dealing with. I do admire your determination, even if it is misguided."

He flicked a lighter. "Cigar, anyone?"

"Sure," said Bob. He walked over to examine his choices.

Atsbee watched him with mild curiosity. "I'm not sure smoking a cigar is a healthy idea for a man in your condition, Bob."

"Why, because I'm fat?"

Atsbee nodded as he lit the end of the cigar, and then examined the end. "You need to shed more than a few pounds, my friend."

"I'll take my chances," said Bob, picking one of the cigars. "You only die once, so you have to make it last."

"It's your funeral," said Atsbee. "Have a seat, Bob."

As Bob returned to take his place on the couch, Atsbee blew a large cloud of blue smoke toward the ceiling. "We've had some problems at Keysoft. Designs have been hacked, confidential corporate information has been stolen. Then a few days ago we learned that a very important military-grade integrated circuit disappeared. Unrelated to this incident, as you might have heard, I am leaving the company. My tenure there is finished."

Bob was not pleased. "That means that all the talk about sponsoring a TV program for me is, was, crap. And following you around for three hundred grand was a lie."

"There was a reason for that little act, Bob. And you're right about the TV show—your comeback will not be moving forward, at least not the way you'd envisioned it. Not to worry, I have other plans for your career."

"Like what? To make me thin? Handsome? Straight?"

I was totally annoyed. "Bob, this is not the time to be negotiating a television deal."

He turned on me. It was the first time I'd seen him angry.

"Oh, get a grip Rick. This is about Reneeeee. No one cares about *my* problems or *my* future. Nooooo. Of course not. We have to save the girl. That's all I've heard for the last hour. Get the girl. Save the girl. Jesus H. Christ on a big stick. I keep telling you, she'll be okay. She knows how to handle herself in these types of situations. Haven't you heard a word I've said all night? Renee. Is. A. Professional. She is going to be fine."

"That's not totally true, Bob," said Atsbee. "There have been some unforeseen complications. She might be in over her head this time."

"See? Even Greg agrees. She's going to be okay."

"That's not what he said, Bob." I sat forward on the couch. "I don't like the sound of this, Greg. Are you telling me you have something to do with what's going down tonight?"

"I have everything to do with tonight's events, Rick. It's been planned for months."

I jumped to my feet. "What the hell are you doing, Greg? You put Renee in danger for some game of yours?"

"Rick, sit down. She's fine at the moment, but she won't to be safe much longer. Scott's at the hotel, but he'll be on his way to her shortly. I want you to know that most of the reason she's in trouble stems from you. Taking that phone in the lobby messed everything up."

I wanted to grab Atsbee by the throat and shake him senseless. I wanted to rewind time, return to my messy house and tell Renee there was no way we could go to the Ritz. I wanted to change so many things, but I couldn't.

"Let's hear it, Greg," I said, slowly sitting down. "And I'm not buying your story about this being my fault. If this is your game, then you planned it poorly."

Atsbee puffed, then continued as if he was in a business meeting.

"Someone in my office was leaking extremely sensitive documents, so we set up a sting. We were going to use a counterfeit military chip as a decoy. Unfortunately someone got hold of the real deal, and if it falls into the wrong hands, a lot of our assets will be extremely vulnerable, especially our multi-million dollar fighters. The sting was to go down during tonight's party, but nothing went as planned. Not only was the real chip in play, three separate groups were trying to get their hands on it. One was headed by Scott and his men, who for some reason, are dressed in black turtlenecks. The second group is a strange team of misfits from the Silicon Valley. Three of their four members have met their demise at the hands of Bob and Rick."

"It wasn't me. He jumped."

"We have the hotel security tape, Bob. Don't worry. It will disappear in due time. The third group is extremely nasty. It is run by a guy named Joey. He and his three men are highly trained, and extremely efficient."

I nodded. "We've crossed Scott's people. They look like a French resistance group."

"Half of them are in the city jail. They'll be moved shortly, but they won't like where they're headed."

"Paris?" Bob chipped in. "I've always wanted to visit Paris in the summer. I hear it's very Frenchy this time of year."

"They'll be getting an uncomfortable suite at Guantánamo Bay."

"Wait," said Bob. "Is that anywhere near St. Croix?"

"As a matter of fact, it is, Bob."

"Oh."

"Greg," I said, "Where is Renee?"

He ignored me and continued. "The phone you received in the hotel lobby was a homing device. Whoever entered the party with the phone was to have the chip attached to their clothing."

"That was dumb," said Bob. "Anyone could have gotten it if they had that phone."

Atsbee pointed his cigar. "That's the first sensible thing you've said all night, Bob."

"Hey, thanks Greg."

"The courier, called RJ, was supposed to drive down from San Fran, get the homing phone, have the chip attached to him, then go the airport and be brought to North Korea. Because you arrived before the original RJ and you were given the homing phone, everyone's timing was thrown off. You avoided the third group when Dan O'Keefe faked an emergency and brought the plane back. That's when Scott's men hustled you away. You were extremely lucky."

"Lucky?"

"You have no idea. Scott's men didn't have a clue what to do with you. He's apparently still unavailable due to being somewhat preoccupied with Traye. Seems she enjoys some of Scott's unusual activities."

"Yuck," said Bob.

"My sentiments exactly. The third group is very different. They would have killed you on sight, no questions asked, but by the time they got to the plane, Dan O'Keeffe was the only one on board. If you ever have the chance to meet a man named Joey, don't. He has a fondness for sharing long aluminum sewing needles."

I thought of the lifeless man from Boeing sitting in that chair with a metal needle in his chest. Apparently Joey was already at work in Half Moon Bay.

Atsbee looked in Ed's direction. "Your co-pilot Dan made an arrangement with Joey to deliver all of you into his hands. When Dan didn't deliver the goods, Joey left one of his metal calling cards. I'm afraid Dan's been grounded, permanently."

"This is all very dramatic, but I need to get to Renee. And I hate to sound insensitive, but where the fuck is she, Greg?"

"About five miles north of here, in a private home. They're waiting for you. We thought the plan was busted when you took off across the golf course. Ended up none of them got what they wanted and so the game is still on. Even at the boat shop, Scott's idiots were only told to detain you until he got there."

Bob was over his disappointment and back in the game.

"Wait a minute," he said, "What is the purpose of this shell game? Now everyone thinks Rick has the chip and you're continuing the charade. Why not tell them the chip is here and nab everyone who shows up? Game over. It's simple."

"It's not *that* simple, Bob."

"It seems very simple. Doesn't it seem simple to you Rick?"

I looked at him. At that point, nothing seemed simple.

Bob was convinced he was right. "You've got these people running all over town chasing this thing. You should catch them in the act. Otherwise what's the point?"

"We *want* them to take the chip," said Atsbee, "It's got a virus. It will infect their systems, and then send a report back to us. We can even download more programs once it's installed in their hardware."

Bob wasn't buying into this one. "Who do you think these guys are, Orange County housewives using dial-up? You honestly believe these bad guys are going to plug that bad boy into their bad-boy network without a bad thought." He took a drag on his cigar and exhaled it into the air, where it mingled with Atsbee's. "Greg, you are crazy-assed stupid if you think this plan will work. Even *I* know it won't work. That's how bad it is."

Atsbee shrugged and matched Bob's smoke with his. "Doesn't matter what you think, Bob. It's all in motion."

I couldn't have cared less about Atsbee's dumb computer chip. I needed to get Renee and make sure she was alright.

"Fine," I said. "Tell me where this infected chip is, and where I can find her. I'll make the trade."

"I thought you'd say that. Ed, are you ready?"

"Always, Greg."

"You're on. Get into your civilian clothes. You're going with Rick to make sure everything goes as planned."

Bob was on his feet. He was upset again. "You're kidding? Ed gets the green light? After everything I've done?"

Atsbee took his cigar out of his mouth and glared at him. "This isn't a stakeout, Bob. These guys don't care about anything, especially you. They are absolutely ruthless and you would be in grave danger if you met up with them, especially if they've seen any of your work. You need to stay here. You're out of shape, untrained, and too big a target."

Bob was adamant. "Not if I turn sideways."

"Even if you turn sideways and hide behind a wall."

"You know, if I worked for you, I'd sue you for fat-man discrimination."

Atsbee laughed loudly. "If you worked for me, I'd fire you for *being* a fat man."

"Where is she?" I yelled, cutting them both off.

Atsbee puffed his cigar again, and pulled a smart phone from his pocket, turned it sideways and squinted. "Right now, I'd said she's about two miles north of here."

"That's on your phone? You know where she is?"

"At the moment, yes." Atsbee turned the display toward me, "These things are amazing."

"Give it."

I took a step toward him. I didn't care if he was the President of the United States. I had to have that phone.

Atsbee laughed. *"You're* threatening *me*?"

"You know it. Give it to me now or I will break you with my hands."

"Ed?"

I heard the sound of a gun's slider loading a round.

"Back away, Rick," said Ed.

I was not moving. And I didn't turn around.

"Fuck you, asshole," said Bob.

"Your finger, Bob?" I heard Ed laugh, "You've got to be kidding."

"Ed, I've owned guns all my life. I'm especially fond of this one. Ever heard of the LM5 Simmering? It's kinda like the 'Little Cricket' in *Men in Black*, or if you're technically inclined, it fires five 32-caliber rounds. I don't think I'll miss from here. Wanna play a game of chicken? Because this gun will spread your kidneys all over this hideous room. Never did care for East Coast Puritan decor, although I do like the window."

Ed laughed again. "You don't have the nerve."

"Ed, put the gun down," commanded Atsbee.

I turned to see Ed glance at Bob, then back to Atsbee, who was signaling to Ed not to act. Atsbee handed me the phone.

Ed lowered his weapon to the floor. "This isn't right, Greg."

Atsbee grimaced. "Bob already has a notch in his belt. So does Rick. I need you functioning. It's going to be a long night."

Bob was right on cue. "Yeah, Ed. Don't push it. I'm not someone to fool around with. Well, sometimes I am...but not now."

I looked at the phone's display. "Is that her?"

Atsbee nodded.

"You're playing everyone, aren't you?"

"It's what I do."

"Apparently you're not that good. Tank, Bob, let's go."

Tank opened his eyes. He'd been sleeping the entire time. He groggily rubbed his face and joined Bob. We backed out of the room, then exited the mansion.

"That was way too easy," I said, heading for the limo.

Bob had fallen for it. "I thought it worked out rather nicely," he said, trying to keep up with me. Tank was a good five steps behind Bob.

"Bob, be realistic. Ed could have killed you in a second. And what about the ugly dude who was behind Atsbee in the Board Room? He had to be somewhere nearby."

"Oh, yeah, forgot about him. He was kinda cute, in a bear sort-of-way. So, do you have a plan, Stan?"

"We'll take the limo."

"Great. I'll drive," said Bob.

"No way."

"Didn't you witness my exquisite skills out there on the course? I was masterful."

"Bob, you killed a guy."

"No, I didn't. He ran off a cliff."

"You can navigate," I said.

As we approached the limo, Barry opened the window.

"Where to, boys?"

"Get out, Barry. We're taking the car." I was surprised at the meanness in my own voice.

Barry was confused.

"Don't you understand English? Get out of the car," said Bob, pointing his gun.

Barry opened the door and stepped onto the driveway, looking like he'd lost his best friend.

I didn't care about Barry's feelings. It was time to save Renee.

Driving Miss Crazy

We were racing along the half-lit coast highway. Sea smell was everywhere, except near Bob who had the odor of an abandoned brewery. He turned around and looked in the back.

"I'm in the wrong part of the bar...I mean car," said Bob.

Tank was recovering, from what, I had no idea. "Can I git you somethin', Bob ol' buddy? Seems we have some 'cellent choices back here."

I was worried about both of them, but it was more important that I kept my ex-roommate semi-sober. "We're on the clock, Bob. This is where you earn your hours."

"Yeah, yeah, I know. But what's that got to do with enjoying life?"

"I'm pretty sure you're not supposed to drink on the job."

"I thought being soused while on the job was one of the few perks of being a private detective."

"I don't think so."

"Haven't you watched those old movies? All the detectives drink. And they drink a lot."

"Those are movies, Bob."

"And I'm an actor. It's all good."

"And what's with the miniature handgun? Next time, just so you know, when it comes to firearms, size matters."

Bob looked at me like I was crazy. "You might want to rethink that statement, partner. I almost shot my cat once with this thing. Hasn't come home since. This baby makes a nasty exit wound, especially in stucco walls. FYI and ASAP, I always keep it with me. A gay man should never travel unarmed or unaware. Keep that in mind if you ever decide to switch teams."

"I'll remember that fun fact."

"Why didn't the turtlenecks find it?" I asked.

"We just emptied our pockets into the can and then they duct-taped us to some chairs. They were totally useless bad guys. And they wasted a lot of duct tape, especially on me. They were much more concerned with you and Renee. They treated us like second-class citizens. I hate it when that happens. Makes me feel...ordinary, like you."

I wasn't about to get into a discussion about haves, have-nots, used-to-haves, and wannabes. Apparently Bob thought he was a "have" when he was really just a "was."

"How we doing?" I asked, glancing over to him.

"Not bad. I could use a bite to eat, though," said Bob, "But I feel pretty good, considering."

"The phone, Bob. Watch the phone. We're trying to find Renee, remember?"

Bob squinted at the device, his face illuminated by the display. "It's kinda hard to tell. It looks like she's about a mile up ahead, or it could be ten, I'm not sure. Hey, wait, you passed her."

I slammed on the brakes and pulled a U-turn with the big car.

Bob grabbed the dashboard. Tank flew across the back of the limo. "I'm okay," he yelled.

Bob was not impressed with my quick reaction. "Rick, be careful. You have to keep a low profile when you're sneaking up on people who shoot other people, especially if you're the people they're looking to shoot."

I had no idea what he said. He probably didn't either.

"We don't have time for subtlety," I said.

"Or food, I presume."

"Bob, where are we going? What's the phone say?"

He stared at the phone. "Take a left down this side road."

I spun the wheel, made the turn, then stopped.

"We aren't there yet," said Bob, still staring at the phone.

"How far, Bob?" I said.

Bob squinted. The way he was acting, I didn't think he could see anything.

"Are you sure you can work that thing?" I asked.

"It's a little blurry," he replied, putting the phone to his nose, "Maybe you should have it checked."

"You need glasses, don't you?"

"I do," he said, turning the phone sideways which didn't help because the screen quickly rotated. "But I can't afford them. That's what happens when you quit your day job - you lose your insurance. Even if you're a comedian, it's not funny."

I grabbed the phone and enabled the satellite view.

Bob was impressed. "Hey, that's cool. How'd you do that?"

"Map options."

There was no time to give him a phone lesson.

"Here's the plan," I said, "We'll go in from the ocean side."

Bob was not well. "I...I thought it was on the bluff."

"It is. The bluff's on the ocean side of the house."

"Ohhhhhhh," said Bob, "Well, I'm not sure I can go with you."

"Why not?"

"I'm afraid of heights."

I should have figured that Bob would surprise me, but I was expecting another joke. "Suck it up, Bob. It's for your country."

"No, it's not. It's for Renee."

"Bob. Let's go."

"Tank?"

No answer. I looked in the back and spotted him drinking from one of the liquor bottles. I decided I couldn't risk having him ruin this operation.

"Tank. Stay in the car. Don't let anyone take it."

"Got it, boss," and he released a huge belch that filled the car with such a horrible smell that it forced Bob and I out of the vehicle.

* * * * *

The phone guided me around several bluff side houses. I glanced behind me. Bob was already breathing hard. Maybe it wasn't such a good idea to bring Mr. Outdoors on this rescue mission. Atsbee had a point: Bob was hard to miss, even in the dark.

"I think you should wait here," I whispered.

"I'll watch the rear," Bob said quietly. "I'm experienced at that." He looked around, and then changed his mind. "You know, I think I'll just go back to the limo."

"Wait. I need your gun."

Bob pulled his weapon from his pocket, handed it over and then headed back the way we came.

I had to assume there were guards, but if they were the remaining turtlenecks, I could probably get her out safely. These idiots had proven themselves to be an ineffectual group.

The phone indicated she was in the back, at the far corner. I moved in that direction, making sure I didn't bump into a guard stationed outside. The window at the far end of the house had a gap at the bottom of the blinds.

There she was sitting on a metal chair in the center of the kitchen, far from any of the counters or doors. All the kitchen furniture had been moved, so if anyone approached her or if she moved, it would be obvious. Her hands were tied behind her back, her feet bound. Mouth taped.

Through a large arched opening that lead into the next room there were two men sitting in the same type of kitchen chair as Renee. They were half-awake and bored. I guessed they were armed, but probably sucked at fighting and shooting. Still I knew from experience it only takes one bullet to ruin someone's day.

Renee looked tired, but unharmed. If I came in the back door it would be a straight shot through the breakfast nook to get her.

As I approached the small back stoop, I heard a lot of shouting over the sounds of the surf. It sounded like a drunken argument, something that would happen in a bar parking lot or a late night boozy city street.

I heard the revving of an engine, a big engine, and then a screech of tires, followed by more yelling.

The two turtlenecks stood up, looked at each other, and then moved toward the front of the house, guns drawn. Before they could get to the window, the entire front wall exploded inward and ripped to shreds as the huge limo plowed into the house. Stucco flew everywhere. The front end of the car rolled into the living room and lurched to a stop, but the engine was still roaring.

Running to the back door, I smashed the window and grabbed the handle from the inside. The limo revved its engine and began to back out, bucking as it tried to free itself of the smashed studs. Large chunks of drywall and glass continued to fall off its dented hood. The turtlenecks covered their heads as more debris fell. A cloud of dust filled the entire house.

Renee and I made eye contact, but there was no time for pleasantries. I untied the flimsy rope. She ripped the tape off her mouth. I tore the tape off her ankles. We glanced into the front room to see the limo back clear of the wall, leaving a gaping hole in the side of the house. The turtlenecks yelled at the car as it continued to move away. We raced out the back door.

I lead Renee along the side of the house. We reached the front and cautiously peeked around the corner.

Bob was reinventing the role he'd played earlier in the evening as the maniac driver.

"It's my brother's car," he slurred, close to tears, a little too loudly. "His wife died of cancer last month and now he's got erectile dysfunction. This is going to kill him. It's the only way he can make any money and he owes thousands in hospital bills and he can't even jerk off. What am I going to do?"

The men had their guns drawn and weren't sure whether to shoot him or give him money.

Renee and I crouched behind a bush at the side of the building.

I turned to her. "I think this is the best performance of the evening. Much more inventive than that pitiful story about his manager ripping him off. It might even be better than your bimbo act."

"You've got to be kidding."

"You were awesome, but the dumb redhead act is a little worn. This is full of high emotion and much more dramatic."

Bob continued to walk in circles, which apparently made him dizzy, because he had to stop and regain his balance.

Renee moved close in and whispered, "I think he's a little too much."

"But they're buying it," I said.

"If it was anyone other than these morons, he'd be used for target practice."

"I think it's time to help him out." I pulled Bob's gun out of my pocket.

"What the hell is that?" she asked.

"Bob's handgun."

"Are you kidding? I wouldn't trust that thing. Don't get it near me."

She was right. What was I thinking? It could blow up in my face.

"I'll take the one on the left" said Renee putting her hand on my shoulder, "It's good to see you, Rick. I missed you."

Not waiting for a reply, she broke into a run and tackled the left side turtleneck, smashing him into the front lawn hard. His gun fired on the way down, but the shot went wild. I did the same to the guy on the right while Bob continued his wailing laments.

"What am I going to do?" he moaned, "It's a tragedy....a horrible, horrible tragedy."

Renee finished with her man, knocking him out with a huge roundhouse punch. She grabbed his gun and dropped the third man running out of the house. I did the same to turtleneck number four behind him. Then I came to her side.

She looked at the limo covered in stucco and splintered wood. "What's with your fucked-up choice of vehicles? Can't we get something with a little more speed and maneuverability?"

I glanced to the next driveway, where a Silverado pickup and a tiny BMW mini sat.

"Over there. Which one?"

Renee turned and looked at the cars, then to Bob, who had uncovered his eyes and realized his job was done. I half expected him to take a bow.

"Bob'll never fit in the mini. We'll go with the pickup."

"Shotgun!" yelled Bob.

Renee and I instinctively dove in different directions to avoid the expected blast. I came up with my gun at the ready.

Bob walked over to me, hands on his broad hips. "What is wrong with you two? I just wanted to sit up front. That's how you do it in America."

I stood up and dusted off my severely worn trousers. "Next time you want to ride up front, just ask." Then I realized someone was missing.

"Bob, where's Tank?"

"In the limo, I guess. Hey, where's Renee going?"

I ducked into the back of the car. Tank was laid out on the long leather seat. It looked like he was asleep, but there was no telling if the collision had hurt him or he was simply passed out.

"Come on out of there Rick and keep your hands where I can see them." This voice sounded familiar.

I pulled my head from the limo and looked into the semi-darkness.

"Scott? Is that you?" I asked.

"You're one big pain in the ass, Rick Johnson."

"Scott, what are you doing?"

"I work the big deals, remember? Delivering that chip to the airport will be my last job. Costa Rica is very affordable these days."

"Don't you have anything better to do than to jeopardize our men in uniform?" I said, hoping to appeal to his sense of humanity.

"I have no idea what you're talking about."

"Scott, the chip is a friend/foe identifier. Selling it endangers our guys and you'll become a class 'A' traitor."

"My bankers aren't real big on paperwork and neither of us cares how I get the cash. Being a live traitor is a much better alternative to an honorable dead man."

"Why don't you go to Atsbee?"

Scott laughed. It was the first time I'd seen him smile.

"How's that working out for you, Rick? Get anything? Did he call you back? No. Greg Atsbee doesn't care about anyone but himself. He's just waiting for one of us to deliver the chip."

"It's his chip, Scott," I said.

"Of course it is, but we're the fall guys. The chip gets stolen, he steals it back, sells it, and then oh damn it's one of those broke ex-roommates. It's business, Rick. Big business. Big Atsbee business. And it's time to take my cut."

I had Bob's mini-gun in my pocket and the turtleneck's weapon tucked in my belt, but I knew I needed to be patient. Scott was going to shoot or make a serious mistake. I had to wait for the right moment.

An incredibly loud growl came from the pickup behind me. Spot lights on top of the cab lit up the area. Scott raised his hand to shield his eyes from the glare. I took that opportunity to dive out of the way. Renee powered the pickup over a small property wall and charged forward. I jumped to my feet and with one move flipped myself into the back of the truck landing hard on the flat metal floor. Tires spun as Renee made a wide turn, ripping up the front yard, barely missing the damaged limo. The wide tires threw thick clods of dirt into the air.

Shots rang out as the truck sped down the street. I kept my head down, listening to Scott's bullets fly by. Some pinged into the tailgate. In a matter of seconds we were cruising the coast highway. Squad cars with their sirens wailing, passed us heading toward the damaged beach house.

Several miles down the road Renee pulled over and I climbed into the front seat.

"Excellent driving," I said.

"I could have done better," crowed Bob from the back.

"Me too," slurred Tank.

Somehow Tank had made the long haul from the back seat of the limo into the pickup during my conversation with Scott without anyone noticing.

"Hey, check it out!" yelled Bob, holding up a half-empty bottle of Smirnoff vodka. "Not one of the world class brands from the limo, but like I always say, if wishes were horses, beggars would play polo."

The two big men attempted to give each other a big high five and totally missed.

"What's a polo? asked Tank.

There was only so much room in this operation for overweight male backup power. I decided to stick with Bob. If I was going to be killed or lose my girlfriend, I was going down laughing. Tank needed to go home.

Renee kept her eye on the road, staying close to the speed limit. We both knew that getting pulled over by the police would be a disaster.

"Bob, about that bottle, I hate to tell you this..." said Renee.

"Oh, come on, Renee. Can't a guy have a little fun? This could be our last night together."

"I realize that, Bob. So in the spirit of friendship, you're going to have to share."

Bob looked wistfully at his prize, took a long swig, and then passed it forward. I handed it on to Renee who equaled Bob's hefty gulp.

"Hey!" complained Bob. "Take it easy. That might be all we have."

"Bite me," said Renee, taking another long drink. "You haven't been tied up for hours."

"Maybe not tonight."

I handed the bottle back to Bob, who quickly downed the remainder.

"Oh, I forgot." Bob said. "It's illegal in California to drive with an open container." He lowered the window and tossed the bottle out of the car.

I looked into the back. "Tank. You need to go home."

"What...what time is it? I gotta get up oily," he said slowly. He *really* needed to go home.

Bob wasn't concerned about his new drinking buddy. "Hey, if anyone sees an open liquor store, I'm starved."

I glanced back at him. "Really Bob? Now?"

"Fish gotta swim, a guy's gotta eat. By the way, where are we going? Someplace fun, I hope. I need a vacation from this vacation."

"We're going to drop Tank off," I said

"And then we're going back to the hotel," added Renee.

I turned back to her. "Isn't it dangerous going back to the place where we were almost killed and where everyone knows what we look like?"

"I've got a couple thousand dollars of makeup, brushes, guns, and ammunition in that room, and I am not in the mood to leave it behind. We'll get our stuff and leave."

"We can raid the honor bar too," said Bob.

"Take it easy, Bob," I said, keeping an eye on the road. "We don't want you passing out. It could be a long night."

"You must think I'm a lightweight."

"Never crossed my mind."

My Alternative Universe

I believe everyone has one love they wish they'd chased, a person they regretted not speaking to, or a situation they'd like to replay. A do-over.

One of my life do-overs was pursuing Jenny. I kissed her in fifth grade and then Tank tanked me. I'd thought about her a lot over the years. What if Tank had said, "Sure, take Jenny to the park, on a bike ride or to the movies." But he didn't and we didn't. Now I was about to meet her again. I was nervous. What if....?

We walked into Tank's kitchen sideways because it was the only way Bob and I could muscle the wiped out Tank through the door. The guy was total dead weight. Renee was behind us, holding the torn screen door open. The house wasn't in very good shape. I'd describe it as a small California ranch wreck.

The only thing I did notice was a lot of stuff relating to model airplanes. There were photos of people holding model airplanes, photos of models, models of models and several oversized models hanging on the walls and in front of the windows.

And there she was - Jenny, the love of my fifth grade life. I could not believe what I saw. That cute little girl had been inflated like one of the balloons in the New York City Thanksgiving Day Parade.

Somewhere behind those dull eyes was that energetic little girl I'd fallen in love with, oh so many years ago.

"Tank? Tank, are you alright?"

Tank mumbled something that sounded like "limo," but there was no telling what language, if any, he was using.

"The bartender said you went off with some troublemakers from the hotel."

"That would be us," I said sheepishly. "Tank helped us out of a tight spot, Jenny. My friend Bob would be dead if it wasn't for your husband. He was brilliant, absolutely stunning."

"My Tank?"

I looked at him slumped against the Formica-covered kitchen table. I couldn't believe it either.

"It's true," added Renee.

Jenny stared at me. "Rick? Rick Johnson? Is that you?"

"Yes Jenny, it's me. How are you?"

There was a change in her expression. She saw herself through my eyes in all her two hundred thirty pounds, her gray streaked, unbleached hair, standing in her K-Mart robe surrounded by twenty-year-old, torn wall paper. There was sadness in her half-smile that told me everything, except why.

"Thanks for bringing him home," she said, trying to hide her embarrassment, "He has an important competition tomorrow. Can you put him in the bedroom?"

"Sure." I said.

Bob and I carried Tank down a narrow hallway, past a couple of sleeping kids and placed him sideways on a king bed with a deep indentation in the middle. We wrestled his shoes off. Whew! *That* was a mistake.

"I can handle it from here," Jenny said. "Please, come back into the kitchen."

When we returned I saw Renee playing with one of the model planes, spinning the propeller with her finger.

I turned to face Jenny, but I didn't know what to say. Neither did she, so we didn't say anything. We looked at our feet. My shoes were a freaking mess and she hadn't done the dishes in days.

"Can I offer you some tea or coffee?" she asked.

The three of us must have smelled like a frat party. We all mumbled a "No thanks."

"I'm sorry about Tank," I said, "We didn't mean to bring him home this way. The night kind of got away from us."

Jenny laughed. "He didn't tell you?"

I shook my head. "I'm afraid we haven't done much catching up. We've been running around town dodging bullets."

Jenny's embarrassment disappeared, replaced by a chuckle. "Tank hasn't slept for days. He's been over at the Ritz building a huge set for some party. He's not drunk. He's exhausted. And he has to get up early tomorrow. Like I said he's got a big competition in the morning."

I wondered what kind of competition Jenny was talking about. Was he in a drinking contest? A hot dog eating event? I was sure it wasn't a triathlon or a volleyball tournament. Maybe it was arm wrestling...or checkers.

"He's entered another dog fighting championship. He's been waiting all year for this one."

I nod like I'm an expert at dog fights. Like most people, I'm full of judgments. I hoped my distaste for his activity didn't show. Bob's fame saved me when Jenny recognized him.

"Hey, aren't you Bob Clay?"

He made a half-hearted attempt at a smile. "Yes, that's me."

"Mr. Clay I want to thank you," she said, walking toward him, "You brought so much laughter into our home when we were experiencing a great deal of sadness. I know in my heart that your humor saved our family."

I thought he was going to cry. He closed the distance and hugged her.

"Jackie..."

"It's Jenny."

"Jenny, that's the nicest thing I've ever heard."

She laughed. "You're lying, aren't you, Bob."

"Yeah, I've been told a lot nicer things, but *they* were lies. You've made my day, Jackie."

"Jenny."

"Sorry I have problems with names that start with J."

He released her. It looked like he was crying, then again, maybe he was faking it. I'll never know.

"Okay," he said, clapping his hands together, "We have to leave because I'm working on a new career and we have a busy night ahead of us."

"Are you going to do a movie?" she asked.

She'd struck a nerve. I know Bob missed the entertainment business, not because of the money or even the fame. He missed being loved and adored.

"Ah, no." Bob stammered, "I'm training to be a professional detective."

Jenny's expression started as confusion then ended in a broad smile. "Of course you are Bob. And you're going to be wonderful." She hugged him again. "And thanks for taking care of Tank."

Renee stepped out of the shadows. "Hi, I'm Renee."

"Hello, Renee."

"I'd like to say something and I hope it's not out of line, but I think raising and fighting dogs is not only illegal, but cruel and despicable."

I was surprised Renee brought this up.

"I totally agree with you, Renee."

"So why do you tolerate it?"

"I'm sorry, Renee, there must be some misunderstanding, I know it's late..."

It was Renee's turn to look confused. "You just said that Tank has to get up early to..."

"...Go to a dog fighting championship," said Jenny, finishing Renee's sentence. She pointed to the ceiling. We all looked up, expecting to see a stuffed Rottweiler or a bulldog. Instead we were confronted with a gigantic model biplane.

"He's been dog fighting with model airplanes for years. I know it's odd, but it's better than running around town causing trouble."

Renee looked back at Jenny. "Tank built that?"

"Took him over a year."

"I think I've said enough," said Renee.

Jenny was totally okay with Renee's mistake.

"I don't blame you, Renee. I would have said the same thing."

Bob was still staring at the model. "That thing's bigger than me."

The coo-coo clock struck midnight. Seeing a little yellow bird pop out of its wooden house was too much for all of us.

In seconds Bob, Renee and I were back in the pickup heading toward the Ritz.

Ritz Spritz

Renee opened the door to our hotel suite, unsure if she'd be greeted by a band of international murderers.

Bob rocked impatiently from one foot to another. "Come on, girl, get a move on. I gotta go," he whispered.

"You should have done your business in the lobby," she said, blocking his way.

"I hate public restrooms," he said, trying to push by. She wouldn't let him pass. Once she was confident the room was safe, she moved into the room. Bob rushed to the bathroom closing the door behind him.

"The stiffs are still in here," he yelled. "What a couple of deadbeats."

"We need to talk," Renee said to me in an ominous tone.

My heart sank. I hated those words. They always meant, "The relationship is over, there's no fixing it and it's *your* fault."

I sat on the now-familiar couch. "Okay, Renee, let me have it. What was it? Let me guess, you're an international spy dedicated to your country and can't have a relationship outside the agency, or was it that you don't like my fighting skills?"

She stood in front of me with a frown on her face. "What are you talking about? We have to get out of this situation and you want to know if we're still together?"

"Uh, yes. I would like to know where we stand, relationship-wise."

"Well, if you look at your actions over the past hours, I'd say we're at an impasse. I sat in a smelly, greasy storeroom and you left me there."

"You didn't want to go with me."

"I said I wasn't going to commit to you if I was being blackmailed."

"No, you said you couldn't have a relationship because of your long working hours and inability to text on the job. Is it my understanding we're back on?"

"Stay focused, Rick. We have work to do. But since we're on the subject, our one-week anniversary is coming up. I hope you got me something pretty."

I wasn't sure what was happening between us. Before I could sort it out, the bathroom door flew open. Bob slammed it behind him. "We're lucky dead men can't smell or they'd be very upset," he said, waving his hand in front of his face.

"Bob?"

"Yes, Renee?"

"Come over here and brainstorm with us."

Bob sat on the couch. Renee pulled up a chair and faced us. "We have to locate this chip and then decide how to get rid of it. We don't want to be looking over our shoulders for the rest of our lives."

"Yeah that's a pain in the neck…"

We both stared at him, which was getting to be a routine in itself.

Bob realized it was time for him to join the grownup party. "Okay, forget I said that. Sooo, back to work. Let's find the chip and give it back to an unarmed, kind person who likes us."

"Stand up, Rick," she said, ignoring Bob, "We need to make a full search."

Bob rubbed his hands together. "Now, we're talkin'. This is better than watching nasty TSA videos."

"Can it, Bob," she said without turning, "Either the Boeing man planted it on you, someone else did, or everyone is lying."

"Or the chip is somewhere else," said Bob, completing her sentence.

"I doubt the body count would be this high if the chip didn't exist," said Renee. "It might be a fake. It might be somewhere else. But my guess is it's somewhere on Rick's body or stuck in his clothes."

"Then why would Greg let us out of his mansion?" said Bob, "That makes no sense."

"No one gave me anything," I said, looking at Renee. "I swear."

Renee began her pat-down, first one leg, then the other. She lifted my coat jacket, ran her hand down my buttocks, then, facing me, reached into my jacket."

"Does this mean you still love me?" I asked.

"I'd love you more if you knew where the chip was," she said, still manhandling me.

I was beginning to like the attention, even though my arms were getting tired. "I think it's in my pants," I said.

"You wish."

Renee patted the lapels of the tux, then reached into the inside of my jacket back near my shoulder blades.

"Bingo," she said, slowly, carefully pulling a thin plastic container attached to the end of a long pin. "Looks like someone planted a computer chip on you, Rick. Pinned to the inside of your jacket."

She held it to her button nose and examined the case closely, turning it around.

"The chip's inside this small plastic box, which is attached to a long barbed needle. Impressive design. You're the carrier, the delivery boy, and you have no idea it's on you."

She peered into the small plastic box.

I put my arms down. "What do you think?"

"I believe it's the real deal. If it's not, we have to treat it like it is. If Atsbee's playing us, so be it."

"What now?" asked Bob.

Renee was still examining the case. "I think this other device is some kind of tracking beacon."

Bob brightened up. "Hey, we could pin it on a dog, or maybe a whale."

I was thinking out loud now. "Renee, if that's some kind of homing device, shouldn't we get it away from us or at least get out of here fast? Have you packed your shampoo? Toothbrush? Hand grenades?"

"Very funny, Rick. Let's leave the comedy to the big man. He's much better at it."

"Thanks, Renee."

She shot him a look. "I didn't say you *were* funny, Bob, I said you were better at it than Rick."

Bob shrugged, ignoring the remark. "So, is it time for the laundry cart?"

"Okay, get the cart, Bob."

"Now we're talkin' serious deeeetective work." He jumped to his feet and disappeared out the door.

Renee watched as the door closed behind him. "I've never seen him move so fast."

"I think he likes the job," I said.

She was confused. "What job?"

"His fake detective job," I explained. "I don't think he wants to be a P.I. He doesn't have anywhere else to go."

"Bob always had hundreds of friends. I saw them on TV."

"Fame is a fickle lover, doesn't pay the bills, and leaves when you want her the most."

"Kinda like you."

"So, now he has no money. No fame. I think we're all he's got."

"That would be sad, having only us to depend on. We're not the most reliable friends to have, especially tonight" she said, lost in thought.

"That's all *I've* got," I said.

"What are you talking about? You have Larry. Evelyn still kinda likes you I bet. You have your friends at Gordon Biersch. You have Tank and Jenny. You have your ex-roommates, including your new BFF, Greg Atsbee."

"Yeah, right," I laughed, realizing she was being sarcastic. But then it sunk in. I didn't have anyone in my life and my fling with Renee was hardly cemented.

Bob returned with a huge laundry cart.

"You see Rick, in this business you have to know how to open doors because the best things in life are on the other side."

"A laundry cart is one of the best things in life?"

"Sometimes a laundry cart is enough. Let's get these stiffs out of here before someone realizes they aren't part of our entourage."

Bob and I put the bodies into the cart, being careful not to rip the fabric lined bottom. We covered them with towels.

"What now?" I asked.

"We'll leave them down the other end of the hallway. Can't leave them lying around here. These bad men are already getting a little ripe. Come on, we've been in here too long."

Renee looked at him with admiration. "Bob, I think you're catching on to this operation."

Bob lit up. "You think so?"

"No doubt about it, Bob."

He grabbed the end of the cart and disappeared into the hallway.

I looked over to Renee. "Ready to go?"

"Let me grab my stuff."

"Get going, agent Gunnison, we are out of time."

Renee stopped. "Who told you I'm an agent?"

"Bob."

"He was trying to be funny."

I smiled. "Bob might stretch the truth, but he has a way of listening in on hotel phones and finding facts. And you basically said you were a spy back there in in the marine shed."

"Bob also has a way of saying anything to get a laugh. I was thinking of being an entertainment agent, but it requires too much night work. That's when I like to kick back."

"And sleep with celebrities all across Europe?'

She stopped cold. "When this is over, you and I are going to have a long conversation," she said seriously.

"Will it include loaded weapons?"

"It might."

She disappeared into the bedroom and started gathering her belongings. "You have no idea, do you?"

"About what?"

"That this is going to be a long, dangerous night. Now help me with this stuff and let's get out of here before all hell breaks loose."

Cat Fight!

We crept down the fire stairs carrying our suitcases and a duffle bag chock of Renee's weapons collection. She opened the door to the second floor, checked the hallway, and turned back to Bob and me. "All clear. Keep it quiet."

"What?" Bob said loudly from the stairwell, which echoed like an empty gymnasium.

"Ssshhhh," I said, equally as loud.

"Enough of the shushing," demanded Renee. "No shushes."

We exited the stairwell and worked our way toward the elevators. Halfway to our destination, a door behind us opened.

"Rick? Is that you?"

We stopped and turned like three stooges caught in the act.

Sticking her head out of the door was Evelyn. Still dressed in her sparkling white dress, she looked beautiful except for the circles of white powder that outlined her tiny nostrils. She rubbed her nose and smiled. In the past she'd do her business in the powder room, which made sense to me considering cocaine was her drug of choice.

We all looked extremely guilty, which of course we were.

"Evelyn. Why aren't you at the party?"

A puzzled look replaced her spaced-out expression. "What happened to your tux?"

I looked down. My trousers were ripped and wrinkled. My shirt was torn, my tie was missing, and my jacket was marred with sand, grass clippings and mud.

"I was out by the bluff and dropped my contacts. Couldn't find them in the grass."

"You wear contacts? That's new."

"I only wear them at night."

"What are you up to, Rick?"

Renee handed her suitcases to Bob, who immediately dropped them on the floor with a dull thud. She walked up to Evelyn.

"Are you Rick's ex-girlfriend?"

Evelyn straightened up and stared at Renee, her eyes unfocused. "And you are..."

Renee offered Evelyn her hand. "Hi, I'm Renee Gunnison."

"I'm Evelyn deWilde. You can call me Ev."

I had no idea what Renee was up to, but I knew she wasn't trying to be Evelyn's next BFF.

"You don't know me, but I'm with Rick now. I have no idea why you'd dump such a hot, sensitive guy for a bald man four times your weight. But hey, it's a free country. How are you doing tonight? Enjoying the party? How's that coke treating your sinuses?"

Evelyn shook Renee's hand politely. "I'm doing well, thank you. I never expected Rick to go for a redhead. Does the carpet match the drapes?"

"There is no carpet, Evelyn. How's life under the fat man?"

"I beg your pardon?"

I came to Renee's side and gently tugged her arm. "We have to go."

Renee pulled her arm free, teeth clenched. "I'm not done, Rick." She turned back to Evelyn. "Next time you get your bloated bed-buddy alone, ask him where he gets his millions, and while you're at it, ask him why his wife isn't anywhere to be seen in this country."

"Wife?"

"He's married, you know, been married for years. Be careful Ev, you're in way deeper than you think." Then she turned to us. "Come on, men, let's go. Our work here is done."

We grabbed our bags and turned the corner. We entered the waiting elevator. As the doors started to close there was a blur of brown and Mojo raced in.

Mountain High

We made our way out of the building through another fire exit that didn't trigger an alarm and approached the valet station from the side of the building. Mojo trotted proudly at my side. It was like he'd never left. My best friend was back. One look at him and even Renee smiled.

The Silverado was waiting at the entrance as we'd instructed. Mojo jumped into the front seat. We threw our luggage into the back seat and drove away. Between some educated guessing and a lot of help from Google maps, we drove up into the Santa Cruz Mountains.

We located an isolated section of the two-lane road that runs the ridge between the Pacific Ocean and the inland Silicon Valley. Renee pulled off the road and backed into a clump of bushes so we weren't visible to any passing cars, although I doubted anyone would be traveling this back road.

It was a spectacular Saturday night. We sat on the ground and leaned against the side of the truck. Far in the distance, the Pacific Ocean reflected the half risen moon. Mojo was excited. He ran up and down the hillside, chasing imaginary squirrels and deer.

Bob tossed a stick down the hillside. Mojo disappeared after it.

"I'd feel better if we dumped the chip and whatever that tracking thing is. The way it is now, we're sitting fucks."

"You mean sitting ducks," I said.

"No, I was right the first time. Keeping the chip anywhere near us is like gluing a target to our foreheads. We should have left it at the front desk with a note."

Mojo returned with the stick, tail wagging. I tossed it back down the hill.

"Unacceptable," said Renee, "Leaving the chip would have put us all in danger."

Bob laughs. "Whew. I was worried there for a moment. I guess we're safe now," he said, opening one of the tiny bottles he'd taken from the honor bar. Then he passed a bag of turkey jerky. I shared some of the treat with Mojo who was already tired of the run and fetch game.

"What's the weapon count?" I asked.

Renee kept her focus far out to sea. She spoke without turning. "We've got two turtleneck handguns, a silenced Glock from the guy in our bathtub, Bob's mystery mini-gun, and two used throwing knives. Then there's my stuff: sawed-off shotgun, four grenades, a pound of C4, four detonators, three AR-15's, two SIG-Sauer hand guns, an M-21 sniper, six bottle rockets, and some assorted M80s and eight cherry bombs."

I could tell Bob was surprised at our impressive arsenal, but he didn't address it. "Why don't we go back to Atsbee and hand over the stupid chip. He's the one who started this. He should finish it."

Renee shook her head. "That guy is a chess player and we're the pawns. He's ten moves ahead of us."

"Not if we go off the board."

This caught Renee's attention. "What do you mean?"

"Chess is a game where all the pieces have a predetermined type of move. What if the pieces could fly, jump over everything, get off the board, run around the side of the table, and attack the player instead of the other pieces. That's a different type of game, and a traditional chess player wouldn't know what to do."

I thought this was a great idea for a movie, not a solution to our current problem.

"Bob," I said, "are you crazy?"

I looked over and saw that Renee was getting sucked in. Mojo put his head on my leg, his eyes switching back and forth between Bob and Renee.

"Wait a minute," she said, "Bob might have an idea."

"Yeah, he's got an idea, like running a guy off a cliff." I countered.

Bob straightened up. "You're not seeing it, Rick."

"No, I'm not."

"It's like putting a guy in a laundry basket. You liked that one, didn't you? Or how about saving Renee at the beach house by driving a limousine through the wall of a house? Couldn't have done that without me."

"You still haven't said anything except that we should cheat at chess."

Renee stood up and faced us. For a moment I thought she was going to lose her balance and fall down the hill.

"Boys, boys, this isn't about you."

I thought the evening was totally about us, but didn't dare say anything.

"Well, maybe it is. A little," she said.

Bob was energized. "I say let's go down to Atsbee's place, put a bomb in his hand, a gun at his head and make him tell us all the players and all the moves. Then at least we'll know what to do next."

"I don't trust that guy," Renee said, "He's playing too many angles, and you know he has some serious protection he hasn't revealed."

Bob was starting to panic. I could feel it.

"We have to do *something*."

"Bob."

"Renee?"

"This isn't the place for you."

He quickly calmed down and looked skyward. "It is a bit cold."

Renee couldn't stop a small chuckle, but she continued. "Look, I think Rick and I are better equipped to deal with this situation."

"So being detective/spy/operative is only for thin people? What's that all about?"

"That's not it at all."

"What is it then? I've saved this guy's life tonight. Yours twice. I've tapped phones, danced in the moonlight and drunk from the vodka stream of life. I've driven golf carts and limos. I've defended my country, and you say I don't belong? You, young lady, are deeeeelusional if you think I'm not qualified to be with you. I'm on the team. End of story. Next subject."

"It's too dangerous," she said.

Bob was not in a joking mood, a fairly rare occurrence.

"It might be too dangerous for you, Renee. Not me. I've heard this excuse to eliminate me from the action several times tonight and it's bullshit I tell you. Total bullshit. Besides, there's something you're forgetting."

"And that is?"

"Just because you two are falling in love, it doesn't mean you have to dump me."

"It's not that way."

"Renee, it's obvious you guys want to play kissy-face. I have eyes, you know. I might be a third wheel, but this wheel is not spinning off anywhere. You're stuck with me."

"Bob."

"Besides, you aren't dumping me now because I have what you want."

"What, an empty bottle of vodka? A couple of stale Snickers bars from an honor bar? Leftover jokes?"

"Hey, that came close to hurting my carefully-protected emotions, Renee. Not to worry though, I've been insulted by much funnier and crueler people than you, like my mom and my producers. But you need me because I have the magic chip."

"Yeah, right. Try something else, Bob."

"Go ahead, look for yourself."

Renee checked her pockets as Bob continued. "And if you don't think I belong with you guys, then you can go sit on a big fat stick, and I'm not offering mine."

Renee finished her search.

"You can't have it, Bob. Give it back."

"Only if you let me stay."

Renee held out her hand. "It's your choice if you stay or go, but if you don't hand over the chip, I *will* take it from you."

Bob stood his ground and looked like he wasn't going to give it up. Renee looked mean, like she was going to do something serious. I was certain that Bob was making a mistake challenging her.

The standoff lasted more than a few seconds. It felt like six years. In one of his few moments of sanity, Bob pulled the chip from his shirt pocket and handed it over.

"Smart move," she said without a hint of thankfulness, "Don't try that again."

Her voice actually frightened me. I never understood how such a beautiful woman with great hair could be so menacing. I glanced at Bob. He held his head low for about a second, maybe less.

"Okay, Renee, you can be the bully and keep the chip. But I have to tell you I've got a plan for catching these jerks and returning the chip with none of us being hurt, chased or tracked down and punished for being involved in this international mess."

"We're clear about this," said Renee, with a tone in her voice that was totally fearsome. Of course, Bob didn't even notice.

"I got it," he replied, "You want to have the chip. Fine."

She was not convinced of his sincerity. "And you'll keep your hands away from it," she said, staring intently at him, "Very far away."

Bob nodded and shrugged. "Oh, definitely. Won't get near the sucker." Then I heard him mutter, "Ungrateful bitch."

There was a pause. Renee turned, ready for battle. Bob stood in front of her, as if he didn't have a care in the world. I think if she physically attacked him, he wouldn't have defended himself. Neither moved a muscle. After a few seconds she lowered her guard. Personally, I think she got bored. Bob gave her nothing to work with.

"Okay, Bob, what's your plan?"

"Well," he said slowly, "I have a connection with the most intense and the smartest people in this country."

"And who might that be?"

"My fans, well ex-fans."

A smile spread across Renee's face. She took a step toward him and put her hand on his shoulder. "Bob, honey, you have no fans. And even if you did, what could they do to help us?"

He regained his cockiness, which pleased me. A dull and motionless Bob Clay was more frightening than an angry Renee Gunnison.

"I maintain an influential, highly unorthodox website with many loyal subscribers. If I call on my people, there will be a nuclear explosion of intelligence and an answer will appear within an hour or two. They are that powerful."

Sometimes I thought this heavyweight guy was simply brilliant, and sometimes I didn't want to be on the same planet with him. He was either right on, or so far off that I honestly believed that he should be locked up.

"Bob, even if it's true about the cerebral powers of your followers, it's 1 a.m. on a Saturday night. No one's waiting for your 911 posting."

"Prime time for my peeps. They'll come up with an awesome solution. I've gotten some of the funniest bits from them."

Renee was not impressed. "Bob, we don't need a comedy sketch. We need a plan for survival."

"What do you think a comedy sketch is?" Bob replies.

Renee was quick with her response. "It's an unrealistic play based on an absurd situation."

"And this is?"

I had to smile. "Renee, it might be worth a try. Do you have a better idea?"

"Personally, I liked the concept of running away the best," said Bob.

Far in the distance, three sets of headlights were winding their way up the hillside. For some reason, they didn't look like happy-go-lucky Saturday night joy riders.

"Get in the truck, boys. We're heading off-road and downhill."

"And why are we doing this?" I asked. "Can't we drive the other way?"

"They're probably coming up the other way too."

Bob and I climbed into the pickup. Mojo hopped in with me.

"Grab onto something solid, lads. We're going where no man has gone before."

She released the brake and gunned the engine.

"You've got to be kidding," moaned Bob as we took a hard left and started down the hillside. "It's a stolen pickup, Renee, not a goddamned space ship."

It's All Down Hill from Here

The angle of the hill wasn't steep enough to cause a problem with the large four-wheel drive pick-up. The Silverado handled it easily. The high clearance, wide tires and powerful engine were designed to go off-road, but I knew an unseen boulder or deep rivulet had the potential to damage the tires or even tip us over.

The light from the half-moon aided Renee's decision-making process as she navigated between scrub oak and outcroppings of semi-hidden boulders. Even though our speed didn't exceed ten miles an hour, we were being thrown around like we were in a giant bouncy toy.

"I...think...this...was...a...questionable...idea," said Bob as Renee evaded a cluster of granite which threw us to the right.

"You wanted off the chess board," she yelled at him.

"Yes, off the chess board, not off the damn map," yelled Bob.

"It's better than getting shot."

"The jury's still out on that one," Bob responded, "I haven't experienced rolling down a cliff in an American-built truck."

I have to ask, not taking my eyes off the obstacle course ahead. "You've rolled a foreign truck *and* been shot?"

"Ya gotta live to understand the things you don't want to do twice. I don't want to be shot again."

"Who shot you?"

"A former friend. We don't talk any more. Oo-ooo, on the left! A road. Take the road!"

Renee turned the wheel and gunned the engine, causing the back of the truck to fishtail. Crashing through a flimsy barbed wire fence, the pickup bounced violently onto the asphalt.

"I love pavement," said Bob.

"This should lead back to the coast road," I said. "Then we can make a run for it."

"You're not serious," replied Bob. "We can't run anywhere if we have some kind of tracking device with us. They've probably got a drone following us. Holy crap!"

"What is it?" yelled Renee.

I was expecting a guided missile to be heading at us.

"Listen. It's from one of my people. His handle is Taskmaster7. He said we need to wrap the homing device in multiple layers of tinfoil or put it in a metal box. This will defeat its broadcast capabilities. Quick, find a 7-Eleven or a supermarket. We'll wrap this sucker up tight, and then we can run away."

"One step at a time, Bob."

* * * * *

The Chevron Stop and Go had one roll of aluminum foil. I ran back to the Sliverado and tossed it to Renee.

"Wrap it up," I said.

Renee started pulling the shiny material out of the box and wrapping the device

"What do we do now?" asked Bob, watching her enclose the device in layer after layer of foil. Mojo was bored. He'd settled onto the seat next to Bob.

"We'll figure something out," she said. "We can get to San Francisco in an hour. Lots of places to disappear there."

"We have to ditch the pickup," said Bob.

"Why?"

"It's too obvious, and eventually someone is going to miss it," said Bob.

"Who's going to miss the truck?" I counter.

"Maybe a neighbor, or the original owner. How about an entire neighborhood that saw a bunch of terrorists shoot up their neighborhood and crash a limo into a house."

"They don't have white terrorists in Half Moon Bay," added Renee.

"You could have fooled me," said Bob. "We've met nothing but Caucasian extremists since we got here. The airport was crawling with them."

"Those guys are thugs and spies, not terrorists," said Renee, looking in the rear view mirror.

Bob turned to her. "Oh? What's the difference?"

"Headgear?" I offer.

"Stop it. Let's get our ride figured out."

Bob looked out the window. At the nearby gas pump was a metallic blue low rider with two Chicano men in bandanas.

Bob turned to us. "What do you think? No one would be looking for us in that beauty."

Renee glanced over at the car. "It's worth a try, but I can't ask. They'd get the wrong idea."

Bob opened the door. "Not a problem for this detective in training."

We approached the two young men with caution. They were as out-of-place in this rural town as Bob and I were in our shredded tuxedos. At first they looked all mean and threatening, but then one of them broke into a grin.

"Yo, dude. You're that funny fag that used to be on television, right?"

Bob played it cool and maybe a bit too uppity. "I prefer comedian or private eye...but whatever works. I was admiring your..."

The guy's expression turned sour. He probably thought Bob was hitting on him. Things started to look a little dicey.

"Your car. I like the way this ride was all, like, done up. You know, rideable," Bob said quickly.

It was a clumsy recovery, but Bob played the awkward geek really well.

"I can't get over this car," he continued, trying to look interested in a motor vehicle. There was no way Bob liked anything mechanical in his life, but he kept faking it. "Any chance we could arrange a swap? Of vehicles, I mean. The big powerful macho Silverado for this smaller, but extremely sleek and highly modified...car."

"What's the deal, homie?" said one of the guys. "You trying to unload a hot ride on us? Where'd you get that gringo pickup truck anyway, and what's in it for us if we do your trade?"

I wondered this myself. Why *would* they want to trade? The guys looked at each other and nodded.

"You know, you got yourself a deal, funny man."

I headed back to the truck to get the keys. I didn't know what was up with that crazy barter, but I knew it was not good.

"What's happening?" asked Renee.

"Bob pulled it off. We're swapping rides."

"We can't go too far with that thing."

"Why, is it broken?"

"No, it's hot. They'd never give it up if they owned it."

"It's not like we own this one."

"You got a point, Rick. Here are the keys. Come back and help me unload the stuff."

The two low-riders walked around the truck. Mojo didn't like them. He growled. Renee took him out the other side of the pickup.

"Bro, this Piece Of Shit is filthy and it's been shot."

Bob came to the rescue. "Yeah, me and my buds have been riding off-road. We like to get to drinkin' a lot and we end up shooting things. We kinda made a few unfortunate choices. But shit, it runs fine. We just drove it down that fuckin' mountain ten minutes ago."

"No way, man. You did that?"

Bob pulled up his tux pants. "Oh, yeah. Love the off-road life. Do it every weekend when I'm not chopping trees or rappelling off a tall mountain, bro."

I wanted to shove Bob for pretending to be Mister Mountain Man. Luckily, these guys were not taking him seriously either. Who would believe a three-hundred-fifty pound guy was a tree-chopping rappelling adventure freak? We all knew that Bob couldn't climb a flight of stairs without risking a heart attack.

I returned to help Renee move the gear into the trunk of the low rider. Renee patted Bob on the back. "Way to go with the negotiating, Mr. Detective."

Bob lit up like a kid on Christmas morning. "You think so?"

She nodded. "You done good, boy."

Bob shook his head. "I'm not so sure. I think I messed up."

"You played it perfectly, Bob." I said. "None of us could have pulled that off."

"I'm never going to fit in the back seat of this thing."

I opened the passenger door. "Not a problem. You can ride shotgun. It's my pleasure, partner. Mojo's already in the back seat."

Before we could get into our new ride, the two guys jumped into the Silverado. They laughed out loud, then spoke at the top of their voices in Spanish. I know it was about us. The truck roared to life.

"Fuck you, asshole gringos," they shouted.

I wanted to yell back, but I knew we got the better deal. And I didn't want them coming back. No do-over for this one.

The Silverado tore down the street with the two guys whooping and hollering, leaving behind a black streak on the asphalt from the spinning tires.

"They're going to ruin that truck," muttered Bob.

The three of us watched the Silverado head north. From the south, two dark sedans sped past us. They both ran a stop sign without touching their brakes.

"Those guys have to be going over a hundred miles an hour," said Bob.

The dark cars caught up to the pickup and forced it off the road and into the side of a hill. Sparks and large pieces of metal flew into the air. There were several bright flashes, followed by a huge explosion.

I looked over to Renee. "Did you leave something in the truck that could do that?"

"I have things that could do that, but it wasn't me."

"They chose poorly," said Bob, watching a column of smoke rise into the sky, illuminated by the fire below.

"Bob, stealing lines from 'Indiana Jones'?" I said, "You're dating yourself."

"Better than dating no one. Hey, let's do something clever, like use this opportunity to escape with our lives. It won't take the bad guys long to figure out those guys are not us."

I climbed into the back of the tiny car. Bob squeezed into the passenger seat.

"This is not going to be pretty," said Renee. She slid the car into gear and pulled out of the gas station, heading away from the growing fire.

Field of Plane

We passed through Atsbee's open gates, drove down the long driveway and arrived at the circular driveway. The sky was just beginning to lightened with the oncoming dawn.

The three of us and Mojo struggled to get out of the small sedan. Bob plopped himself down on the thick, well groomed grass. Mojo came to his side. Renee and I joined him and we all looked at the mansion facing us.

"I think you and Mojo should stay behind," said Renee after a few moments of silence.

I was shocked. I turned to her. Her beautiful red hair reflected the sky's glow. No woman had ever struck me as so special.

"I don't think I can do that, Renee."

"Bob and I will take the chip and make the deal. You stay out here and if we don't text you every three minutes, you can blow the door off. But we need someone out here and Bob's not the one."

"I *am* the one. Just not that one."

"See? Besides, we don't want Mojo in the line of fire. It's the best."

I was getting a little blurry and figured she was probably right.

She stood up and went to the trunk. We'll take some weapons in, but you'll have the C4 and rifles. Stay alert and we'll be out in a few minutes if all goes well. You ready, Bob?"

Bob struggled to his feet. "Come on, Renee, let's finish this thing."

I returned to the car with Mojo. As I settled down in the driver's seat, my mind moved into Army Ranger mode, looking in every direction as Bob and Renee headed for Atsbee's front door.

Once Bob and Renee disappeared into the house, I drove around the circular driveway and stopped where Barry parked the limo a few hours earlier. I figured I could spot anyone approaching from there, get to the front door quickly, and if necessary, make a quick getaway with Bob and Renee.

Mojo was done. He passed out in the back seat. Between being with Evelyn, the ride down the mountainside and consuming the three half eaten tacos he found under the front seat. He clearly needed a break.

I slouched low in the car, watching the phone. I don't know if I fell asleep or zoned out. When I came to my senses there was a guy standing at the window with a gun in my face.

I guess I wasn't a Ranger anymore. Mojo didn't even move.

"Let's go, Rick."

I stumbled out of the car and a second man shuffled around the back of the vehicle. All I heard was a noise behind me, then *wham*.

* * * * *

I woke up in the back of an Escalade or an Excursion or an Exclamation or some kind of car that starts with an E. My head was pounding. My mouth was dry. I felt sick and I stunk, badly. The big car stopped and the door opened. I was dragged onto a dirt road in the middle of nowhere. The sun was much too bright. They pushed me away from the car into a field. I stumbled a few feet into the tall grass.

"Tough luck for you, Rick," said the guy wearing a shirt with a pocket patch that read "Mike." Was he some kind of mechanic? Did he steal Mike's shirt? Who was Mike anyway? I hadn't slept. I had no weapons, and the two ugly men standing in front of me didn't like me.

I looked skyward. There were two hawks or buzzards wheeling in the distance. Had something died over there? It didn't matter. My problem was here, on the ground.

Then I heard the noise. So did Mike and his friend. It was like a mosquito, but a lower pitch. We looked around. Our eyes met again.

"This is where you finish your ride, Mr. Johnson."

I was thinking that I should plead my case. That I was innocent. It wasn't me. That I've never seen a computer chip. That they've got the wrong guy, but somehow I knew those ideas sounded incredibly lame and would probably piss them off.

"You've got the wrong guy."

"I don't think so."

The noise was getting closer, but we ignored it.

Off to the side, one of the buzzards drifted in a wide circle as if waiting for an unsuspecting prey. Then it disappeared. I tried to talk my way out of it again.

"I'm not RJ."

Mike smiled. It wasn't friendly. "We know you're not RJ. Scott was supposed to intercept him and we were supposed to kill Scott. But you messed everything up."

I know this would make sense to someone, but it wasn't me.

"I'm sorry. I didn't mean to get in your way. I'm not in your way now. Maybe I should just move on down...this road here, okay?"

"Take one more step and we'll shoot you, a lot. Where's the chip?"

"What about my friends?"

"The girl's hot, but not all that smart. And the fat guy's a nerd. He thinks he was some kind of TV star."

I wasn't asking for a review of my current relationships and I certainly wasn't about to explain Bob's résumé. I tried something else.

"The chip is with Greg Atsbee in his house. If I get it for you, will we be okay? No hard feelings?"

The dark objects in the sky weren't birds. Now I knew what was circling overhead. But now they were heading directly at me and the car. One was a very big, double-winged plane, a crop duster. Following behind it was a single-winged aircraft, some kind of fighter. The planes were probably the source of the buzzing I'd heard. Then I realized they weren't real, they were model airplanes. Big ones. Really big ones.

"You get us the chip and we'll be cool with everything," said Mike.

"No get-me-backs?" I asked, my mind trying to stay with the conversation and keep a blurry eye on the wacky machines.

"What the fuck is a get-me-back?"

"You know, when you get the chip, you promise you won't kill everyone because you're mad and you don't want any witnesses."

"You're right. We should kill your messed-up friends, but we won't—if you get the chip to us, everyone will be fine. We'll let you all go and you can go anywhere you want."

Mike looked at his partner with shifty eyes like he was going to burst out laughing. If I gave them the chip, everyone I loved would be toast, burnt toast, with lots of holes in them. I wasn't even sure they were going to let me try to get the chip. Chances were I'd be left in that ugly field. My body would probably not be found for months, if at all.

"Okay, asshole, we'll give you one chance..."

Mike never got to speak another word. The biplane came screaming in at a billion miles an hour. I threw myself to the ground. The bottom wing of the plane took Mike's head clean off. The plane spun off like a cartwheel into the field. Mike's headless body wavered for a moment, then collapsed to the ground.

Mike's friend turned and met the second model plane head-on. He was thrown back violently, with the propeller grinding into his face. In seconds, I was covered in blood splatters.

If you never see a guy with a plane stuck into his face, you're not missing anything.

I got up and rummaged through Mike's pockets. I gagged more than a few times, but this totally disgusting task was necessary. I had to get back to Atsbee's mansion in case something went down. Despite being around severe injuries in the past, for some reason I'd lost my immunity to this type of carnage.

Mike's body was still twitching when I located the keys. I looked up and spotted more trouble—two men were heading toward me. Big men. Could this get any worse? I picked up Mike's gun and prepared to shoot, except the sun was in my eyes, I couldn't see anything and my head was pounding like an old jungle movie. I backed up and moved behind the big car, squinting. Then I saw them.

One of the guys was Tank. This guy was a rescue magnet.

"I knew it was you," he said, catching his breath, "Who else...wears a tux in a field with two ugly guys acting like they're going to wipe you off the face of the earth?"

"It looked that bad?"

He straightened up and took a deep breath, "You weren't going to last much longer. What are you doing, Rick? You are one crazy bastard."

"Tank, you killed them."

Tank looked at his handiwork.

"Wow. That's pretty...bad. We didn't mean to. We were just trying to scare them."

"I think you got a little too close, but it's okay."

"Is it?"

I gave him a big hug.

"You bet it is."

"Oh, hey, this is my best friend, Crazy Eddie."

I looked in Crazy Eddie's eyes. He was crazy all right. This guy should have been dating Evelyn.

Crazy Eddie shook my hand so hard it made my head hurt even more.

"Great to mcct you, Rick. Heard all about last night. That was somethin', huh?'

Eddie was still shaking my hand, but he was looking to his side at the two bloodied bodies. One of the inert figures had Eddie's plane buried in its face. "Ffffuuukkk..." He said it like it was a mile-long word. "You know what, Tank?" he said.

"What is it, CE?"

"This is because of that metal sheeting we put on the leading edge of the wings."

Tank turned to him. "Naw. With that angle of attack, they'd be headless regardless."

"I don't think so, T. The added weight of the metal combined with the extra rivets created a front weight differential that caused an increase in the down slope speed. They'd still be dead, but they'd both have their heads attached."

"Ed you're not considering the wind factor from the onshore breeze that should have countered the additional weight. Besides, I was aiming high."

"Not high enough, T."

Tank looked at the dead men. "You're right about that, Ed."

Having settled their technical discussion, Tank turned to me. "Bet these assholes are part of the gang that took your chick, huh?"

"You guessed it." I hoped that was enough information for him.

Eddie spotted the gun in headless Mike's friend's hand.

"Hey, Tank, you weren't kidding. These guys were going to kill your friend."

Tank was irritated. "I told ya, Eddie. Rick's been running around all night, haven't you, Rick?"

"All night long," I said, trying not to break into a Lionel Richie song. I was not only exhausted, I was bordering on insane.

"What are we gonna do, Tank? My plane is all...bloody. Now we can't be in the competition."

Tank wasn't paying any attention to the planes. He was staring at the carnage.

"This was like that movie...do you know which one I'm talking about?"

"*North by Northwest*" I offered.

"Shit no. This was like *Midway*."

"Guys, you have to get out of here. Gather your planes and any pieces you can find and leave. I doubt anyone saw what happened. I have to go back to Atsbee's place and get Renee."

Eddie woke up from his stupor. "Atsbee? I thought he was dead."

Tank's all over this one. "Eddie I told you, that's a guy named Gatsby and he lives on Long Island where they invented Iced Tea. This is a different guy, remember?"

"Ohhhhhhh, yeah."

I couldn't delay any longer. I had to get back to Atsbee's. I hop into the big black "E-something" and drive off, hoping Eddie and Tank know enough to get far away from the scene of a crime.

Rescue Rooter

I gave a final glance to Eddie and Tank as I turned the large black car around. They were picking up their planes and I was pretty sure Eddie was going through their pockets. They would have left their fingerprints all over the place, but what do you expect from a guy who goes by the name of Crazy Eddie?

I checked my phone. There was a message from Bob. It said, "All finished. Deal done. Come get us."

Following Google maps directions, I pulled up in front of the house. The low-rider was parked where I left it. The first thing I did was check on Mojo. He was still asleep. I guess I hadn't been gone too long. He looked up and as soon as I opened the door, he jumped out ready for action.

I considered filling my pockets with explosives before going in to Atsbee's mansion. Instead, I went to the trunk and picked out a couple of handguns. If all was well inside, there was no need to blow up Greg's house. I hoped I didn't have to do much running or shooting. My head hurt and I was still pretty fuzzy. Mojo, unaware of the danger that could face us, trotted along. I had no idea what to do with Mojo. Leaving him behind made no sense. Bringing him into a potential shoot out wasn't a great idea either. I decided to let him decide on his own. He's a smart dog. Smarter than some humans I knew.

The front door was unlocked. I entered slowly. Muffled voices drifted down the hallway. I made my way to the large room. Bob was sitting on the couch, alone. He glanced in my direction. I could tell by his sad eyes that all was not well. There was blood on the floor and on the couch. Something had happened. I was hoping that Renee was okay. I assumed that she was somewhere close by, or she was doing some other spy thing. No matter, I refused to panic. I was too exhausted. Mojo stopped and growled.

"It looks like I'm too late," I said to Bob.

"You're not late, Rick. You're right on time." I recognized Scott's voice coming from behind me. I winced inwardly.

"At ease Mojo," I say. He obediently sat and stayed quiet, looking up at me for more instructions.

"What's with the blood, Scott?" I said, not bothering to turn.

"Your man Atsbee had a little accident."

I turned slowly, not wanting anyone to overreact. Greg was standing next to Scott holding his bloody arm. Behind him were two more men. They grabbed Greg roughly, shoved him past me and pushed him onto the couch. He was in pain, but from the placement of the wound, I figured he would survive.

"Sorry, guys," said Atsbee. "I didn't expect this."

Scott's hatred of Greg was all too apparent. "Of course you didn't expect this, Greg, because every one of your stupid tricks failed. You didn't swap the chip. You didn't get the culprit who was stealing your corporate secrets, and now our old friend Rick Johnson is going to hand over the chip so I can get it out of the country and settle my debts."

"I don't think so, Scott" I replied.

"Rick, it's a little late to be playing the hero. Not only will you watch Greg bleed to death, but then you'll watch our overweight roommate die in front of you, simply because of some moral duty that you can't perform. I will have that chip whether you give it to me, or I take if off your body."

"I'm not overweight," Bob protests. "I'm just...big boned."

Scott's laugh was actually cruel. "Keep believing that, fatso, because in a few minutes it won't matter. You'll be on a permanent diet. Now, Mr. Johnson, I'd like you to meet the real Richard Johnson."

A short man with long sideburns walked into the room. It took me a moment to recognize him. It was the guy who was making a scene at the valet station the night before.

"This is the man who was supposed to receive the chip in the hotel lobby. So, if you want Greg and Bob to live, you'll hand it over."

I glanced around the room. Renee had to be somewhere close by. Even if she was, there wasn't much chance she could mount an effective rescue, considering there were two goons, Scott, and now this wild card named Rick Johnson all armed and very serious. Any one of these derelicts was capable of causing serious injury.

"What a surprise. It's a little gun party." This was a new voice. I turned to spot Evelyn's boyfriend, Saul Weinstein.

"Saul, you shouldn't be here," said Scott.

Weinstein pushed the two goons aside and walked into the middle of the room.

"I thought I should check on our flight arrangements, Scott. Matter of fact, it might be time to add a person to the manifest."

"There's no room, Saul. I don't think you have a visa for where we're going."

"I'm getting on that plane, Scott."

"I seriously doubt it."

I turned and recognized the one-eyed man from the lobby. He was still wearing his stupid trench coat, holding a gun, and his working eye was rolling around in its socket. There were far too many weapons in the room. Bob was probably disarmed. Atsbee was no help. I had at least four guns trained on me.

"This looks like a Mexican standoff," said Weinstein.

I couldn't tell who was on whose side. There were too many players, and Atsbee probably had strings attached to each of them. It was time for him to start acting like a real puppet master.

"There's no standoff," announced the one-eyed man. "RJ will be taking the package to the airport as planned. Saul, you can accompany, that's been approved. Evelyn will to stay."

Saul nodded. "She was never to be included."

It all made sense now. Weinstein used Evelyn and now he was escaping. Where to? Korea? Dubai? New Jersey? I'd hoped that Saul would be immersed in a full-on Evelyn DeWilde experience. Maybe he had and that was why he was fleeing.

Scott was all business. "The chip. I need the chip."

"So do I," said the Cyclops in a raincoat.

Giving up the device would have endangered thousands of American lives. Refusing to hand it over would have resulted in my being killed or injured and they would get the chip anyway. Luckily, I didn't have to make that decision.

"Here," said Bob. "Take the stupid fucking chip. It's caused nothing but trouble."

I stared at Bob, holding the device, still wrapped in tinfoil.

"Who wants the chip on a stick?" he announced. Every eye in the room focused on him. He sensed it, and I was half surprised he didn't revel in all the attention. Bob tossed the foil wrapped chip on the coffee table. There was this magical moment when everything was okay. No one was being shot, chased, or hit by a radio-controlled plane, and the chip was in no one's control.

The moment passed quickly.

"RJ, take the chip," said one-eyed Matrix Man.

"Me?" I said.

"Not you, idiot—the real RJ."

The short RJ crossed the long living room. I was expecting everyone to race him to the chip like children at a birthday party, but no one moved. He picked it up.

"Bring it here," said the Cyclops. Scott watched RJ carefully. So did Weinstein. Even Greg eyed him.

RJ walked back to the Cyclops holding the chip in front of him as if he was in a church procession. "This tiny gold mine is going to make us all rich," he said.

The one-eyed man smiled, took the chip with one hand and shot RJ in the chest with the other. Twice. I'm pretty sure he was dead before he hit the floor.

"You're such a fool, RJ," said Matrix Man.

Scott turned to his muscle men. "Get the casket," he said.

The two goons left.

"Rick, you and the mutt, sit on the couch"

I walked across the room, signaling to Mojo to follow me. He obediently sat at my feet as I joined Bob and Greg.

"Bob? What's happening?" I whispered.

He shook his head. "No idea. I came late to the party."

"Who shot you, Greg?"

Greg nodded toward Bob.

"You're kidding. Why?"

Greg shrugged. "Stay focused, buddy," he whispered. "That chip is going to cost a lot of lives if they take it."

I did a one-eighty and watched the proceedings. Matrix Man secured the chip in RJ's pocket. He looked up, all proud of himself. "Custom officials don't like bodies. Our deceased little RJ will slide into any country we want. This will be his shining moment." He slapped the dead RJ on the chest. "Good job, little man."

My brain was beginning to ramp up. I had to get that chip and I had to find Renee. But I was in this screwed-up room with a bunch of armed traitors.

"Hey, Johnson," said Scott. I turned to face him.

"Don't even think about doing whatever it was you were planning," he said.

Something changed. It was me. I had to do something.

"Lucky for you, you're too tall for RJ's next move," he said, nodding at the small casket.

"Are we done here?" said Bob, "I'm hungry."

Greg was slumped on the couch which had turned a deep crimson color. He must have lost more blood than I'd figured. The goons were putting mini RJ into the casket. Scott had his gun trained on me.

"Okay, let's get this show on the road," said Matrix Man, "Once we get RJ on the plane, we can finish this."

I knew what "finish this" meant. None of us were getting out of the room alive.

Two explosions! Outside. Big ones. The ground shook. Another one! Everyone ducked. Guns were cocked. The goons ran down the hallway.

Scott looked at me. "I'm going to say this only once, Johnson. Stay on that couch. Brian, guard the casket and shoot those fuckers if they try to go anywhere."

Scott headed toward the front door followed by a very nervous Saul Weinstein. Then, all I heard was gunfire. Automatic weapons. Atsbee passed out. Only Matrix Man was left, hovering around the casket, looking in every direction, like he had a choice with that eye.

Matrix Man heard something on the other side of the room. He slowly moved in the direction of the sound, his gun held out in front of him. Then I heard the familiar sound of a silencer, twice. Pffft. Pffft.

Nothing happened. Matrix Man looked at his chest, then looked up. Renee appeared and Matrix Man crumpled.

"Everyone okay?"

"Atsbee's shot," I said, "He needs help."

"I'm good," said Bob. "Did you bring food?"

"They put the computer chip in the casket," I said.

Renee rushed to the pine box. She opened the lid and rummaged around. She put something inside, or took the chip. I wasn't sure. She closed the lid. I had no idea what to do. Mojo did. He walked across the room and greeted Renee like an old friend.

"It's not here," she said rubbing Mojos' head. "Whose Escalade is out front?"

"Mine, for the moment," I said.

"Get Atsbee out of here. There's a hospital down the road a mile from the airport. Follow the signs. I'll get you out the back. Come on."

"What about all that automatic weapon fire?"

"I set that up. They're shooting randomly."

I wanted to ask how she did that, but it didn't matter. We got Greg to his feet. Renee led us around to the far end of the living room where there was a side door. Outside, Bob and I carried Greg to the car. He was much lighter than I thought he'd be. I realized that attitude and power aren't very heavy.

I looked down and there was trusty Mojo, trotting alongside me, like he was heading to the park. There was no sign of the bad-boy gang, but there was a large hole in the front yard. Smoke drifted skyward. Sounds of gunfire came from inside the house.

"Where are they?" I asked Renee.

"At the far end of the mansion. I locked the security, ignited an incendiary device, then set up some delayed gunfire. They're pretty confused and they will have a hard time getting out of there."

"What are you going to do?" I asked.

"I'll either stop them here or cut them off at the airport. I have to get that chip. You go get Greg out of here before he dies."

Renee ran back to the house. I was unhappy I didn't get to say goodbye, but I understood. Business before pleasure. In a fit of brilliance, I ran to the low-rider and popped the trunk, grabbing a stash of weapons.

Mojo and I raced back to the SUV. I opened the rear hatch and threw the weapons in. Mojo leapt past me as I closed the rear hatch. I ran around to the front, jumped into the driver's seat, started the car, and headed for the main road.

The hospital was minutes away. We got Greg out of the Escalade and onto a gurney. Then, the questions started. Bob mumbled a mishmash of gibberish about finding Greg in a ditch and then revealed to the orderly that this was the world-famous tech leader, Greg Atsbee. While the attendants were digesting that information, I headed for the exit. They'd figure it out. My job was to get to the airport and make sure that chip didn't leave the ground.

"I'm coming with you," Bob announced, waddling through the automatic doors.

"You don't have to," I said. I wasn't sure how much help Bob would be, but I wasn't about to discount him. This fat man had been saving my life all weekend.

"Rick, this was my quest," he said climbing into the passenger seat.

"Bob, you don't have a quest."

"I'm still coming with you. Besides, I have no idea what a quest is. I do know we have to shoot those planes...with guns, preferably big guns."

I reacted before thinking. "What are you talking about?"

"If they have holes in them, they can't fly very far."

We peeled out of the hospital parking lot. I didn't know why shooting up multi-million-dollar planes seemed wrong, but Bob had a point. If we riddled the jets, they'll be unable to fly very high or very fast or maybe not at all.

We didn't have much time, so I crashed through the airport's rear perimeter fence.

One of the planes was moving. I had to assume it was the bad guys. I saw someone on the runway. It was Renee! I had no idea how she got here. But there was a bigger problem. She was aiming a weapon at us. I drove toward the runway watching muzzle flashes come from the automatic weapon she was firing. I heard pinging of bullets hitting metal. The ground in front of the SUV was torn up by gunfire. She must have hit the tires because the car started to wobble. Then I lost control and the SUV slid to a stop on the grass.

I managed to unhook my seat belt and pushed upward with everything I had. The door was heavy, but I managed to push it to the side so that it stayed open on its own. I climbed out of the car and jumped to the ground. Mojo was right behind me.

Renee was pointing an M17 at me.

I returned to the back of the SUV, opened the hatch, and grabbed two rifles. Big Bob was stuck trying to climb out of the car with little success.

"Don't come any closer," yelled Renee.

Bob managed to exit the car and fell to the ground in a heap.

"Why is she shooting at us?" he said, standing up and brushing grass clippings off his tattered tux jacket.

"No idea."

I tossed him a rifle. "Here."

"I don't know how to use this!"

"Figure it out!"

"Stop!" Renee yelled.

I wasn't interested in her at the moment. My job was to make sure the plane did not leave the ground. From this distance and this angle, I figured that any shot would bounce off the side. Bob and I started moving toward the runway. I turned to my faithful canine.

"Mojo. Stay."

Of course this time he chose to ignore me and ran along with me.

"Last warning!" she shouted.

"What are you doing?"

Renee took aim. I jumped to the side. Mojo leapt with me. He thought it was a game. I heard bullets zing by. They were close. I think she missed on purpose.

Then I heard Bob grunt. I was on the ground looking up. He was staring at his shoulder. He staggered forward, took another round, and fell to his knees.

"I'm hit," he said, "The bitch shot me!"

I looked back at Renee. She was going to shoot again. The plane was taxiing to the far end of the runway. Renee hit Bob a third time, this time in the other shoulder and he tipped over. I crawled to him. Mojo came to his side and started whining.

"Don't let them get away," he gasped. "I hate getting shot. Do it for my sake, Rick. A dying man's request."

I thought he was being overdramatic, but didn't say anything.

The jet was at the end of the runway. I stood up. I heard another shot fire. This one hit me in the thigh, knocking me back to the ground. The jet began its takeoff. I was on my side. I aimed my gun at the plane, but I knew it was going too fast and the bullets wouldn't penetrate. I fired all my rounds. Nothing happened. The jet lifted off the ground with a roar and turned west. I'd failed.

I crawled back to Bob. He was doing better than I expected.

Renee ran to us. I was hurting now. A lot. I was pretty sure she was going to kill us. I looked for Bob's gun. It was nowhere to be found. Mojo greeted her like a long lost friend. That dog did not have a mean bone in his body.

"Renee! How could you? Don't you know what's gonna happen? And you shot Bob!"

Renee laughed out loud.

"Bob's fine."

"You shot him three times."

"So?"

Bob struggled to his feet and started taking his clothes off. "I knew it would come to this."

I couldn't believe what I saw. He was wearing a full body armor suit under his street clothes.

"It's about time someone shot me," he said.

"Is this some kind of joke?" I screamed. "You and Bob set me up? This is totally fucked."

"Oh lighten up Rick, you were just going to sit on your couch and go bankrupt anyway. And look, you got your dog back."

Renee pulled a phone from her pocket. Bob and I watched her dial.

"Isn't this phone thing getting a little old?" he said.

"You used me. Both of you." I said through the pain.

Bob shrugged and walked to her side. "You got any spare change for the candy machine in the lobby?" Then he turned to me. "Rick, I gotta say, I told you almost everything that is going on. I even told you about the espionage thing."

"You didn't say anything about working with Renee."

"I told when we were driving on the golf course that I had to keep *some* secrets. Besides, you got some danger action, *and* you got your Mojo. Still missing that finger, though. Nothing we could do about that."

Renee smiled that knowing-smile, but it appeared that the chip was heading out to sea.

"Renee, why did you let them go?"

"Not to worry, Rickster. What I have here in my hand is no ordinary cell phone," she said proudly, "It's a *smart* phone. It can be programmed to do lots of things. It can call other phones, but sometimes it can be used to trigger an explosive device. Watch the pretty lights, boys," she said, pointing her phone in the direction of the jet.

She pressed send. Nothing happened.

My leg was killing me. My head was hurting, Mojo was licking my face and Bob had lost a hundred pounds in the last two minutes.

"Are you sure you know what you're doing?" he said.

Renee looked at the phone. "Here's the problem."

"The problem is that you're crazy," I said.

"I'm not crazy. I'm just dyslexic. I called my dry cleaner by mistake. Watch."

She pressed send again. A moment later there was a huge explosion in the distance.

Renee turned to us. "See? No more chip. No more bad guys. All gone."

"You blew up the plane?" I asked.

"I put a pound of C4 in the casket. We had to let them take off, Rick. I couldn't find the chip and I didn't know who had it. This way the chip is gone, the bad guys are gone and we're home free."

"I don't feel so free," I said, holding my leg.

"I'm feeling a lot lighter," said Bob, looking at the pile of Kevlar lying on the ground.

Renee looked down on me with a huge smile.

"Buck up, Rick. You're a trained soldier. You've been shot before. Let's get you to the hospital. Maybe you can stay with Greg. He's got a nice view of the airport."

R & R

Greg Atsbee and I spent that Sunday afternoon in the local hospital. A couple pints of blood, a short surgery and we were ready to rock and roll. Accompanied by a team of his personal medical experts, along with Bob, Ed, and Renee, we piled into a specially outfitted chartered bus and headed up the coast to Greg's other mansion, the one that wasn't blown up.

During the hour-and-a-half drive to Atsbee's place on the San Francisco Bay, he told us how to answer the hundreds of questions that would be coming our way.

"The bad guys chased us, tied us up, shot us. We don't know why. Then the plane blew up. Do not deviate from that. You know nothing and saw nothing. I'll take care of the rest."

I repeated that mantra over and over during the next two weeks. After the circus of government spies, interrogators and insurance adjusters left the premises, Bob quietly disappeared. So did Renee. Even Ed was back flying planes. Mojo was the only participant left in Atsbee's house.

I stuck around the mansion taking advantage of Greg's rehab personnel until I could walk reasonably well. Eventually, I knew it was time to move on down the road, but I had one more thing to do before leaving - a one-on-one luncheon with Greg.

277

I limped down the huge stairway and entered the dining room that reminded me of "Citizen Kane." I sat to the right of the head of the long oak table.

Over the past month I'd dined with members of the CIA/FBI/NSA and some other acronyms that mean nothing to me. But this meal was special. This was where the guy in-the-know wrapped everything up.

"How are you today, Rick?"

"Getting ready to leave. Gotta face the music down south."

He lowered his eyes. "It's been nice having you around." I could tell he was sincere. When he was in his corporate mode, he stared right through you.

As soon as Greg was seated, waiters appeared from side doors and started serving. We made a short toast and traded small talk about the current wind conditions in the bay, the whitecaps and the city view. Then I dove in. It was now or never.

"So, you said I could ask some questions about that night."

Greg stopped mid-bite of a perfectly cooked salmon piccata.

"All right, but I reserve the right to not answer."

"Who was on the plane when it blew up?"

Greg stared at the paneled wall for a moment, then started moving his fork in the air like he was counting the people in their seats.

"Let's see, there was Traye, Sam Weinstein, Scott DeVore, a North Korean general, the general's assistant, the pilot, co-pilot, and that little guy in the casket, but he was already dead. By the way, that information is not to leave this room. The cover story is that a missile test failed. That will be the end of it.

As far as you and the rest of the world are concerned, that plane never existed."

"Wow," I said, realizing this was a pretty wide-ranging cover-up. Then it dawned on me why the government guys kept asking so many questions. They probably didn't know anything.

"What about the damage to the house where Renee was being held, the one that Bob rammed with the limo?"

Greg smiled. I almost got the impression that he was proud.

"You never knew, did you?"

"I was kinda busy dodging bullets."

"I had a team following you all night. They weren't a very effective fighting group, but they were spectacular at clean up. From the time you killed that guy in your hotel room until Renee nailed the raincoat man in the house, my guys were deflecting and diverting housekeepers, picking up people who'd fallen from cliffs, paying off bellmen. They were lying to the local police, Homeland Security and the FAA."

"But we blew up the front of your house and the house on that bluff where they were holding Renee was totally trashed," I said, trying to get him to answer the original question.

"It was a drunk from my party. Stole one or our limos—smashed into the house and disappeared into the night. He ran away. No usable prints. And my house? A gas leak and some leftover fireworks. My guys patched the bullet holes in less than two hours."

"Didn't any of the turtlenecks talk?"

"They never made it to the Homeland Security office. Another sad story of a hit and run. That one happened over the hill in nearby San Jose. Blocked the 101 for three hours."

I looked at him. "This operation sounds a lot bigger than moving a computer chip offshore."

Greg was back to digging into his meal, pausing only to talk to his plate.

"What went down that night was the destruction of a large scale commercial and military intelligence operation. Not only did we interrupt the theft of classified materials from Keysoft, it led us to a lot more espionage cells around the Bay Area. By the way, you were always being watched, but technically, you were on your own."

"Then why all the questions from the spooks? They weren't watching, too?"

"They had their own surveillance room, but we controlled what they saw. This entire operation was coordinated with very few people in the know."

"And that makes you..."

"The boss of the few people in the know. You, on the other hand, had no idea how many alarms went off when you took that package in the hotel lobby. Even Traye, who was using Scott like nobody's business, panicked. Ironically, it was her idea to invite you and Bob, which turned out to be her undoing."

"What about Renee?"

Greg stopped eating, put his fork down and wiped his mouth. There was a kindness in his expression that I couldn't read.

"Renee's not an escort. She has only one purpose in life - to protect this country. The minute Renee caught wind of what was happening, she kicked into high gear. But you're asking something different, aren't you?"

I didn't care about some stupid chip, Traye, or the levels of bureaucracy that were involved that night. I wanted to know where I stood with Renee. More importantly, I wanted to know where Renee was.

"Do you know where she went?"

"I'm afraid not."

I let it drop...for the moment.

"How much money did you give to Cayuga?"

This one took him by surprise. He glanced at me with a puzzled look, then decided to go for his salad.

"You're testing my patience, aren't you?"

I wasn't afraid of Greg Atsbee. I wanted to find out what kind of man he was.

"I gave them just over twenty million. But we only publicized six because any more would be pretentious, don't you agree? I mean, Cayuga was not that large an institution."

Apparently Greg Atsbee was generous as well as modest.

"While we're talking about money," he continued, "I thought Tank performed quite heroically. Not only was he the crew chief on the hotel construction, he helped you rescue Bob and Ed, and saved your life in that field. He and Jenny will be moving into a much nicer house, and there will be an ample college fund when their kids come of age."

I decided right then that if there's such a thing as reincarnation I wanted to come back as Greg Atsbee.

"What about Bob?"

"He's okay. He's feeling a little guilty about his little faux pas, but I've got something in the works for him that I think will perk him up."

I couldn't believe it. Bob had shot Greg and Greg hadn't mentioned it, not once.

"This ordeal must have taken a lot out of you," I said impulsively, "Are you okay? Is there anything I can do for you?"

He looked at me, shocked, but he knew what I was saying. I cared about him. I couldn't buy him a jet or a better meal than we were having, but damn, I owed the guy. He was the one who hooked me up with Renee.

"I'm fine, Rick. Thank you for asking. I have a surprise for you."

I wanted to act all cocky and say that I loved surprises, but like Renee said, I'm not that funny.

"Oh, what is it?"

"The fact that you risked your life and probably saved thousands of our troops when you intercepted that chip, made it pretty obvious that you deserved a reward of some kind, so I had my staff go to bat for you. Your bankruptcy is off the records, your parole and convictions are gone, wiped clean."

He slid a manila envelope in my direction.

"This is a small thank-you, for everything you've done. Put that in a reasonable investment and you won't have to worry about your finances ever again."

Greg stood and offered me his hand.

"It's been a pleasure, Rick. But all good things must come to an end. I'm leaving this afternoon. I'll be starting a new job that will be very time-consuming."

"The pleasure was all mine, Greg. Whatever it is you're doing, I wish you all the best."

"Thanks, Rick. Maybe we'll see each other again sometime."

I doubted that, but it was nice of him to say it. With that, Greg Atsbee disappeared.

I opened the envelope. Greg Atsbee might have left the room, but a chunk of his money was still there, in my hands.

Greg's List Not Craigslist

It'd been about six weeks since I'd seen Greg Atsbee. He called and invited me to his Beverly Hills home. What else did I have to do, count my money? I'd already done that, about twenty times. I still found it hard to believe that I was rich, so when Greg called, I went.

I parked my Mustang in the oak-lined driveway. At the massive oak door I was met by a real live butler wearing white gloves. He led me to the back of the house. On the way, I passed beautiful artwork: sculptures, pictures, statues. There was a fountain in the middle of one of the rooms.

We arrived at a cozy room full of leather furniture and photos of recognizable celebrities from every artistic industry. It was basically an upscale man-cave. Bob was sitting in one of the brown leather chairs. I hardly recognized him without his body armor. He got up and we bear-hugged.

"How's the leg, Rick?"

"Ready for action, Bob. How about you?"

"Got a whole new routine. Doesn't include any weapons or stakeouts. Actually, Greg's figured out how to get me back on stage without causing a riot or a national protest."

"That's great news," I said. "Where is he?"

"Mr. Atsbee will be here in just a minute," offered the butler, who was standing by the door.

"So what have you been up to?" I asked.

"Been livin' large off Greg's thank you check," said Bob, "It's a special guy who you can shoot and he'll still give you a couple million. Actually, I think it saved his life. Those bad guys didn't like him and were glad he was in pain."

"You might be right, Bob," said Atsbee, walking into the den, "Probably kept them from finishing me off right then."

We all shook hands. We were the winning team. It was a special moment.

"Hello, boys."

We all turned to face Renee. Wearing a short green summer dress, I'd never seen her look so good.

"Excellent," said Greg. "We're all here. We can get started."

Bob returned to the leather chair. I settled in on the couch. Renee sat next to me as if we were back at my ugly condo. I was immediately suspicious. I wasn't going to fall for her seductive tricks. My body totally ignored this concept and wanted to drag her to the nearest bedroom. But I'd changed. I wasn't acting on impulse any more. I guess we'd all changed in one way or another.

Greg dropped his CEO game and was acting more like the host of a neighborhood barbecue.

"First of all, thanks to the three of you. You were great and I'm glad I could get you back together again. So, there's the new information that I wanted to tell you. Bob, not only are you going to get an HBO special, you've got a tour of Europe being scheduled."

"You're kidding."

"Kid you not. I'm the executive producer."

"Who's promoting it?"

"The U.S. government and they have much deeper pockets than me."

Bob was confused. "What is it, some kind of USO tour?"

"It's a little different than that."

I immediately knew there was something up with this "news." When you combine "government" with "entertainment" and "deep pockets," it's probably something suspicious, underhanded or both.

"You've started your new job," I said with some doubt.

"That's right. And I'd like you and Renee to travel with Bob, as co-executive producers."

"You want us on the dark side," I said.

"I prefer to call it being undercover."

Bob became even more excited. "This is great. I love working under covers. Makes everything so much friendlier."

"What about Mojo?"

"You dog? Not a problem," replied Greg, "He's welcome."

This sounded fairly interesting to me. I'd been sitting around twiddling my thumbs for weeks. It was about time to get something going and this actually sounded fun.

"What do you say, Rick? The job's pretty simple. Mostly surveillance and observation. With a little brush-up on your training and some fancy new equipment, a tour of the continent would be rather appealing."

I looked at Atsbee, always the puppeteer, always in charge.

"I'm game," I said, "I'll go anywhere and do about anything if Renee's in on it."

"And if she's not?"

"I'd have to pass."

"Renee? How about it?"

We all looked at her. She waited a moment before she spoke, shifting her focus from Atsbee to Bob and then ending on me.

"I don't think so," she said finally. "It won't work."

"Of course it can," I said.

Greg put his hand up. "Wait a minute, Rick, let's hear her out."

"I've been doing a lot of thinking about this and either I'm in a relationship or I continue doing what I've been trained to do. Trying to date and working puts too many people at risk, people I care for."

Greg seemed to understand. "I realize this kind of work can be dangerous at times, but I'm offering you a simple assignment. We're not going to war. It's a surveillance job with a few other minor chores."

Renee laughed out loud.

"You are so new to this game, Greg. These guys won't give a damn about your safe plan or protecting your people. They call us assets, by the way. When they want something done, they want it done, their way. Even if it's the dumbest idea you've ever heard. I've gotta go, but thanks for the offer."

She got up, crossed the room and hugged Bob.

"I'll miss you, big guy."

"I'm not *that* big."

"You're not that small either. I had a great time. I haven't laughed so hard since you were on television."

"I'll miss you too, Renee. Thanks for everything."

"Greg," she said, shaking his hand, "I wish you luck. You have a lot to learn about your new partners. They don't work like a board of directors. They're more like a board of dictators."

She came back to me. I stood up. She kissed me lightly on the lips. Her green eyes met mine. "Rick Johnson. Believe in yourself. You're a better man than you can imagine."

"Awwww, how come you didn't say that to me?" said Bob, ruining my moment, again. What else was new?

Renee turned to him. "Because no human being could possibly be as spectacular as you think you are, Bob. And just so you know, I am the closest thing to mortal perfection that you'll ever meet."

Bob didn't get it. Renee turned back to me. We hugged again. She ran her hand down the side of my face, then turned and walked out of the room.

I remembered the wave that flattened me when I was a young boy. I survived that pummeling, and knew that I'd survive this one, too. It would just take a lot of time to heal.

Atsbee slapped his hands together.

"Okay, you two, let's take a few days off and then we can talk about the tour details."

I turned to him.

"I told you, Greg, if Renee's out, I'm out."

Greg nodded. "I was hoping it would work the other way around; that she'd sign on to be with you. I offered her a lot of money, but you know that's not a motivator for her. If you change your mind, you know how to contact me. There's no one I'd rather do business with."

"Hey..."

"Except Bob, of course."

I smiled and shook both their hands.

"Good luck, Rick," said Greg, and I left the room.

A Different Kind of Trouble

Everywhere I looked in my condo there were reminders of Renee - in every room, in every chair, and on every countertop. We'd talked, laughed and made love all over the place. I tried to ignore it, but I just couldn't.

My over-eager realtor scheduled an open house the second Sunday after I'd listed my condo. There was no way I could be around while people poked and prodded through my stuff, so I left for the afternoon. My first instinct was to head for Gordon Biersch Brewery, but then I remembered that's where Renee and I had first met.

The Pickwick was an old-school bowling alley in the nearby town of Burbank. Spacious, and often half full, a person could lose themselves in the rows of wood-lined lanes. Even if there was a kid's birthday party, there was plenty of room and the noise of the creaky machinery masked everything.

I rented a pair of oddly colored bowling shoes, bought a beer, and chose a sixteen-pound ball, being careful to avoid the red ones. They reminded me of Renee's fiery hair and her emerald green eyes.

After a few games I'd worked up a sweat. The tips of my fingers were starting to ache. I was on my third beer. It felt good to focus on something that wasn't a painful memory.

I heard the sound of a bottle hitting the floor. I was fairly certain it was mine. I turned around and locked eyes with a brown-eyed brunette.

"Oh, sorry," she said in a British accent, "Was 'at your beer?"

I nodded. "Yeah, it was."

My guard went up. I took nothing for granted anymore. I scanned my immediate surroundings for anything that could be used for a weapon. The only thing I could come up with was the sixteen pound blue bowling ball in my hands.

It was obvious she wanted to talk to me. I hoped that's all that was about to happen.

She offered her hand. "Jean Whitten," she said.

Maybe she wasn't going to kill me after all. I carefully placed the ball back on the return.

"Rick Johnson."

"Pleased to meet you, Rick. Sorry about your beer."

She looked around. We were alone at the far end of the building. She turned back to me.

"So, Rick, where's the girlfriend?"

I shrugged. "Gone. Haven't heard from her in a while."

"Guess that means you're back on the market."

I could swear I saw a twinkle in her eye.

She continued. "This guy I know, Bob Clay, is going on a European tour. He's looking for a few good men. Would you be interested in coming along?"

I thought I'd settled all this with Atsbee weeks ago. "Is this how you find prospective employees, scrounging around in old bowling alleys?"

She smiled. I sensed something familiar, but I couldn't place it.

"It's worked in the past. Just so you know, a few people have spoken highly of you. One of them said living without you was like having a hole in her life. Didn't make much sense to me, but she said you'd understand. Anyway, would you consider joining the team?"

These people were relentless. I was about to refuse yet another time. Then I looked down and spotted a huge scar across the back of her hand.

I paused a moment and then smiled.

"I wouldn't miss it for the world."

The End

www.ingramcontent.com/pod-product-compliance
Lightning Source LLC
Chambersburg PA
CBHW061943170626
46813CB00006B/2512